ZOMBIE
-IN-CHIEF

ZOMBIE -IN-CHIEF

EATER OF THE FREE WORLD

A NOVEL TAKE ON A BRAIN-DEAD ELECTION

SCOTT KENEMORE

TALOS

Talos Press books may be purchased in bulk at special discounts for sales promotion, corporate gifts, fund-raising, or educational purposes. Special editions can also be created to specifications. For details, contact the Special Sales Department, Talos Press, 307 West 36th Street, 11th Floor, New York, NY 10018 or info@skyhorsepublishing.com.

Talos Press® is a registered trademark of Skyhorse Publishing, Inc.®, a Delaware corporation.

Visit our website at www.talospress.com.

10 9 8 7 6 5 4 3 2 1

Library of Congress Cataloging-in-Publication Data is available on file.

Cover design by Anthony Morais

Print ISBN: 978-1-945863-21-9
Ebook ISBN: 978-1-945863-22-6

Printed in the United States of America

THE TYCOON

He was, really, not *so* bad.

If only they could see this. If only they could put down their signs and quiet their clever chants for a moment and actually *talk to him*. Speak with him one-on-one, like real people. Then they would doubtless see him the way his friends did. The way his business associates and employees did. The way the rich and famous all over the globe had come to see him.

He would look into their irascible, protest-mad eyes, shake their unwashed hands, and then the remarkable, magical force that had carried him this far—that had made him a billionaire, and television star, and placed him at the helm of one of the most-respected brands on earth—would surely cast its spell over them.

Surely.

But for whatever reason, such simple solutions were never possible.

Instead, this. Always this.

As the Tycoon sat in the $5,000 leather office chair at the top of the tower that bore his name, he could look straight down into the public circle below where the thousands of demonstrators had gathered.

Their protest chants and signs were rather nonspecific. They said that the Tycoon "had to go," that he didn't care about America, and that he was a fraud. But what were these declamations, really? What were these claims? They were not action-items you could check off once they had been completed. Rather, they were abstractions.

Though his familiarity with "using computers" remained cursory at best, the Tycoon managed to launch an internet browser on his laptop and scroll through the day's news headlines. So many were about him. But, again, these stories also seemed to have been written by people who just did not understand. People who—if he could only meet *personally*—would surely come around. But who, as it stood, misunderstood him utterly.

The Tycoon's friends and advisors had told him that the primaries would be the difficult part. That securing his party's own nomination was the true test. It had to be, they said. The party needed to examine him with a fine-toothed comb. Needed to review his performance under every condition. It was not personal, he was assured. Yet the process was necessary because anything *they* might find, the opposition party would *undoubtedly* locate. If he went in to the general election untested, there was no telling what might happen.

And so, though it made him cringe and itch all over, the Tycoon had allowed it. The muckrakers had gone to work, and they had found muck aplenty. In his business dealings. In his personal life. In his memberships and associations. It had been a feast for the carrion crows. They'd found things he'd forgotten about entirely! Things from his distant past—he was now reckoned to be about seventy years old—that had not even been transgressions at the time. They had simply been how things had been done back then!

So much had been found.

And *none of it* had hurt him.

If anything, this unearthed litany of failings and foibles had made the Tycoon a stronger candidate. To the voters, he now appeared more real. More authentic. A straight-shooter who didn't pussyfoot around when it came to what he thought, or said, or did. To the astonishment of his primary opponents, the American electorate seemed positively starved for a man of his temperament. The things they had been told they "could not do" anymore? Well, he did them. He had done them for years—sometimes on camera, in front of audiences of thousands. He had dismissed the "rules" with a wave of his hand. He called the other side agents of "political correctness," and, with those magic words, had made them disappear.

And it wasn't just talk. He *showed,* through his bold acts and actions, that it was all—all of it—the emperor's new clothes. That in fact you *could* impersonate a handicapped reporter. You *could* enforce all immigration laws. You *could* ignore the petitions and concerns of groups you found annoying. You could do *all these things!*

The Tycoon showed his party that perhaps they had forgotten this simple fact. You *could* do it! Here—he seemed to say in his speeches and rallies—hold my beer. (This was a figure of speech, of course. The tycoon did not drink. Alcohol.) Watch, now. I'm going to do it. I'm going to say it. I'm going to show you that the magic spells the other side has used to control your thought and speech and behavior were never really magic to begin with. And we can dispel them simply by not believing in them anymore.

And so he had. And so they did. And they loved him for it.

This had demonstrated to his party that he—above all others—was the man for the job. And so he had swept the primaries almost entirely. Now he would be coronated at his party's convention, and then there would be only one obstacle left.

Her.

The former first lady and secretary of state. The Tycoon's advisors told him not to underestimate her. He had learned to give as good as he got during the primaries, but her attacks would be different, they told him. She came from a dynasty known for dirty tricks. He could expect them to come fast and thick.

Her opening move had been to announce that her party was thankful—yes, *thankful*—that the Tycoon had been nominated to face her. His party was in such disarray, she said in a press release, that it had nominated the weakest possible candidate. It had nominated the man with the least experience and the most scandals. The man who put his foot in his mouth every time he spoke.

Thinking on this, the Tycoon pushed his chair back from his gilded desk and laughed a deep belly laugh. As she was in so many things, his opponent was so close . . . yet so far off at the same time.

It was not his own foot he put into his mouth. It was other people's.

Feet, yes. Feet were a fine place to start. An acceptable appetizer, definitely. But there was so much more. So many other wonderful parts to enjoy. So many different courses to the meal. Arms and legs. Fingers and faces. And of course brains. Brains. *Braaaaaaaaains.*

The word reverberated inside the Tycoon's mind like the last strains of a symphony.

Brains.

Than which, there was nothing higher or better. Why did one get up in the morning? Why did one go to bed at night? Why did one do all of the horrible, degrading, frustrating things that the world required?

Brains.

Brains, and brains again. Always brains. Ever brains.

The Tycoon was not the only one with this predilection, of course. He was not the only person of prominence whose tastes ran to the flesh of the living. But the others—in his opinion—had thought small, so far. That was their problem. They had been content to haunt abandoned hospitals and derelict shopping malls. To emerge from misty bogs at midnight to feed on unlucky villagers. To abscond with the mourner who dawdled a tad too long after the funeral, and then to retreat once again beneath the cemetery landscaping.

These were not bad souls, necessarily. But they lacked a fundamental ambition. They failed to think in matters of scale. To have brains occasionally was one thing, but to have them with great regularity? To install systems that would allow you to get them again and again, whenever you wanted? *That* was true success. As a celebrity billionaire, the Tycoon thought bigly upon these things. He had considered the path toward such a goal for many years. And eventually, he had determined there was no better way of achieving it than securing the presidency.

At his rallies, the Tycoon's supporters held aloft home-made signs praising him for foregoing a life of ease, for risking his name and his fortune, and for subjecting himself to the slings and arrows of national politics—all because he so loved his country.

And they were half-right.

He *was* taking a gamble. But it was not out of patriotic love for his country (or any other country in the world—despite what they liked to imply regarding his relationship with Russia). Neither was it out of anything so crude and commonplace as selflessness or compassion. Instead, it was out of the simple need for more. Not more power or recognition. (Goodness knew, he had enough of those already.) But the need for brains. More brains.

The two syllables pounded inside his head, day in and day out, like the heartbeat he did not have.

More brains!

More brains!

More brains!

And not just for him, but for *all* members of the walking dead. For all zombies everywhere! Whether they sauntered through the corridors of power in starched shirts, or lurched aimlessly and half-naked in forgotten misty burying grounds, they were all his people. *He* needed more. *They* needed more. And they would have it. Despite what the scruffy protestors outside his office said. Despite what his elitist political opponent said. Despite, even, what the prognosticators within his own party said—who looked at predictions and poll numbers and always shook their balding, flabby heads dejectedly. The men (and a few women, too) who wheezed: "But *even* with the bump we'll get at the convention, it's going to be a real challenge to catch up to her . . ." The ones who suggested that the best outcome possible—the *true* victory—might be to use the notoriety arising from his presidential run to start a TV network. And besides, they assured him, the system was rigged. He shouldn't take it personally. Someone like him had never had a serious chance. Someone like him . . .

If only they knew the half of it.

Who he *really* was. What he *really* wanted.

But soon they would. Soon all of them would.

As the Tycoon stared down into the mass of protestors gathered outside his skyscraper, this was the one thing in the world he felt he knew for sure.

THE REPORTER

"**A**t this point, there's no way he can win."

Jessica Smith nodded thoughtfully and seriously at the prognostications of her boss, a veteran reporter some twenty years her senior. He smiled a world-weary smile and held the door for her as they strode into the largely-empty arena.

Preparation for the convention was behind schedule and more disorganized than anyone wanted to admit. The contractors in tool belts and hard hats—when they realized that the first convention reporters were actually arriving—rolled their eyes and thanked their lucky stars that they were not the project managers who would ultimately be blamed for the disorganization and delay.

Despite the ongoing challenges and holdups, some of the trappings of a political convention *had* been achieved in a sort of rudimentary way. American flag bunting hung from windows and walls. The stage in the center of the arena was still under construction, but columns and platforms were beginning to come into existence. Hurried carpenters rushed to and fro. Instead of the Muzak so typical in these venues, patriotic music was being piped into the parking garages, stairwells, and elevators. All in all, it rather gave Jessica the feeling of something constructed by a foreign (or possibly alien) culture that had never before seen an American political convention, but had been asked to give it a go anyhow.

Jessica had landed her position with this elite, East Coast news outlet directly after graduating from journalism school. She had beat out literally thousands of applicants for it, and knew how lucky she was. In a time when newspapers across the country were dying, or merging, or merging and then dying, her employer was one of the last powerful papers that had—kind-of, sort-of—remained profitable.

Jessica had been interested in American politics since before she could remember, and journalists had always been her idols. So far in her brief career, she had covered regional politics and written about city council and mayoral races in New York City. But she had only seen national political conventions on TV. They had always looked extravagant and exciting. (And like they had been produced and built by people who actually gave a damn about what they were doing.)

As the senior reporter who supervised her—George Cutler was his name—paused to regard a crude, stock image of a bald eagle that had been tacked to the door of a press lounge, he smiled sympathetically at Jessica, like a father whose child has just met the deflated, alcoholic mall version of Santa Claus.

George shook his head and moved down the hallway, trudging deeper and deeper into the half-built convention space. Jessica followed. They passed arena staff vacuuming floors and cleaning bathrooms. Several away teams from special-interest groups and civic organizations were also present, hurrying to set up displays and erect banners.

George spoke confidentially and quietly, as though he and Jessica were educators discussing a student who would have to be held back a year.

"As you know, I've been to a few of these—and this is your first one, so maybe you can't tell—but this is *not* typical."

Jessica nodded thoughtfully, but said nothing.

"In American elections, the candidate who spends the most money wins about ninety-five percent of the time," George continued. "Just look around. What does that tell you about what's happening here?"

"He says he's still putting his fundraising team together," Jessica tried, as they passed a large *papier-mâché* elephant so crude it could have been created by a child. "After he gets the convention bump, that might get more potential donors excited. Could be that's when they plan to start the real push for cash."

George smiled as he shook his head, as if to say Jessica had found a solution that was technically plausible, while still managing to still be very unlikely.

"Even the regular donors know he's not going to win," George said. "Sure, they'll make some contributions in the days ahead, but they'll be token gestures. Favors to a friend. There's no way, Jessica. He is going to lose the general election by a landslide. Have you heard the old Louisiana political axiom: 'To lose, he'd either have to be caught with a live boy or a dead girl'? Well at this point, I think they could catch *her* with both of those . . . and she'd still beat this guy. And his party knows it. Think about it. It's the week of the convention, and they haven't even announced who is going to be speaking.

Why? That's because they still can't find anybody who wants to get on board this sinking ship. It's embarrassing for everybody. They're embarrassed to be doing this, and we're embarrassed *for* them. But we all still have to do our jobs. That's the way the world works."

"So then . . ." Jessica struggled. "So then . . ."

"So then why are we even here?" George asked with a grin. Jessica nodded timidly.

"For one, we're getting a paycheck," George said. "Whatever else may be true, that certainly is. The real news won't be what happens on the stage. It'll be out in the streets. This week, I want you to think human interest stories, Jessica. That's the best we're going to get. Why do people want to vote for this clown? How did a sick joke powered by misogyny and internet memes ever make it so far? *That's* what we've been sent here to ponder."

They passed down another carpeted hallway and into a section of the arena that contained very small media conference rooms. George and Jessica would be walking *past* these; they were reserved for the lowest of the low when it came to news organizations. They housed bloggers, agenda-driven publications, and nonprofits with newsletters. The tables in these rooms were small and crowded closely together. The reporters—such as they were—would be cramped. The lighting was grim and institutional.

Glancing inside these rooms, Jessica felt thankful all over again to have secured a position at a top-tier newspaper. Jessica looked over this competition, such as it was. And that was when she saw him.

Jessica slowed her gait and eventually stopped walking entirely. She rubbed her eyes with her free hand. Was she really seeing this?

She was.

"Tim Fife?" she called incredulously.

He looked up from his laptop. He did not see her immediately, but he smiled at the sound of her voice. He looked like a man tasting a familiar flavor or smelling a favorite scent. Jessica lingered in the doorway to the small side conference room.

Eventually he saw her and stood, revealing blue jeans that had seen better days and a black t-shirt that read "*Humpty Dumpty was pushed!*" Somewhat alarmingly, he also wore a white plastic brace around his neck, as though he had recently suffered an injury. There was a mustard stain—a fresh one—starting at the edge of his mouth and making its way down over the brace, and onto the shirt. He had not shaved in two or three days.

"Jessica!" he said, pushing back his chair.

Jessica smiled and hastily glanced back up the hallway for a moment toward her colleague.

"George," she called. "I'll catch up with you!"

George nodded and continued on his way. Jessica warily entered the dingy conference room. Tim bounded over, lunging step after lunging step, and Jessica gave him a hug.

"Tim, what're you doing here?" she asked.

"The same thing you are, I expect," he said with a smile.

"It's been so long since I've seen you!" she said. "You were always so much fun to have in class—so lively and full of interesting ideas—and we all missed you so much after you left the program. Are you doing okay?"

"Oh, this?" he said, gesturing to the brace that framed his head like a sixteenth-century ruff. "Old injury. Acts up every now and then. The doctor said I should wear this whenever it hurts."

"Oh," said Jessica. "But I meant, how have you been since . . . since I last saw you in New York?"

Tim had been a member of Jessica's class at the Columbia University Graduate School of Journalism, but had dropped out before the end of their first year. It was not entirely unheard-of for students to leave the program. Sometimes they discovered they simply didn't like journalism, winced at the dim career prospects, or just didn't get along with the professors. In Tim's case, it had been the latter. Sort of. Outside of his studies, Tim had been operating a mean-spirited political gossip blog in his free time. A professor had learned of this, taken Tim aside, and strongly encouraged him to discontinue the project if he expected ever to be employed by a respectable news organization. Tim had found this a rather shortsighted view of the situation, and had separated from the program not long thereafter.

"I've been fine," Tim said with a glint in his eye. "More than fine, if you really want to know! I'm doing *quite well*. I heard about *your* job, though. Wow! That's the real brass ring. Congratulations."

"Thanks," said Jessica. "So, who are you here with? Are you still doing your . . . your . . ."

Tim smiled to say that she could relax. He had heard it all before.

"My trashy political website?" he finished her sentence. "Yes and no. It kind of got folded into something else."

Jessica raised her eyebrows inquisitively and hopefully. Perhaps things had not gone so poorly for Tim.

"I'm now part of TruthTeller," he said. "I have my own regular column about politics, plus I get to do in-the-field reporting. It's a really nice arrangement."

Jessica's eyebrows strained under the weight of this new information, and eventually buckled. Her whole face fell.

"TruthTeller?" she said, her voice falling to a whisper. "But that's that . . . *fake news* website, right?"

"Well people call us that," Tim said, nodding. "But for every door it closes, it opens ten others. TruthTeller is a place where we can ask the questions that others won't ask. Can't ask. We pick up and look underneath the rocks that others won't even touch. Sometimes we don't find anything . . . but sometimes we do. It's freeing. Very exciting, too. I feel like we're on the leading edge of some revolutionary things."

"And it's run by that angry shouting man, yes?" Jessica said. "The chubby one who's always selling nutrition supplements?"

Tim nodded sheepishly.

"Well . . . as my colleague was just saying to me . . . a paycheck's a paycheck, right? That's why we do this. They *do* pay you, yes?"

"Yes," Tim said. "And that's good, because Columbia didn't forgive the loans I took out . . . even though I didn't finish."

"Oh," Jessica said. "Right. I didn't even think of that."

Jessica's father was a stockbroker who had retired at 50; her mother, an orthodontist to the stars (or at least their children). Jessica's tuition at Columbia had been taken care of by her parents, who had also seen fit to house her in a doorman building in Morningside Heights for the duration of her studies.

Jessica suddenly thought of George and glanced back down the patriotically-decorated hallway.

"Gosh, I ought to get back with my boss, but we really should catch up some more," she told Tim. "It's so nice to see you again. And so surprising! Maybe we could get dinner or a drink sometime this week."

"Yes," Tim said hopefully. "That'd be great. Here . . ."

He began fishing about inside the front pocket of his jeans. Moments later, his greasy fingers had located a business card, only slightly stained with mustard. It looked homemade— printed on a personal printer and cut, inexpertly, with a pair of kitchen scissors. Tim pushed it into Jessica's palm.

She gripped it awkwardly and brought it up to her eyes.

Tim Fife
Senior Political Content Creator
TruthTeller—"Where the Truth Will Find You"

His email and phone were listed beneath that.

"Thanks," Jessica said, thrusting it into her pocket. "Great running into you, Tim! Being here is all so strange. It feels surreal. I have no doubt this is gonna be a crazy week!"

Tim's face grew eerily still. His heavy breathing fell to a Darth Vaderian murmur. The mustard on the side of his face caught the light from the fluorescent fixture above, and seemed to glisten with supernatural power.

"You have *no idea* how crazy," he whispered ominously. "You have no idea."

THE FAKE NEWSMAN

As Jessica Smith departed, Tim Fife straightened his neck brace and returned his ample body to his chair. Only as he sat back down did he notice that the medical device—and indeed, much of the front of him—bore a thin but prominent stripe of yellow. He resolved to clean it off at his first convenience, but not immediately. For the moment, there were more pressing matters at hand. Tim opened his laptop and began to type.

They were living in times of wonder and astonishment. Every sign pointed to this conclusion. Every star that shone seemed to consecrate this idea with its slow arc across the sky. These days had never come before, and they would never come again. This was all unique.

Tim's responsibility was to help his readers understand this simple but vital fact. This election was not like others, because in this election *the whole story was not being told.*

There might have been wars waged on the public's access to information at other junctures in history, but never to such a degree, never in such an organized way, and never with so many involved in the conspiracy. In previous generations, it might have happened accidentally. But now there was now a horrible *intentionality* to it. The truth—not just about one thing, but about many—was being intentionally held from the people. The digitization of information had made this withholding possible. Collusion no longer needed to occur at secret midnight gatherings. It could all be executed and coordinated remotely, and 'round the clock.

That was why the resistance needed to use these same tools. It needed to be digital, nimble, and unafraid.

As the smell of her perfume began to disappear from the conference room, Tim felt genuinely sorry for his J-school colleague Jessica. The world was changing and moving on. Institutions like hers had failed to notice. Sure, he could momentarily envy her salary and prestige, but how long could it last?

Jessica had signed on with one of the finest and most respected producers of buggy whips . . . but the era of the automobile was dawning. You could smell the gasoline on the wind. It was coming. Tim Fife was sure of it.

Seeing Jessica had been a distraction—a welcome one, but still a distraction. Tim tried to refocus. He forced himself to return to the task at hand. Now was not the time to be sidetracked. Not by old friends, or even by old friends who were attractive young women. His work was so important. At times, Tim could be overwhelmed by the sheer magnitude of the responsibility that fate or God or the universe had placed upon his neck brace. The future of the world was at stake. Literally the world. For the next four years, at least.

Before Tim could ruminate further on the importance of his charge, he was interrupted by the arrival of the rest of the TruthTeller convention team. They were a pair of men who— aside from a deep and abiding dedication to fact-finding at any cost—could not have been more opposite.

Ryan Hoffwell was loud and large. He wore his hair even longer than Tim did. His t-shirt was even more filthy. And he outweighed the already-portly Tim by a good hundred pounds. When Tim stood next to Ryan, he felt thin and handsome.

Dan Kieffner was the other TruthTeller representative. Dan was in his early forties and did not like to talk about his past. He was tall and bald. He had a leer that bespoke a capacity for violence. He did not dress "well" by any precise understanding of the term, but could usually manage to find clothes that were appropriate to the situation (which was more than could be said of Tim or Ryan). Dan had muddy tattoos that ran along his arms, the kind that were usually administered for free by a roommate during a stay as a guest of the government. And "the government" turned out to be the two words you *did not* want to mention around Dan. Worse than any slur or slander, reminding Dan that—across the world, in every nation, in every place you went—people tended to be *governed* . . . made him halfway insane. For this reason, Tim Fife had been surprised when TruthTeller management had designated Dan as a member of the team that would be covering this convention. (Usually Dan wrote about instances of government overreach: Police shutting down a kids' lemonade stand for lack of permits. A township that required licenses for professional dog walkers. Mandated government certifications to paint someone's fingernails. That sort of thing.) Since arriving in Cleveland, Dan had seemed even quieter and more disturbed than usual. Privately, Tim wondered if Dan had been sent along by management in the hopes that—if he could not report on it—Dan would perhaps *make* the news. By going crazy. (Everyone expected something to happen at the convention. Maybe that "something" was going to involve Dan Kieffner.)

The trio settled back into their chairs. As was typical, it was Ryan who spoke first.

"I brought doughnuts," he said. "They had doughnuts in a room over there. A sign said they were for reporters, so I totally took some."

Tim looked up expecting to see a plate of doughnuts, and found that Ryan had snagged an entire box. Well, Tim thought to himself, at least it was only *one* box.

"Who was that lady?" Dan asked, opening his laptop.

"Just an old friend from J-school," Tim said. "She's here for work too."

"She's down the hall in one of the *nice* conference rooms?" Ryan observed. "Sounds like a member of the *establishment* to me."

"Eh, she's not so bad if you get to know her," Tim said. "One of the good ones."

"You were in a co-ed . . . J-school?" Dan asked suspiciously. "The 'J-school' I went to, we were segregated into cell blocks and never got to see women."

"Journalism school," Tim said. "Not—"

"Oh," Dan said. "Never mind then . . ."

The trio ate doughnuts and checked their emails. Truth-Teller headquarters would often send suggestions for stories to file, but the reporters also received their share of news tips directly from readers and private sources. It was these informal tips (and the green light to follow up on them, if one so wished) that made working at TruthTeller so different from other reporting jobs, and—at least in Tim's opinion—so much fun. When you wrote for the *New York Times* or the *Chicago Tribune*, there were topics upon which you'd automatically take a pass. New photographic evidence that members of the British royal family were actually lizard people, for example, did not tend to be pursued by those outlets. Conspiracy theories at all generally seemed to be quite scarce between their pages. TruthTeller, which did not have pages—at least not the kind you could stick things between—was different. Some conspiracies, it suggested, might very well be true. Others, which were such whoppers that even regular readers of Truth-Teller found them hard to swallow, still received attention *via* reporting on the phenomenon of the conspiracy. "*We're* not saying that there's good evidence that the Federal Reserve is controlled by shape-shifting aliens, but a lot of people seem to *think* there is. How could this be? What's really going on? And how could the mainstream media—the MSM, for short—have failed so utterly to tell you about this phenomenon?"

It was upon this final question where TruthTeller really hit its stride. TruthTeller positioned itself as a trusted friend who you could count on to shoot straight and treat you like an adult. MSM news outlets felt they were performing a service by "protecting you" from news that was too wild or outrageous. But had you asked to be treated like a child? To be fed the pablum of censored, safe, gentle news?

Or were you an adult who deserved to hear the *whole* story?

Tim and his TruthTeller colleagues endeavored to make readers feel as though they were.

And so Tim scanned his inbox, looking for the next lead full of danger, intrigue, and suggestion. Many tips contained interesting speculation, but no new information. Even more frequently, the tips would involve topics that TruthTeller had already done to death. Sometimes, what Tim saw disturbed or confused him. Sometimes it bored him. Many tips quite simply made no sense at all.

In recent days, one of the recurring messages he'd been instantly dragging to his "Delete" folder had concerned information that one of the major party nominees in the next presidential election was a member of the walking dead. These tips appeared to come from multiple sources, but that meant little to nothing. Many tipsters with agendas often sent in the same information using multiple identities and email addresses. Tim had taken to ignoring the emails with the screaming subject lines like: "DEFINITIVE PROOF: Candidate is a Zombie! —TruthTeller must publish!!!" It was too fantastic, even for him.

Thus, is was not Tim, but Ryan, who brought it up.

"Are you guys seeing the zombie thing?" he asked between bites of second doughnut.

Tim and Dan grunted yes.

"I'm starting to think there could be enough for a story," Ryan said. "I dunno. Maybe a few hundred words?"

Tim stopped clicking and leaned back in his chair.

"Really?" he asked Ryan. "We're not exactly starved for content right now. We're *at* the convention. Anything could happen. Everybody is here. You really want to spend your time on a supernatural angle?"

"Yeah, but . . . do you ever just get a feeling?" Ryan asked.

Ryan was going right for the big guns.

Of course Tim got feelings about stories like this. Of course he did. It was one of the reasons why he worked at TruthTeller, despite the lousy pay and the lack of professional respect. Tim understood on a deep, primordial level that you could sometimes get a special *feeling* that something needed to be reported on. And when that happened, you needed to be free to do it.

"Sure," Tim said, adjusting his neck brace. "I know all about getting feelings."

"Well, I'm getting the feeling that this could be usable," Ryan said. "Zombies are a new angle. They bring so many things to the table. Religion, mysticism, violence. I dunno. The more I think about it, the more I like it."

"I've seen those same emails, but I haven't read many," Tim admitted.

Tim toggled into his garbage file to see if some might still be there.

"It's just . . . I dunno," Ryan said. "I think there's space to make some interesting connections to the candidate. There's his charity work in Haiti. The trips with a billionaire donor to a vacation home on what the locals call 'Zombie Island.' And of course the rumors about what goes on at his club in Florida. That's not a few hundred words?"

Tim shrugged. Perhaps Ryan had a point. While there would be angles aplenty to pursue on convention week, perhaps a conjectural piece about the undead would be the right thing to get their gears turning.

"Do you want to take it?" Tim asked.

"I mean, you can if you want to," said Ryan.

"Really?" said Tim. "*You* were the one who had the feeling."

"I didn't necessarily mean it was the right story *for me*," Ryan said.

"Yeah, okay," said Tim. "Then maybe I will."

Tim slowly pulled together the related emails. The messages had been addressed to him, but had obviously gone to the entire TruthTeller staff. The spray-and-pray method. Hey, when you had a scoop like this, you wanted to leave nothing to chance.

Tim looked over the grisly inventory the tipster had sent. It included a bulleted list of all the reasons why the major party candidate was actually a zombie, and promises of "iron-clad" photographic evidence to be shared at a later date and in person.

Tim shook his head, smiled, and hit reply.

THE TYCOON

Ohio was more than just a "swing state." That was what his advisors had told him. Instead, they said, Ohio was like a

small version of the entire country. Like a little America, min-
iaturized and dropped in the middle of the cornfields. It was
half urban and half rural. Half conservative and half liberal.
It had college towns; gleaming, growing cities; rusting, dying
wastelands; and acres and acres of farmers and Amish and
4-H. Parts of it were flat, but parts out east were practically
West Virginia hill country. Parts were black, and parts were
whiter that white, and there were enclaves of other ethnicities
too. All manner of religious devotions were observed, from
the casual to the all-consuming and cultish. The Tycoon's
advisors had told him these things, he guessed, to make him
feel as though the place was at least 50% on his side. It was half
of everything, they reasoned, so it must be half with him.

He wished, now, they'd merely left it there, with that single
idea. But no. Unable to contain themselves, they had provided
embellishments. Painted vivid verbal pictures of all the great
variety that the state offered. Really fleshed it out.

And now the Tycoon understood that there was *nothing*
here to which he might truly relate. The duality of the place
did not suit him at all. For a man raised amongst the skyscrap-
ers of New York, the idea that the cultivators of these immaculately square patches of farmland—which he could see so
vividly from the window of his airplane—were the ones on *his*
side? Were *his* 50%? The notion seemed insane. Impossible.

It was in these moments that the overwhelming depres-
sion took him, and the Tycoon wondered if the talking heads
on the Sunday morning political shows might know something after all. That he would never impress these voters, or, at
least, never excite them to the degree needed to win the day.
That he could not relate to their tractor pulls and their church
bake sales and their weekend hunting trips. (The Tycoon had

stepped aboard a tractor only once in his life—to prove it was safe—after a farming operation owned by his father had suffered a spate of OSHA violations. Religious institutions were also not well-known to the Tycoon, for he experienced a slight but steady burning sensation whenever he set foot inside one. Weekend hunting trips, however, might be the place where a little common ground could be found. . . . Something about hunting *hunters* had always been deeply satisfying to him. There was an irony involved.)

The Tycoon's advisors were ambitious, cutthroat men. Generally, he liked these traits. But it could also make them a bit overeager and pollyannaish. These advisors had assured the Tycoon that any rifts here in the heartland (where he did not connect with voters) would be ably bridged by his running mate. The Tycoon hoped that this was true. That the Governor of the adjacent Hoosier state was indeed the man for the job.

Why his advisors had selected the Governor was no mystery. The Governor of Indiana had proved just what could be done with (and *to*) a place like that.

Under his watch, Indiana now dumped more toxic chemicals into its waterways than any other state. More than West Virginia. It also maintained some of the largest coal-fired power plants in the world. The coal plants in the thirty-mile stretch around Evansville alone released more greenhouse gas than any other municipal area in the USA. By the reckoning of some agencies, no other state now contributed more to climate change.

Back in the early 2000s, the Hoosier state had been a large investor in (and subsidizer of) wind power. Giant wind farms dotted the fields between Indianapolis and Gary. When the Governor had taken office, he had cut those programs entirely. He had also made Indiana into a right-to-work state, busting up the unions wherever he could. But beyond any formal adjustment to policy, the Governor had also ushered in remarkable changes to the culture. Made it a place where they weren't all up in your face with the artsy stuff and the transsexual gender-business, and so forth. The Governor had passed laws that let businesses forbid service to anybody they liked, as long as the urge to do so stemmed from a "religious conviction." And all this, somehow, magically, in a state that had fought with the North in the Civil War. It was as though this Governor had smuggled a state from the Deep South north of the Mason-Dixon line, convinced everybody to drop their accents, and passed it off as part of the Union.

That was an accomplishment. The Tycoon did not doubt that this man was capable. Hell, this man deserved a medal!

By why? *Why* had the Governor of Indiana done all of these remarkable things?

That was the remaining question which puzzled the Tycoon.

For what did such a man *want*? His appetites were famously few. The Governor did not overeat. He did not smoke. He did not seem to drink. Whenever the governor danced with his wife, he held her at arm's length. They looked like teachers at a Catholic high school, demonstrating the acceptable distance for students before prom. (The Tycoon, when he danced, held his wife close. So close it could make observers uncomfortable. This came not from any intoxication with his wife's anatomical gifts, but rather from his total dedication to the role. He must position himself as a groper and an ogler. He must leak tapes of locker room japery. He must make comments even about the shapeliness of his own daughter. All so that the truth might never be guessed—that his flaccid zombie penis had not worked *in that way* since he had become a member of the walking dead and lost any blood pressure entirely.)

In sharp contrast to the Governor, the Tycoon was *ruled* by desire. Once implemented, his plans for the country would result in a hedonistic blood orgy the likes of which the world had never known. The Tycoon's every step inched him toward this scenario of excess and carnal satisfaction. But the Governor? Did he truly seek only to sit on the porch beside his matronly spouse, sipping unsweetened iced tea in the shadow of the coal plants? Was that a consummation devoutly to be wished? Was that *anything*? Even men who were not zombies—normal, healthy men—wanted more than those things.

What *did* the Governor want?

A limousine brought the Tycoon from the private airport where his plane had landed to the hotel that would serve as his headquarters for the convention. The Tycoon smoothed his hair and checked the Scotch tape on his tie. Then he exited the car and made his way into the parking garage elevator that would take him up to the executive suite where the silver-haired leader of the Hoosiers was waiting.

What indeed?

The elevator doors opened directly into the suite. It was not as fine as the executive rooms in the hotels that bore the Tycoon's own name, but it would do in a pinch for the Midwest. The Governor was already there. He sat on a couch, reading from a Bible so old it had doubtless been his grandfather's.

The Governor smiled genially at the Tycoon, closed the book's paper-thin pages, and stood. His broad smile revealed pearly, almost perfect teeth, unstained by tobacco, wine, or impure thoughts.

The Tycoon shook the Governor's hand hard, and found the Hoosier's grip surprisingly soft and yielding. But this man rode motorcycles! He split wood with axes in campaign commercials! Yet his handshake was weak and his skin felt as though he had not done a day's real work in his life. (For his part, the Tycoon loathed handshaking. Making his peace with the humiliating practice had been one of the most challenging parts of the campaign. People who knew him knew that he disliked shaking hands. For years, he had cultivated a reputation as a germophobe. His enemies and detractors, meanwhile, characterized his aversion to pressing the flesh as a sign of his contempt for the poor and working class—as the sign of a man who saw average Americans as riddled with disease and contagion. Little did they guess the truth. That the Tycoon avoided touching others because *he was contagion.* He was the deathless flesh that should not walk, but walked still. And he worried—with every how's-your-father, up-and-down pumping of his wrist—that the person shaking his hand might notice how cold and lifeless it was. Might fail to detect a pulse. Might feel the settling of the blood that had not been properly pumped by a heart in many years. [This same subterfuge explained the Tycoon's penchant for sporting a healthy coat of foundation wherever he went. Let them call him an orange Creamsicle. More importantly, let them blame it on his vanity and pride. But most of all, let no one suspect that his makeup concealed the corpse-pale sheen of the unliving.])

And so the Governor of Indiana wore no makeup, and also did not even attempt to muster a strong handshake. No matter, the Tycoon decided as he released his grip. The Governor would still serve a purpose. Useful idiots often did.

Both the Tycoon and the Governor understood the way in which they were meant to counterbalance one another. The Tycoon was associated with the hedonism of the 1980s, but the Governor of Indiana could reassure voters that these days of youthful indiscretion were far, far behind him. On the other side of the coin, the Governor himself was an outright bore. A goddamned human sleeping pill. The Tycoon's colorful antics would show the electorate that the next four years would not be completely devoid of mirth and excitement.

The private moment between the two men did not last long.

Into the room stepped Jay McNelis, chief media advisor and manager of the Tycoon's campaign. He would be the one ghostwriting the speech the Tycoon would deliver on the final day of the convention. However, the Governor's own staff had insisted on writing the vice presidential nominee's remarks. McNelis had convened this meeting to ensure that the candidates were—at least figuratively—on the same page.

Handshakes out of the way, the three men sat around a circular oak table. (Fine for Ohio, thought the Tycoon. Yet he would never have such a drab, functional item in any of his own hotels.) The candidates listened as McNelis outlined the function of the speeches that they would give. The future vice president should outline the problems, McNelis explained. He should bear the bad news, and describe everything wrong with America that the Tycoon could fix. Then, the next night, the future president would ride into town on the white horse. *Here* was the solution. *Here* was the hero arrived to save the day. That would be the function of the Tycoon's remarks.

As McNelis spoke, the Tycoon nodded along and tried to pay attention.

McNelis was famous for his stewardship of a successful news website, and brought many skills to the table. The Tycoon had worked with him to formulate all the main policy points of his platform. Though McNelis was both oleaginous and wise—a Harvard MBA and a career on Wall Street attested to that much—it had nonetheless taken him many months to piece together that the master he served might be something other than alive. And while McNelis was one of very few who "knew" about the Tycoon, he still did not seem to fully grasp the motivation behind the Tycoon's platform. The world the Tycoon wanted to create.

The Tycoon preferred it that way. He would trust McNelis as far as he could throw him.

McNelis opened his laptop and prepared to begin. His complexion—which hovered somewhere between W.C. Fields and greasy, rancid meat—glistened in the reflected light from his computer screen. The Governor of Indiana bowed his head like a man in church preparing to receive a blessing.

"Alignment is key, gentlemen," McNelis began. "Voters do not expect you to be identical, but they need to see you stand together on the issues that matter. You come from different places. You have different jobs. Different life stories. That's fine. But on the key stuff, they need to expect the same things from *both* of you.

The candidates nodded.

"So let's do the list one more time, shall we?" McNelis said, looking over the top of his glasses at both men.

The Tycoon smiled. He loved the list. He loved it all the more precisely because McNelis and the Governor sitting beside him had no sense of what it actually meant. What the actual project was.

"First and foremost, the border wall," McNelis began. "We don't say this explicitly, but it really is the foundation of our platform. It's the core. In your speeches, you can't talk about it enough. Border wall. Border wall. Border wall. It's the symbol of everything we hope to accomplish."

Yes, the Tycoon thought to himself. *The border wall. That wonderful, wonderful wall. Which will keep all those delicious people* in, *where the zombies can get them. No escape to Mexico. No escape at all.*

"Right behind the wall is a complete overhaul of our healthcare system," said McNelis. "You both need to touch on that for a significant portion of any speech. You need to characterize the current system as broke and bloated. Unsustainable. Making people sick and bankrupt. Say that doctors don't like it. Say that it's too confusing for the average American to use. But the good news is we're here to fix it! We're going to have it right-sized in no time. We're going to repeal *and replace.* Always make clear that there will be a replacement. We'll figure out what it is later."

Oh yes, the Tycoon thought. *Anything that made Americans hale and hearty and free from disease had to go. People were so much easier to catch when they were sick or injured or had lingering medical conditions. It was simpler for the zombies when the humans were hobbling along on homemade crutches or confined to wheelchairs. The weaker and sicker the better. Healthcare absolutely needed to be eliminated.*

"Next, voters hate political correctness," McNelis said. "I'm sure you gentlemen do too. Let the voters know it! We need to paint the other side as more concerned with pronouns than with policies that will improve people's lives."

The Tycoon understood that, at this point, Newspeak was probably too ingrained to counter effectively. But no matter. The Tycoon had decided to use it to his advantage. When the populace became aware of the murderous, brain-eating zombies in their midst, the president himself would ensure these "differently-alive" Americans were not discriminated against, were not "othered," and that their "vibrant, dynamic culture" of murder and carnage was respected just like any other. After all, colonialists had kept zombies literally hiding in the shadows for centuries. Were they not the *most* in need of restorative justice? Was not it time for them to shamble forward with their rotting heads held high, to take their place alongside other Americans?

"Then there is the biased, liberal media," McNelis said. "You need to remind the voters that the media is not treating you fairly. Their coverage is always prejudiced against you."

"Them!" the Tycoon snapped, quite unable to control himself. "I hate them so much! They've been against me my whole life. Just because I'm successful!"

"And don't forget the media's war against the church," the Governor piously added. "They've taken every opportunity to slander and criticize Americans of faith. You saw what happened in my state when I signed that legislation—you know, the one allowing people to practice their faith as they saw fit. By not serving gay people. The media went crazy! It wasn't the good people of my state. *They* were fine with it. It was the media! Always making something out of nothing. Always stirring up trouble."

"So true," said the Tycoon, nodding his head sympathetically. "So *very* true."

The Tycoon truly did despise the mainstream media, but only because it was in the habit of telling people true things. For all its incompetence, the mainstream media was—now and then—accurate. And that *would not do* during a zombie outbreak. A news agency that would correctly inform the populace where the zombies were and in what direction they were headed? Outrageous! But because the Tycoon realized he could not stop them entirely, he believed his best course was to dilute them. To cast doubt on the veracity of their reports. And to provide Americans with alternative news outlets, featuring alternative facts. (These outlets would one day provide alternative broadcasts in times of national emergency, with different takes on where the zombies were, what they were doing, and whether they were really anything to worry about in the first place.)

"It all comes back to personal freedom," the Governor said confidently. "The freedom to believe what you want to believe. In each and every sphere of your life. Nothing more American than that."

McNelis and the Tycoon nodded along vigorously.

Not all parts of personal freedom suited the Tycoon. The Tycoon realized, for example, that more personal freedom meant things like the freedom to own firearms. And few things annoyed zombies more than being taken out with a clean headshot. Even so, the Tycoon had calculated that the present course still worked in his favor. (From what he could tell, neither major American political party ever took a significant step toward banning guns. However, the opposing party was reckoned as *wanting to.* For this reason, gun sales actually went up when *they* were in power—based on the unfounded fear that they *might* pass restrictions . . . and so one ought to get while the getting was good. In this way, it seemed to the Tycoon that running as a member of the party that wished to provide unrestricted access to firearms might help ensure that there were *fewer* in the hands of civilians when the dead really did begin to rise. Sometimes the way forward could be a little counterintuitive.)

"Finally, then, there is *globalism*," McNelis said soberly. "That is the last major tentpole of our campaign. You hate globalism. It is everything your opponent represents. She is a globalist to her core. Everything she has ever done provides evidence of that fact."

The Tycoon and the Governor nodded along.

"We're running for President and Vice President of *America* . . . not of *the world*," the Governor chimed in. "It is the people of America who will elect us. We must put America first in all things."

"Yes," said the Tycoon. "And I intend to use my powers of negotiation to make sure we negotiate better deals for America. If other countries won't play ball, I'll show 'em the door. I'll show 'em there's a new sheriff in town who means business. Big business."

The Tycoon smiled in what he hoped was a confident, convincing way. The Governor seemed to buy it.

America must be first, the Tycoon reasoned. It must be first at the expense of all others, and at the cost of alliances and allegiances. Isolating America in geopolitical terms was just like building the wall. It was the 3D-chess version. When the dead rose and the carnage began, other countries should not be tempted to intervene or assist. They must understand America's conviction to go it alone. To refuse all help, *whatever* the circumstances.

McNelis seemed very pleased by their alignment around these core messages of the platform. The three men spent several minutes more reviewing talking points for the upcoming speeches, but all seemed to be in accord.

As they prepared to adjourn for the evening, the Governor asked the Tycoon if they might speak privately for a moment. He suggested the balcony of the suite. McNelis—ever alarmed at the notion that anything substantive could be decided in his absence—looked on warily as the two candidates opened the sliding glass doors and walked out onto the cheap stucco balcony. The Tycoon gave McNelis a stern look to say he should relax. (He knew McNelis would do no such thing. It was physically impossible for the man.)

The Governor pulled the glass door shut behind them. The hotel was not tall like buildings in New York were, but there was still a nice view. The wind whipped up. The Tycoon's hair was tousled. The Governor's remained as still and solid as something carved from Indiana limestone.

"I just wanted to take a second," the Governor began awkwardly. "I know that we haven't really chatted since this whole thing got started. What we just did in there . . . We may have been 'aligning' on the principles of our platform, but it doesn't really feel like we're being genuine with one another, does it? Being real?"

Could it be? Was this puritanical man—famous for being so hard of heart—secretly a softy who wanted to be pals? The Tycoon began to wonder . . .

"Yes, of course," the Tycoon said. "I regret we haven't spent more time together. That's my fault. When I'm president and you're vice president, we'll be working closely. We can make up for lost time."

"We've both been busy since the campaign got started," the Governor said in a consolatory way. "It's nobody's fault. I wonder though, if it would be possible for us to do a little of that this week."

"A little of what?" the Tycoon asked, confused.

"You know, spend some time together," he said. "Maybe have you out to Indy. I could show you the governor's mansion."

Alarm bells went off in the Tycoon's head. Alarm bells that warned that he was about to be very, *very* bored.

"Love the idea," the Tycoon said. "Love it. But tell you what . . . You're sick of this Midwest weather, right? I've been here just a few hours, and I'm already sick of it. Let me sweeten the pot. Let's do it at my place down in Florida. Your family . . . have they been to Florida before?"

"We went to Disney when the kids were younger," the Governor said.

"They'll love my place!" the Tycoon said. "It's nothing like Disney World. Except for the good parts—the parts your family liked. It has those parts. Golf too. And the weather's fantastic."

The Governor nodded carefully. It was clear to the Tycoon that there was something he wasn't saying.

"I just . . . As you know, I'm a man of faith."

Here it comes, the Tycoon thought. (He was not quite sure what "it" was, but knew it would also be boring.)

"I do," said the Tycoon. "I do know that. That's why I picked you. One reason, anyway."

"I hope then, that, in Florida, there'll be an opportunity for us to speak privately and at length," the Governor said. "I would never be able to be a part of something that went against my faith or what I believed in. I'd really like to see inside your soul."

The Governor smiled his winning, game-show-host smile. The one that had gotten him elected to congress and then the governorship. The smile that *always* worked (on Hoosiers, anyway). The smile that had been honed over a lifetime.

It was at this moment that the Tycoon realized he might truly have a problem.

This man who gave every appearance of being a gentle, pious innocent might *actually be one*. His determination to move America in the direction of a 1950's sitcom might be earnest and honest. And such a soul might prove less than malleable when it came to making the kind of policy decisions that would make the United States ripe for takeover by legions of the walking dead.

The Tycoon also noted that it would be difficult to work alongside a man who wanted to see into his soul, because the Tycoon was not entirely sure that he had one. (The question of what a zombie's inner life might be composed of was an elusive one, even to zombies themselves.)

The Tycoon took a moment to steel his resolve, and to remember all his victories. He had confronted men like the Governor before, and he had always found a way to come out ahead. He had always charmed them. When necessary, he had beaten them.

The Tycoon had just defeated scores of candidates to win his party's nomination. He could surely do this small, final task, he told himself. Compared to winning the primaries, making some small adjustments to his running-mate should prove—if not a cakewalk—at least within his wheelhouse generally.

The Tycoon liked to say that deals were his art form. He smiled his own winning smile back at the Governor. He had the feeling he was about to make the deal of a lifetime.

THE REPORTER

The first day at the convention site passed quietly for Jessica Smith. After finding the workspace they had been assigned, she and George reviewed assignments for the rest of the week. George remained intent that Jessica should pursue human interest stories with a local angle. How did everyday Clevelanders feel about the convention? What were the issues *they* cared about? Did either major party candidate seem poised to actually make a difference in their lives?

Local first responders could also be interviewed, George suggested. Did they anticipate a terrorist attack? Would it be homegrown or foreign? Would there be rioting in the streets?

Aware that she was still a cub reporter, Jessica tried her best to read George and to agree with him whenever it seemed appropriate to do so. From what she could tell, George's chief concern was not that they would find themselves underequipped to cover all of the convention week's exciting events, but that nothing worth covering would emerge. No "real news." Just horrible nonsense and puffery.

"I hope you like reporting on freak shows," George said at one point. "Because that's what this is going to be."

Jessica had half-smiled at this, unsure what it meant she should do. (George, for his part, assumed his use of the word "freak" had brushed Jessica's millennial sensibilities the wrong way. He reminded himself to be more careful of his wording in the future.)

Despite the week's grim prospects, Jessica reminded herself how lucky she was. It could always be worse. She thought again of poor, overweight Tim Fife. At least he had found a job *somewhere*.

After sleeping fitfully in a frozen hotel room with a noisy, overactive air conditioner, Jessica rose before dawn to begin her first full day at the convention site with limited hopes and a sense of dread gnawing at her belly. She showered, made up her face, and then returned to the shabby hotel room desk where she had left her laptop charging. That was when she chanced to glance in the direction of the door.

And saw it.

A dull gold envelope—not yellow, but gold—had been slid underneath. Had it been there minutes before when she had wandered to the bathroom in the half-darkness? She could not be certain.

Wondering if it could be a missive from the campaign (or even from the hotel itself), she rose and retrieved it. She examined both sides, but found no logo or imprint. Undoing a clasp and opening the envelope, she found a piece of stationery within. On one side had been scrawled:

Kidd's Bar
Strongsville
Noon Today

Jessica wondered what to make of this. Was it a joke? A request for a date? A warning of an impending terroristic action, of which the police should be notified immediately?

Then something else. Something else still inside the envelope.

Jessica scowled and looked closer. Then reached inside.

She withdrew a photograph of the billionaire tycoon that
the party would nominate as its candidate on the final day of
the convention. In the photo, he was seated in a well-lit out-
door setting at night. It reminded Jessica of an exterior lounge
at a fine (if somewhat garish) hotel. The photo had been taken
secretly, and the subject clearly believed himself unobserved.
He was wearing a suit with no tie. Before him was a table, set
for dinner. There were dishes and plates and glasses of water.
And what he was eating was, very clearly, a human hand.

Jessica smiled. Then frowned. Then smiled again.

This was a test. The kind of thing George and the boys
did to bust the balls of cub reporters. George had probably
planted it in the middle of the night. He would be waiting for
her excited call or text about it. Jessica decided she would not
even give him the satisfaction of mentioning it during their
breakfast meeting.

Jessica continued to dress and gathered her things. Yet
as she did so, she could not shake the photo from her mind.
Finally ready to begin her day, she checked her watch again
and decided there was enough time to give the novelty image
a second look. The sun was rising now, and she threw open
the hotel room curtains and let the natural light augment the
glow from the nearby desk fixture. She held up the photo and
looked at it again.

She began to get the feeling that something was not right.
Or rather, not wrong.

She was no expert at image alteration, and knew that what
did or did not "seem Photoshopped" was not a bar by which a

reporter ought to judge anything. Not in the twenty-first century. At the same time, the image did indeed appear genuine. It was, in a way, perfect in its imperfection.

Jessica tried to imagine the scenario under which the photo could have been taken. Had the billionaire been funning at a Halloween party? Had someone placed a hand in front of him as a joke? Had he been eating the shaved hand of some exotic primate?

But no . . .

That *was* a human hand. The picture had been taken from a distance, but the detail was there. The fingernails. The hair on the knuckles. A man's hand. Not a monkey's.

Jessica pulled up a web browser and did an image search for anything related to the candidate eating a hand. Nothing. Searches for a candidate eating other parts of a human likewise drew a blank. Jessica even searched for photos of the candidate eating dinner, hoping to find the original manipulated image. But this returned only familiar PR pics, all of them staged. (Even so, Jessica carefully inspected the food arrayed on the tables before him. There was not a hand anywhere to be found.)

Something told Jessica that she was about to cross a point of no return. That she needed to stop and get down to breakfast with her boss if she wasn't serious about this. Time was a-wasting. But that same something in her couldn't leave it alone.

Jessica next searched the internet for Strongsville and Kidd's Bar. (She had heard of neither.) These, at least, proved real. Strongsville appeared to be a pleasant suburb. And nothing about Kidd's Bar seemed sinister, other than a one-and-a-half-star average on Yelp. The reviews mentioned rude bartenders and no TP in the johns, but no cannibal acts.

Jessica picked up the photo and examined it once more in the dawn's early light. So strange. So thoroughly puzzling. Yet *so* apparently real.

Abruptly, her side vibrated and she jumped.

Jessica looked at the face of her phone, and immediately picked up.

"Hi George," she said.

"Everything okay?" he asked. "I had that we were going to meet for breakfast fifteen minutes ago. It's no problem, but you're never late to anything. I thought I'd better call."

"Sure," said Jessica. "Time just got away from me. Sorry."

"No worries," said George. "Are you feeling all right? I don't want to be nosy . . . but I can hear something in your voice."

Now, the moment of truth. Jessica decided that if she was going to fall for a prank like generations of cub reporters had before her, she might as well fall hard.

"Actually . . ." Jessica began cagily.

"Yes?" said George.

"I've got a lead I'd like to follow up, if it's all right with you. Something . . . Something that I think might have a good human interest sort of an angle. Like you've been talking about. I think it could show what the common folks around here are thinking when it comes to all this convention brouhaha. There's more, but I'd like to keep it under my hat for the moment. Hopefully, I can surprise you with something good later today."

"Well . . ." George began.

Jessica physically winced. She waited for him to make a snide comment about not believing every story that's literally slipped under your door. (Or perhaps he'd make a pun about how he had to "hand it to her" on this one.)

But instead, George said: "Okay, yeah. That sounds fine. I don't have anything more important for you at the moment. Will you be going somewhere?"

"Out to a suburb," Jessica answered warily, still waiting for this to be revealed as a ruse. "I'll need to take the rental car, but I can be back by early afternoon."

"All right then, kiddo," George said. "I'll catch you then."

And he hung up.

Jessica lowered her phone and stared at it. She waited for the text that would read: *LOL Got You.*

But it never came.

Jessica gathered her things and prepared to depart.

THE FAKE NEWSMAN

For all of Tim Fife's considerable girth, only trace amounts of it could be attributed to alcoholic beverages. He almost never drank. Whenever he went in for a physical, the physician invariably clucked disapprovingly at Tim's weight, pulse, and blood pressure, yet his liver function was always pronounced "fine." (Tim did not make checkups a regular habit. This was not out of any real doctor-phobia, but because it was hard to trust mainstream science. Every day it seemed TruthTeller discovered something new or previously overlooked about the benefits of leeches, ear candling, or colloidal silver. Why most physicians chose to ignore these marvels was deeply confusing to him.)

When Tim did drink alcohol, it was usually a sip of wine during the holidays while visiting extended family. He almost never drank in bars. He *certainly* never drank in bars before noon.

And so it was with considerable awkwardness that he sat at the back table in the only truly shabby tavern in this otherwise well-maintained suburb of Cleveland. In front of him was a ginger ale for which he had been charged five dollars. You could buy two two-liters of ginger ale for that much, he thought to himself. Why did people come to these places?

Tim was not the only person inside the tavern at this hour, which was much to his relief. The bar was at least partly designed for overnight shift workers who might get off at seven or eight in the morning. Consequently, many of the men riding the barstools were feeling little pain as the noon hour neared. Tim watched them. They did not return his glances. Only the bartender gazed over from time to time, sizing up the hefty, neckbearded newcomer, and wondering if he ought to be out and about in a brace like that.

Tim stirred his ginger ale and waited. The bar was an old building with a tin roof, so his smartphone got very little reception. He could not browse the web or even check his email.

A few moments later, she walked in.

Tim was struck dumb with awkwardness and surprise. Perhaps she would not see him. He had taken a table in the darkest corner he could find, but as Jessica Smith stood in the entrance of the dark bar—holding the door open as she surveyed the grim interior—the natural light invaded every corner. It lit up Tim's neck brace like an incandescent lion's mane. It was one of the first places her eyes went.

Jessica's face registered surprise, confusion, and then anger. Her face fell into a scowl. She looked back out to the parking lot for a moment, as if contemplating departure. Instead, she shook her head and stalked over.

She looked like a cross mother, annoyed at having been called by the school to pick up a misbehaving son.

"Is this your idea of a *joke*?" Jessica said. "I have an important job with real responsibilities, Tim. I'd like to keep that job, if it's okay with you."

She hovered above his table, glowering down at him.

"Jessica, please . . ." Tim said.

Some of the men on the barstools glanced over and smiled. A few put their hands over their mouths and whispered, wondering what there could be between a woman like that and a man like him. Tim could feel himself turning red.

"I should have known this was more of your stupid celebrity political bullshit," Jessica continued, her hand fishing in her bag. "I just don't know why you thought it was okay to use it to waste my time."

Jessica tossed something onto the filthy barroom table. Tim looked down. It was a dull gold envelope. He had no idea what it was or what it meant.

Before he could ask about the envelope, a strange gnarled hand reached down and grasped it. Tim hurriedly glanced up and saw that the hand belonged to a man—probably in his late seventies—sporting a plaid shirt and a navy blue baseball cap with VIETNAM VETERAN stitched across the front in gold thread. The stranger had the face of the kind of men who had been telling Tim for his entire life to straighten up, fly right, and/or take a lap. Tim prepared for the reprimand that would surely follow. For a stern voice to ask them what in the hell their problem was, and to advise them to "Take it outside."

Instead, the mysterious man said: "Good, you're both here. Now we can begin."

The three of them sat together around the barroom table. When they spoke, it was in quiet, confidential tones.

"So . . . *you're* KEKLord69?" Tim whispered.

The man appeared to belong to that final generation proud of its unwillingness to use technology. And yet the man nodded vigorously to confirm that this was indeed his handle.

"You can call me Francis, though," the man said.

"And you're the one with indisputable evidence about the—"

Francis cut him off.

"About the *thing in my email,*" Francis said, talking over him. "Yes. That. That precisely."

"And so, why is *she* here?" asked Tim.

"Yeah, why *am* I here?" said Jessica. "And what the hell is with that photo? Did *you* put it under my door?"

Francis smiled and glanced to the side evasively, to indicate that he almost certainly had. It did not seem impossible. At a political convention, an older man in a veteran's hat could basically go anywhere.

Tim's eyes went back and forth between Francis and Jessica, not entirely understanding.

"Maybe you should show him?" Francis said.

"What?" Tim said. "Show me what?"

Jessica slid the golden envelope across the table. Tim picked it up, opened it, and carefully extracted the photograph inside.

"This is from the same photoset!" he said in astonishment. "It's from the same group of photos you sent over email, Francis. Except . . . except you didn't send this one. And now I think I understand why. Goodness gracious! It's the clearest of the bunch."

The photo of the Tycoon chowing down on a human hand stunned Tim so much that he dropped the photo back to the table. Francis quickly gathered it up and placed it back inside the envelope.

Tim's surprise swiftly turned to envy and anger.

"Wait . . . why did you think you could send that to her, and not to me?" he asked defensively. "*I* work for TruthTeller. She's the one with the fake news media! With the outlet backed by corrupt, globalist-funded—"

"I know, I know," said Francis. "That's why I had to *give* her that photo—all but hand-deliver it. With TruthTeller, I knew you would believe me at my word. The photo in that envelope has never been uploaded to a computer. It's never been emailed. And it's only been printed out the once. I don't need to tell you the kind of people that would want to prevent something like that from coming to light. And what they would do to ensure that it didn't."

Tim nodded, understanding completely, and savoring the dangerous intrigue.

Jessica turned to Francis and said: "I understand *him,* but why *me*? Why not contact my boss?"

"Because you're new and don't know any better," Francis said. "You're here, aren't you? Do you think any reporter who'd been on your staff even a few months would have followed up on something like this?"

Jessica looked unsure.

She said: "Possibly. It could happen."

"*Sure* it could," Francis said.

Tim smiled.

"Okay, so how did you get these images?" Tim asked.

"And I'm guessing there are more?" Jessica said.

Francis nodded.

"These photos were taken by someone in my organization," Francis said to both of them. "By someone who risked life and limb to get them."

"Your 'organization?'" asked Tim.

Organizations within organizations were one of Tim's specialties at TruthTeller. The more secret and more organized the better. He all but salivated when he heard someone use the "o" word.

Then Jessica asked the question that Tim realized he should have started with.

"Who are you, and what do you want?" Jessica said.

The older man leaned back in his chair and smiled. He looked not to Jessica, but to Tim as he gave his answer.

"You have heard—I am sure—of the Knights of Romero?"

Tim made a sound like air escaping from a punctured tire. Then he finished with a loud snort that was half excitement, half sleep apnea.

"The knights of what?" Jessica said, looking back and forth between them. "Hey. Hello? What aren't you telling me?"

"The Knights of Romero," Tim said quietly. "They're supposed to be an ancient order that has worked in secret across the centuries to keep humanity safe from zombies. Like, they've put down zombie uprisings over the years. Worked to quell outbreaks. And they keep it all very hush-hush."

"Zombies?" Jessica said doubtfully.

Tim smiled and shrugged.

"I mean, I'm the *last* person who wants to dismiss something," Tim said. "But the evidence I've seen for the Knights of Romero has been patchy at best. Every few years someone will swear that something was actually the Knights working behind the scenes—an old corpse found with a fresh cleaver in its head—but . . . I dunno. I have a little trouble buying it."

Jessica grinned.

"And this from the guy who always swore the moon landing was faked, Hitler lived until 1975, and members of the British royal family are actually lizard people."

"It's not *many* members," Tim clarified. "Two or three, tops."

"I don't know about lizard people, but the Knights are *very* real," said Francis.

"I mean, I'd like to believe you," said Tim, turning back to the older gent. "What makes you sure?"

"Because I'm a member," Francis said.

Tim raised an eyebrow and adjusted his neck brace. He had a series of questions he'd learned to ask over the years when confronted by information that seemed, even for him, a bit too fantastic to credit. He had honed the ability to dig deeper without offending his subject.

"Tell me . . ." Tim began carefully. "Are there . . . *other* members of the Knights of Romero, or is it just you?"

"Of course there are," said Francis. "Don't be ridiculous."

"And if I wanted to meet some of these other members?" inquired Tim.

"I'm hoping to arrange that directly," said the man.

Tim nodded cautiously. So far, so good.

"Hang on," said Jessica. "If your organization is a secret one, then why have you contacted us?"

Francis's face grew stoic.

"Because there are some things even we cannot do," he said. "You have seen the photos. You know what it will mean if this man becomes president."

"I don't actually," said Tim. "But I can imagine, I guess."

"He's not supposed to win," Jessica added. "I mean, the polls show he's way behind. Like, *way* behind."

Francis frowned seriously.

"Even so, it's not a risk we can be willing to take," he said. "The stakes are just too high."

"Why have you contacted the two of us?" Jessica asked.

"Because you represent the whole spectrum," Francis said. "You're real news and fake news, or fake news and real news—depending on who you listen to. One of you is with a print publication that started on the East Coast back in the 1800's. One of you is a web-based getup that wasn't around last Thursday."

Tim opened his mouth to object, but Francis gave him a look to say that he was speaking figuratively.

"Point is," Francis continued, "if *both* of you report the same thing, then folks across the country'll be more likely to believe it. Everybody, from all locations and political affiliations, will see that this is real. And that's what needs to happen."

Tim did not quite know what to say. Jessica put her head in her hand thoughtfully.

"You'll have to give us more than one photograph, you realize," Jessica said. "It's nice, but it's not enough. If you're pushing a narrative about zombies—zombies, for goodness sake!—you're going to have to give me a little more."

"I mean, I'd run with just this," Tim said. "If there're other photos, that's great, but I'd say TruthTeller is going to be on board."

Francis smiled.

"I anticipated this," he told them. "So I'm going to provide both of you with more evidence—*irrefutable* evidence—which you can study as long as you'd like, photograph to your hearts' content, and share with your organizations."

"Okay," Jessica said cautiously. "What evidence?"

"A lot of things," Francis said, seeming, now, to grow a bit defensive. "Witnesses who've seen this happening firsthand, and who are willing to go on the record. Video and audio recordings. And a real-life zombie we're keeping at our safe house. You can study him all you wish. Just don't get bit."

Tim looked at Jessica. He inclined his head slightly to the side to ask if she was game. Jessica grinned back at him. Her expression said she hadn't come all this way to ask a bunch of farmers what they thought about a border wall.

"All right then," Francis said, pushing back his chair. "I'm parked in the back of this bar, and the safe house is not ten minutes away. Y'all can ride with me."

"I've got a rental car," Jessica said. "Can I follow you?"

Francis shook his head.

"My people . . . the other Knights . . . they're expecting me to return solo. They might get antsy if it looks like I was tailed."

"I took the bus here," Tim volunteered. "So I'll ride with you, Francis. That's fine."

"It's both of you, or nothing," Francis said sternly. "We need to establish trust if we're gonna do this thing. I need y'all to show me that you trust me. After all, *I'm* trusting *you*."

Tim looked imploringly at Jessica.

"All right, we'll ride with you," she said. "But how long will we be gone? My boss will wonder about me."

"Less than an hour," Francis said, heading for the back door of the bar. "Don't worry. Your car won't get ticketed or towed. This ain't New York City."

Francis held open the back door, and they walked out into the late-morning sunshine. Behind the bar was a small parking area. The air was crisp and cool, and seemed doubly so to Tim after spending time in a dingy tavern where the furniture still smelled like smoke (despite a ten-year-old ban). Francis headed toward an old red Plymouth parked under a tree. The area behind the bar was covered in gravel but not paved. There were no other people in sight.

What happened next happened very fast.

All three of them heard the alarming *SHUSH* of a car going too fast down a gravel road. They turned in time to behold a large white SUV pulling around the side of the bar. The windows were down, and the vehicle was full of intense-looking people. Men and women. At least a couple of them were holding automatic weapons.

Tim heard Francis say: "Aww, what in the hell . . ."

Then Tim glanced over and saw the old man reaching into the front of his high-waisted pants. A moment later, he came out with a Dirty Harry revolver—the barrel at least ten inches long.

"Oh Jesus," Tim said. "What are you . . ."

He could not tell if he fell to the ground reflexively, or if his knees simply gave out under the sheer weight of the terror coursing through him. Whatever the case, an instant later he was facedown on the ground, his plastic neck brace clattering against the gravel.

Then someone in the SUV started shooting. Tim heard several distinct pops. Francis started shooting back while sprinting for his car. The man was old, but he could still run quickly. Jessica shrieked. The SUV's tires *SHUSH*ed to a halt and the doors opened. Tim heard new footsteps racing across the gravel. Still essentially prone, Tim tried to inch himself back in the direction of the bar's back door.

A strange, male voice called urgently: "Get her! Get her!"

There were more gunshots, seemingly from everywhere. Then the male voice suddenly cried out in pain. Tim risked looking up.

He saw a group of strangers bundling Jessica into the white SUV. One of them, however, was now lying facedown in the gravel. A man in late middle age, by the looks of it. He had been shot by Francis.

"My God; he's dead!" cried one of the SUV people.

Just then, the sound of first-responder sirens began to wail in the distance.

Tim looked the other away across the lot and saw Francis leaning against his Plymouth. He was covered in blood and seemed to have been shot in several places. Yet he was still alive. He held his long-barreled revolver close to his chest and breathed hard.

One of the SUV people suddenly darted in Tim's direction, as if intending to close on him. Francis came out of cover, leveled his long revolver, and shot at the man. The gravel in front of Tim exploded.

The man from the SUV hesitated. He looked back at the rest of his group. They had just pushed Jessica—resisting and screaming—into the back of the SUV. The sirens of the first responders grew louder and more distinct.

"Just leave him!" an angry female voice cried. As Francis took another shot at him—hitting only the gravel once more—the man ran a zig-zag pattern back to his compatriots. He jumped into the back of the vehicle where Jessica was. The tires churned violently, and the SUV pulled away. The fallen man was left behind, unmoving and prone.

As the SUV drove out of sight around the side of the bar, Tim glanced frantically back to where Francis was resting against the car. Abruptly, the older man's chest stopped heaving. His head tipped back and the weapon fell from his hand. He had succumbed to his wounds.

"Oh . . . shit . . ." Tim whispered quietly.

He was astonished, disoriented, and breathing hard. He pushed himself up onto his hands and knees, then forced himself to stand. His neck brace fell away and clattered to the gravel in several parts, but he hardly noticed. His adrenaline raced. What should he do? What had just happened? What fate awaited Jessica Smith?

He tried to think.

The sirens drew closer. He looked at the two dead men lying across from one another on different sides of the lot. Then he heard a noise behind him. It was the bar patrons. A few had summoned the temerity to crack the back door a bit. Soon they would see him, if they hadn't already.

Tim had only one idea; he must flee.

There was a second side entrance to the lot behind the bar, not far from where Francis had parked his Plymouth. Tim made for it. Not accustomed to moving at great speed, he surprised himself by managing a slow but steady lope. He heard the curious cries of the bar patrons behind him, but did not turn back. He ran. He ran and ran. By lucky chance, the emergency vehicles—he could not see them, but assumed police and fire—pulled up to the front of the bar and stopped there.

Tim escaped unmolested into the wooded yards beyond.

THE TYCOON

"**W**ell, what do you think?"

It was a question he had asked of many top leaders of commerce and industry. Of A-list movie stars and people in the Rock & Roll Hall of Fame. Of literal princes and princesses. And of course, of women. Of so many women. (In his pre-undead days, of course.) More women than he could count. More than he could remember. They tended to blend together over the years. To meld in his mind until they were all one woman.

The Governor put his hands on his hips and leaned back a bit, taking it all in.

The immaculately manicured lawns. The beaches and pools and spas. The exquisite event spaces. The breathtaking Spanish architecture.

The Tycoon's private club in Palm Beach was internationally famous. Elite local families paid six figures to join. Yet for all its luster and glamour, no one seemed to have any sense of its *true* purpose. What the facility was truly designed to be and to do. The patch of land it occupied was in one of the oldest settled parts of the United States. It was practically part of the Caribbean. And the Caribbean? That was where the undead had started. Where darkest arts had first raised them, and where they had then gestated for centuries. The Tycoon's private club was more than a secret sanctuary for the undead. It was their beachhead on the mainland. Their center for *recruitment*.

The Tycoon looked into the Governor's eyes and wondered. Seriously wondered . . .

The warm afternoon wind whipped up and rustled the palm trees and grass. Small lizards, about the size of human thumbnails, scuttled across a nearby railing. The waves lapped peacefully in the distance.

"It's really neat!" the Governor pronounced.

He turned and gave the Tycoon an innocent smile.

The Tycoon's eyes wondered if there was not something more? But the Governor continued only to nod and to smile. That was indeed the diagnosis.

Neat.

The Tycoon let out a deep, unnecessary breath. His question of what people thought had elicited a bevy of responses over the decades. But "neat" wasn't among the ones he'd heard before, at least not from anybody over the age of eight.

"Can't get this kind of view in Indiana, eh?" the Tycoon said, pressing for more.

The Governor shrugged noncommittally.

"You might be surprised what we can get in Indiana," the Governor said. "The moonlight on the Wabash can be pretty special. But no, we don't have palm trees or sea breezes. This is really neat, what you've got here."

Now we were up to "really neat." Slow progress, but progress nonetheless.

"Perhaps we could take a walk down by the water," the Tycoon said. "You won't need your coat. My man here can take it."

They had come directly on the Tycoon's plane from Cleveland, and still wore their jackets. The Governor dutifully surrendered his coat to a waiting valet. Then the pair began to stroll down the ornate flagstone path that would take them across manicured lawns to the club's private beach. Security observed them from a great distance, nearly invisible.

"There's something I was hoping we could talk about," the Tycoon said as they walked. "I want to come to it directly, because I can see you're a straight-shooter."

"Good, yes," said the Governor. Then he let out a small yawn and smiled apologetically. Both men had been working hard, and had slept little on the plane. But the Tycoon knew what he had to say next would jostle his running mate back awake.

"Imagine you had never seen a house before," the Tycoon began. "Far-fetched, but imagine it. Now suppose that some-one took you to the worst part of a major city—a real slum—and showed you a house that had holes in the roof, cockroaches and termites scuttling across the floors, and walls covered in black mold. Would you want to live in a house? Would that appear desirable to you—supposing, again, that you had never seen one before in your life?"

"Where was a living in, if I didn't know what a house was?" said the Governor. "I must be living in something, right?"

"Hell, I don't know . . . a cave," said the Tycoon.

"Well," said the Governor, stroking his bare chin. "A cave does sound better than roaches and mold and all that."

"Good," the Tycoon continued. "Now imagine you had never seen a woman. Like the fellow from that musical with the pirates at the beginning. Anyhow, you've never seen a woman,

and then you meet the worst kind of hag. Warts everywhere.
A beard. Her gums are black and green. Use your imagination
from there."

The Governor continued to smile his million-dollar smile,
but was obviously troubled by the request.

"Can you say that you would be interested in one for . . .
you know. . . to take as your wife?" asked the Tycoon.

"You're not asking if it would make me . . . *like men
instead*?!" the Governor said, recoiling in shock.

"No, no, no," the Tycoon quickly reassured him. "I don't
mean that. Let's say it's imagine yourself with this hag woman,
or nothing at all. Being celibate."

The Governor squinted his eyes in a way that said he was
processing.

"I suppose I can imagine that," said the Governor apace,
forcing himself to grin. "I'm not used to thinking about things
like this, but I suppose I can picture it. And I guess I'd likely
tell that woman thanks, but no thanks."

"Good," said the Tycoon. "Now I'd like you to tell me what
you think of . . . when you think of a zombie."

The men were silent for a moment. The only sound was
their expensive shoes against the flagstones.

"I *don't* think about zombies," the Governor eventually
replied. "Why should I do that?"

"But if you *did*," the Tycoon pressed. "If I asked you to do
it right now . . ."

"Look," the Governor said, beginning to withdraw. "When
I said the two of us needed to spend more time getting to know
one another, I didn't mean—"

"*Answer the question*!" boomed the Tycoon.

The Governor was taken aback. The perfect grin fell from his face for an instant. (It was *only* for an instant, but the Tycoon's eagle eye caught it.) Then the Governor smiled again, as though nothing was, or had ever been, amiss.

"Why, I suppose I'd think of something that was dead, but still walking around."

"Good," said the Tycoon. "Yes. What else? Tell me, what does it look like?"

"It's probably falling apart," the Governor said. "It's dead so . . . so it never heals when it gets hurt. Wounds stay open. Its skin is probably ripped up. It could be missing eyes and teeth."

"And how does it smell?" asked the Tycoon.

"Oh, not good," said the Governor. "Not good at all."

"How does it move?" asked the Tycoon.

"It doesn't walk normally," the Governor said, seeming to grow more confident in his description. "It stumbles. It can't walk fast or run. It . . . maybe it sticks its arms out in front of itself when it walks, like it's feeling its way forward."

"Can it talk, think, read?" asked the Tycoon.

"Why are you asking me all this?" the Governor said, bewildered.

The Tycoon regarded him severely.

"No, it can't do any of those things," said the Governor.

"And *why not*?" said the Tycoon.

The Governor thought.

"Because it's a zombie," he said.

The Tycoon smiled again.

"Now think again about that house covered in mold and roaches, and the woman who makes you want to puke just to look at her," he said.

"I don't understand," said the Governor.

"Of course you don't," said the Tycoon. "But that's fine. That's fine. We are only beginning. I know we are overdue for lunch. But perhaps you will allow me to show you one thing more before we dine. Something that I believe will make everything much clearer."

The Governor made a motion that said "lead on."

The Tycoon did.

THE REPORTER

Jessica was surrounded by strange people. She had not been able to follow precisely the twists and turns the white SUV had taken after it had pulled away from the bar because someone's hands had been in her face, and she had been struggling violently. Then she had been hooded. Sometime later in the ride, her hands had been bound.

But now they were somewhere else.

They had exited the car, and she had been hurried down at least one flight of steps. Her hood was removed and she found herself in what appeared to be a partially-finished basement. The floor was concrete and there was a water heater in the corner. There was also a table upon which several automatic firearms were resting. Jessica had been placed on a dilapidated couch, the cushions spongy from years of use. In front of Jessica stood two women and one man. They wore jeans and sweatshirts. They looked exhausted, sweaty, and alarmed.

One of them—a woman in her thirties with long black hair tied back—stepped forward.

"Who are you people?" Jessica asked.

"We are the people who just saved your life," the woman said.

"And it cost us one of our own," the man grumbled. He was built like a football lineman, tall and thick. He crossed his arms in frustration.

"Saved my life?" Jessica said. "You were the ones who were shooting. Do you know who I am? I am a reporter with the political bureau of—"

"We *know* who you are," the woman said. "That's why we came . . . to save you."

"But who was that fat guy?" the man asked. "The one in the neck brace? We didn't have any intel on him. It messed everything up. Was he somebody you just met at the bar?"

"That's my friend Tim Fife," Jessica said, after thinking of no reason why she should lie. "He is a journalist also. In a way."

"Well he screwed things up, and now a friend of ours is dead," the lineman barked.

"No, he didn't," the woman with the long hair disagreed. "That was not his fault."

"What is happening?" Jessica asked.

"We're here to keep you safe," the woman replied. "We went to rescue you. Frankly, we weren't sure it would work. What we'd do if we actually got you out of there . . . well, maybe we didn't think that far."

"Well we're that far now," Jessica said. "Can you at least untie my hands? I don't have a gun or anything."

The trio looked at each other. Then the woman who had not yet spoken stepped forward. She was very young and pale, and had a nearly-shaved head. As Jessica looked on, she reached to a tactical belt around her waist and pulled out an evil-looking collapsible blade. She motioned impatiently for Jessica to hold out her hands. Jessica obeyed, and the young woman sawed through the rope.

"Thank you," Jessica told her, pulling her hands apart and freeing the remaining rope from her wrists. "Now, can you *please* tell me what's going on? I'm not asking as a reporter. I'm asking as a person."

The trio exchanged another look. Young woman with the buzz cut and the linebacker both nodded. The woman with the long hair spoke.

"We are called the Knights of Romero," she said.

Jessica gave a look like she smelled something funny.

"What?" the reporter said. "I just met one of the Knights of Romero. He was Francis, that older guy at the bar. The one you shot."

"This may be a little more complicated that you're antici-pating," the woman with the long hair said. "There *is* a group called the Knights of Romero. And it's us. Our mission is to prevent the rise of the undead. We work behind the scenes. When we're doing our jobs right, nobody knows that we exist."

"*I* know you exist," Jessica pointed out.

"Today was a setback," the woman said. "In more ways than one."

"Francis . . . if that was even his name . . . had given Tim and me information about a politician being a zombie. Why would he do that?"

"You have to understand that the zombies' number-one fear is being exposed," the woman said. "If the existence of the Knights of Romero were to become generally known, then the public would understand that they—the zombies—also exist. Francis was part of an operation run by the undead to make sure that doesn't happen. He worked for them, as part of their intelligence gathering service. But we have been monitoring that intelligence service closely. The undead are tricky, but we can be trickier."

"What are you talking about?" said Jessica. "I still don't understand what is going on."

"The fact that certain people in high places—politicians, for example—might be zombies is an idea bandied about now and again on the internet," the woman told Jessica. "But it sounds crazy. It's dismissed. It gets lost in a wash of other wild theories and guesses. The undead aim to keep it that way. Of all the thousands of theories that people spend their days blogging about, the zombies are only concerned about one. They aim to ensure no reporter ever truly investigates it. So how do they do that? One effective approach is to entrap interested reporters and literally kill them. That's what our intelligence said 'Francis' was doing. If you haven't figured it out yet, he was going to drive you somewhere secluded and put a bullet in your head. Why do you think he had that gun?"

Jessica had no response.

"You, and apparently your friend, were to be 'taken care of' because you took the bait—the kind of bait they send out to reporters on a regular basis," the woman continued. "Whoever follows up is killed."

Jessica suddenly felt green and stupid all over again.

"When we—through our monitoring and counterintelligence—realized what the undead were planning today, we decided you had to be saved," the woman continued. "I hope you'll appreciate that we took a serious risk in doing so. And that one of us is not here anymore because of it."

Jessica looked up into the faces of the remaining trio. They all looked genuinely anguished. Jessica hung her head.

"There's still so much I don't understand," Jessica said quietly. "Why here? At a political convention in Cleveland?"

"Our organization has been watching several key figures in contemporary American politics recently for signs of undead behavior," the long-haired woman said cautiously. "We haven't wanted to believe it could be true—that they could ever get so close—but what happened this morning brings us nearer than ever to confirming it."

"Are you saying the politicians at the convention are zombies?" Jessica asked.

The sentence felt preposterous even as she said it.

The trio nodded back at her seriously.

"Which ones?" Jessica asked.

"We don't yet know," the woman said seriously.

"But . . . but . . . surely, people would be able to figure it out," Jessica protested.

Suddenly, the quiet young woman with the short hair spoke up.

"Oh, *would* they?" she barked sarcastically. "Are you some kind of expert on zombies or something? Is that what you are? An expert on zombies who was so stupid she fell for the dumbest trick in the book?"

"Now, now, Trish," said the woman with the long black hair.

And so Jessica knew at least one of their names.

The lineman spoke.

"Tell me, miss," he began. "Just what *do* you know about zombies?"

Jessica looked back and forth. It seemed so obvious. Everyone knew about zombies, right?

"Err, they're the walking dead," she eventually answered.

"You've got that much," said the man. "What else?"

"They eat people," Jessica said. "Maybe their brains, especially?"

"Yes," he said. "Go on."

"They're rotting and stupid and they smell bad. They moan. They can't run. They can't read. They're kind of in a stupor all the time. They—what? Why are you all giving me that look?"

"Those things haven't been true for a long time," the lineman informed her. "Those are stereotypes—fictions the zombies themselves perpetuate. It's not the truth. Not anymore."

"Zombies have changed," the woman with the long hair said. "They've evolved. Gotten better. Do you know about the Red Queen—the evolutionary theory? It's based on stuff by that Alice in Wonderland guy. The Red Queen must run as fast as she can just to stay in the same place. In the natural world, the same thing happens. There are plains in Africa where lions have been chasing gazelles for thousands and thousands of years. But each year the lions get a little faster, and so do the gazelles. The slowest lions don't catch enough gazelles to eat, so they don't pass on their slow genes. Same with the gazelles. Only the fast ones live. It's like an arms race that never ends. And it results in very fast lions and very fast gazelles."

"So what does this have to do with—" Jessica began.

"Zombies?" said the woman. "Everything. Zombies that are slow and dumb and stumbly have tended to get killed by humans over the years. Humans were also evolving and improving. First, whenever zombies popped up, we fought them with branches and rocks. Then with swords and bows and arrows. Now we fight them with sniper rifles that can pick them off at damn near 1,000 yards away. As the centuries have gone by, we've gotten better. But the thing is, *so have they.* Doing an impression of a zombie by sticking your arms out and drooling is like impersonating a human by dressing in animal skins and carrying a wooden club. It hasn't been that way for a long, long time."

"How?" asked Jessica. "How does a zombie 'advance' exactly?"

"The strains of the zombie virus that get passed on are the ones that allow them to remain sharper, faster, cleverer. That let them pass as human. They walk, think, talk. See, zombies have developed their own camouflage."

"I don't understand," Jessica said. "If they do all those things, are they even still zombies anymore?"

The lineman spoke up.

"Yes," he said. "They're still zombies because they still want to eat people. And they're still undead. They can't be killed through normal means. Those core traits never change."

"That's right," agreed the woman with the long hair. "A lion who lived 100,000 years ago would come off as a handicapped cur compared to the lions of today. But know what they'd both still have in common? A taste for gazelle. That *never* leaves."

"So the zombies can blend in with regular people?"

"Some of them, yes," the woman said. "To catch them out, you normally have to find them engaging in something unique to their species."

"You mean something like this?" Jessica said.

She reached into her pocket and carefully withdrew the photograph of the Tycoon eating a human hand.

The woman accepted it. She studied it for a long time without speaking, then showed it to the other members of her trio.

"Wow," said Trish. "This is what they used to bait you? Brave on their part. I'll give them that."

"That looks real," the lineman said. "Like, really real."

"Some of us have suspected *him* for a long time, but never had any proof," Trish said. "Maybe it should have been more obvious to us. The loping gate. The orange makeup. The dislike for reading."

"Contemporary zombies *can* read," the lineman explained to Jessica. "It's just not pleasant for them."

The long haired woman began to pace.

"If this is real . . . if this is real . . . oh my God."

"There have been rumors of gatherings at his estate in Florida," the lineman said. "We've seen spotty intelligence before. Never something this good. A few blurry cell phone videos of people eating people. A dinner table laid out with something vaguely humanoid—and *still moving*—on a serving tray in the center. But it's always looked fake. Like something some of his political enemies cooked up for a laugh. I'll be damned if it looks that way now."

"We need to think about how to use this to our advantage," the woman with the long hair said. "This could be the opportunity to strike a very big blow."

It suddenly seemed to Jessica that the Knights had much to discuss. She began to stand up.

"Whoa," said the lineman. "Where do you think you're going?"

"Look, I'm a reporter and I have a job to do," Jessica said. "I appreciate everything, but I need to get back to where I'm supposed to be. Unless you want my paper filing a missing persons report on me? The cops tracing my cell phone location history? Do you want that?"

The woman with the long hair approached Jessica. Stood close.

"I think you understand what we did for you today, and what it just cost us," she said. "I know you're a reporter, but I also hope you understand that I can't let you write about this."

"I'm not going to," Jessica said. "I'm not going to write about *you*. But what about the fact that the next President of the United States might be a zombie? I can't ignore that."

"I won't ask you to," the woman said. "Write what you have to write *based on your own research*. But not based on this. Not on what just happened."

"Fine," Jessica said. "I can do my own digging. It should be easy, given that now I know what to look for."

"All right then," the woman said. "Also . . . don't go anywhere, okay?"

Jessica was unsure what this meant.

"Where would I go?" Jessica asked. "I'm in Cleveland until the convention is over."

"Good," said the long haired woman. "Because we may just be in touch . . ."

THE FAKE NEWSMAN

Tim Fife and his associates sat in a secluded corner of the hotel lobby, huddling confidentially. A nervous excitement ran through each one of them. Ryan's nervous tics sometimes jostled his belly as though he were being physically electrified. For all three, Tim's tale had been revelatory because it confirmed that, at long last, one of their more remarkable leads had proved . . . if not precisely *true* then at least . . . something!

"They just came and took her?" Ryan asked, vibrating steadily.

Tim nodded.

"They pulled out their machine guns, killed Francis, and threw her into the back of the SUV."

"Any idea why?" Ryan pressed further.

"That's what I'm trying to figure out," Tim said. "Maybe they worked for the zombies. Could be they were there to take out a Knight of Romero, and Jessica and I just got in the way."

"'Worked for the zombies' is a phrase I never thought I'd hear," offered Dan, leaning back in his chair. "What do they pay you in? Severed ears or something?"

Dan seemed positively jealous of Tim's encounter. Probably because it had involved the proximity to extreme violence.

"Look, I'll be the first to admit we're in uncharted territory here," Tim said. "There could still be a lot we don't know."

"There most *definitely* is," opined Ryan. "Like, why did they abduct Jessica and not you?"

Dan said: "You mean other than the fact she's good looking, much easier to carry, and comes from a more prestigious news organization?"

"Yeah," Ryan said. "Other than that."

"Isn't she also from a rich family?" Dan said.

They turned to Tim.

"Yeah," Tim said, "but something tells me this wasn't kidnappers randomly interrupting the Knights of Romero. That's crazy. It has to be connected."

"I've still got my old emails archived from people claiming to know about the Knights," Dan said. "I'll pull them right away. They were never leads I followed up on. Now I wish I had."

Dan was too excited by these developments to remain still any longer. He rose from his chair and began to pace around the corner of the lobby.

"Maybe we should go back there and look for clues," he continued. "We might find something useful. We can at least take pictures for the article."

"The article?" said Tim.

"Yeah," said Dan. "The one you're obviously going to file, like *immediately,* giving TruthTeller the world exclusive verifying the Knights of Romero."

Tim nodded and spoke carefully.

"Maybe I shouldn't be the one to go back to that bar. The cops will be looking for me. The people in the bar would have ID'd me, right? Hell, my neck brace got left at the scene of the crime."

"With your DNA all over it," Ryan said.

Tim looked at him defensively.

"What? You drool. I can't be the first one to tell you that."

"Anyhow," Tim continued, "when we file the story, I want to make sure we have all of the facts straight. I want to get some confirmations before this goes any farther."

Ryan and Dan looked at each other. What Tim was describing was not the TruthTeller way. (*That* way was to shout news the very moment you had it—before it had been fact-checked in any manner—in screaming red headlines across the face of the page, insinuating and implying connections to every person possible.)

"Normally, I *would* want to get something up on the site immediately," Tim said, "but these are not normal times. And I don't just mean that I was present at the abduction and probably have police looking for me."

"There's no probably about it," Ryan said, holding up his phone. "The *Plain Dealer* says two Caucasian males are dead after a shooting at Kidd's Bar, and a third, possibly injured, fled on foot. Slowly."

"It *does not* say slowly," Tim insisted.

Ryan retracted the phone before Tim could get a closer look.

"Anyway, this is a national political convention," Tim continued. "This is different. If there are powerful people connected to this shit, they might actually be in town. Physically here. I want to take this as far us the chain as we can before we pull the trigger. If we let on that we know what happened today—and have a reporter who was personally involved—people are going to be a lot more cautious. We want them to be the opposite."

Ryan and Dan both opened their mouths to object. Tim cut them off before they could.

"Look, I'm as sick as you are of the f-word. Being called 'fake news' all the time is grating as hell. But how do we shake that? One way is to break real stories that are too true for anybody to ignore! We run what we've got now . . . we've got a lot of sensation, and a lot of pieces that don't fit together."

"Yeah, and also a lot of clicks and views and advertising dollars," Ryan sputtered. "Can you imagine how much the boss would like that?"

"Yes, I can," said Tim. "But I can also imagine how much the boss would like it if we sat on this story for a few days, did some investigative reporting, and broke the biggest political story of the year. That would do more than get views. That would transform TruthTeller forever."

Ryan and Dan seemed to consider this seriously. Sensing he was making progress, Tim continued.

"And if we could connect this to someone here at the convention—if we could really do that, and uncover proof of what's going on—well . . . I'm not saying we'd win awards, but we'd win awards. All these 'real' journalists with their fancy degrees and corrupt globalist bosses would lose, and we would win. They wouldn't *want* to give us the Pulitzer. But they would *have* to. Think about how good that would feel."

Ryan and Dan did. Irrepressible, irresistible smiles crept across their faces. Forcing your way into the club that had excluded and derided you for so long was a deep, primal fantasy, not lost on any of these gentlemen.

"The other thing we have to think about is Jessica's safety," Tim said. "I know you don't like her. I know you think she's the establishment and so forth, but she's really not a bad person."

"The story in the *Plain Dealer* doesn't even mention her," Ryan said. "Do you think the cops know she was even there?"

"I'm not sure," said Tim. "I don't think anybody in the bar saw her being taken away. I was the only witness."

"Well then, we need to tell the cops," Ryan said.

"*You* do," Tim said. "Anonymously. We'll call it in from a hotel phone in a spot where there's not a security camera. I'll give you all the details I remember. But . . ."

"But what?" Ryan asked.

"But something tells me if anybody is going to figure out what happened to her, it's going to be us," said Tim, a faraway look in his eye. "If they wanted to kill her, she's already dead. If they kidnapped her to get a ransom from her wealthy parents, then that'll come out on its own. But I don't feel like it's any of those things. I feel like there's something going on here that the police aren't even going to see. I think it's up to us."

"What's the next step for the story, then?" Ryan asked. "I mean, the kind of reporting you're suggesting . . . is not what we typically do. You might have to show us how."

"Don't worry," Tim said confidently. "That shouldn't be a problem. I learned a thing or two before I dropped out of J-school. And I know just where we're going to start."

THE TYCOON

They were in some sort of boardroom. Tastefully appointed. Well-lit. Leather chairs around a long polished table. Flat screen televisions set into the walls. The Tycoon stood at the head of the table, like a man making a presentation at a business meeting.

"In a way, we are not divorced entirely from the traits of your savior," the Tycoon said.

The Governor nodded back. It was nearly all that he could do. This was because the Tycoon had had him tied to a chair.

The Tycoon was accustomed to making this presentation to potential initiates. However, in almost all cases, he did so when he believed they were willing to join his organization. The Tycoon had seldom needed to make much of a case for the *benefits* of joining. And he had *never*—that he remembered—had to make his case to a person he thought might be actively resistant.

But today was different. The Tycoon was not necessarily inviting the Governor to join the legion of the undead, but he was asking at least for the man to make peace with it. The Tycoon believed that the Governor might be a hard case when it came to bringing him around, but he did not think the task would be impossible.

Nonetheless, restraint had been a necessary precaution.

The Governor's disturbing smile had never left his face. It stood there even now. His expression said that he was still willing to allow that all of this had been some strange misunderstanding. If the Tycoon would only have his men loosen the restraints and let him go, this could all be overlooked . . .

"I apologize that we needed to tie you up," said the Tycoon, acknowledging the Governor. "Have no doubt. You will be released in time. We just need to get a few things out of the way first."

The Governor continued to smile. He would do almost anything to be the next Vice President. The Tycoon hoped he would do this as well.

"As I was saying, your own savior died and rose again," the Tycoon said. "He instructed his followers to eat the flesh of the dead. To drink his blood in remembrance of him. These are all established facts. So you see, we are, already, playing in the same . . . ballpark."

The Tycoon had never attended religious services on any regular basis. When he tried to address audiences of the faithful in their own lexicon, words often failed him.

"What ballpark is that?" the Governor asked. "I don't understand."

The Tycoon nodded.

"I find that demonstrations can work wonders," he said. "They're much better than words. Say it with words, and people might not understand you. But say it with action? That gets them every time."

The Tycoon stepped to the side of the large conference table where an intercom waited.

"Bring it in!" he called, depressing a button.

"Yessir," an unseen voice came back.

The Governor smiled curiously.

Moments later, the side door opened. Two men in suits wheeled in a large clear tank of water. It was big enough for a man to fit inside. The Governor—who had been to Las Vegas a time or two (for political conferences only, of course)—was reminded of the tank into which a magician on the Strip had submerged himself. And like the ones in Vegas, this tank appeared to have been built as some sort of showpiece. The edges were gilt and the top had been emblazoned with the Tycoon's family name. Ambulatory stairs were wheeled in next, and placed beside the tank.

As the Governor looked on, the Tycoon began to disrobe.

"Think of this as a baptism," the Tycoon said, kicking away his shoes and pulling off his socks. "I usually don't do this personally anymore. But for you, I'll make an exception."

One of the men in suits brought out a silver tray and held it up to the Tycoon. On it was something small and flat and rubbery. The Tycoon nodded to the attendant, who picked it up from the tray. It was a bathing cap. The attendant carefully placed it onto the Tycoon's head, making sure to get every part of his hair inside. (The bathing cap was also emblazoned with his logo.) By the time the cap was firmly in place, the

Tycoon had stripped down to a pair of gold lamé boxer shorts. The attendant next handed the Tycoon a tablet computer that had been placed inside a tight fitting plastic bag. The Tycoon grabbed it, and waved his hand to show that now they were through. He had everything he needed.

The attendants departed, and the Tycoon began to climb the ladder. The Governor still looked on, rapt and smiling. Soon, the Tycoon stood at the top of the tank. He dangled his toes into the water, testing the temperature.

"You may not be able to see your own watch, the way your hands are tied," the Tycoon observed. "There's a clock against the wall. Count inside of your head if you begin to think it might be fast."

With that, the Tycoon slowly lowered himself into the tank. There was a soft splash as the Tycoon's head passed underneath the waterline and stayed there. The clear walls of the tank allowed the Tycoon and the Governor to make eye contact, which they did. The Tycoon waved to the Governor, then pointed once again to the clock on the wall. The Governor, dumbfounded, simply nodded back.

At which point the Tycoon turned his attention to the tablet in the plastic bag. He turned it on and began depressing buttons. If the Governor had not known better, he would have sworn that the man was browsing the web and Tweeting.

The Governor was so confused that he did not think about the clock on the wall until two full minutes had passed. Only at that time did he begin to discern these goings-on as more than simply odd. For one thing, the Tycoon did not appear to be breathing. No bubbles escaped around his nostrils. Was this indeed some magic trick, the Governor wondered. But the Tycoon had never given the slightest hint of being the kind of man who needed to perform for his guests. What was more, he did not seem like a man with the patience to study an art form like prestidigitation.

The Governor watched the second hand of the clock on the wall and tried holding his own breath. He could hardly get past a minute and ten seconds before the need to breathe became unbearable and he started gasping. Astonished, the Governor kept timing. The Tycoon distractedly typed and scrolled on his phone. Minutes passed.

Five minutes.

Six minutes.

Ten.

Twelve.

When a full fifteen had passed, the Tycoon finally looked up from his tablet. He knocked on the glass to make sure he had the Governor's attention. He gestured over to the clock. Horrified and confused, the Governor nodded enthusiastically to say that, yes, the Tycoon was making his point.

Moments later, as if on cue, the suited attendants reappeared. They carried a tray piled high with towels and fresh clothing. Placing this bounty onto the conference table, they ascended the portable ladder and helped the Tycoon climb out of the water. They toweled him off and dressed him in a new suit of clothes. The Tycoon's omnipresent makeup had come off during his submersion. This gave him a stark, cadaverous aspect that made the Governor feel as though he did not like to look at him.

One of the attendants opened a case filled with orange foundation and gave the Tycoon a good dusting. It was uncanny how quickly this base coat restored the Tycoon to fighting shape. The Governor blinked, hardly believing his eyes.

Next, the Tycoon pulled one of the leather office chairs out from the conference table. He slowly and deliberately wheeled it over to where the Governor was tied. Then he sat.

The Tycoon did not speak for a very long time.

"You're breathing very rarified air right now, do you know that?" the Tycoon said after this pause. "Very few people have seen what you've just seen. And a lot of them are dead."

"Speaking of breathing . . . how did you do that?" the Governor asked. "I haven't seen that trick outside of Vegas."

"I did what I always do," the Tycoon replied. "Which is not breathe."

"You don't *breathe*?" the Governor asked, aghast.

"I suck in air to talk, because that's the only way *to* talk," the Tycoon clarified. "But I don't have to do it. Not like you do. I'm different. Special. Now, to return to what I was saying . . . Most people who have seen what you've just seen are applying for the most selective level of membership at our resort. At that level, after the application has been tendered, there are only two possibilities. You can join or you can die. You, Governor, are the first man who will not be required to follow either of those outcomes. But it is important that you understand just what is happening here."

"But I . . . I don't think that I do," he said. "What *is* happening here? Why don't you breathe? What is going on?"

The Governor's assured smile fell away. He began to vibrate in his chair, struggling against the restraints. The Tycoon shook his head in frustration.

"I don't know if presidents always tell vice presidents everything," the Tycoon said, "but we are our own men. We each do what we need to do. Maybe all you need to understand for the moment . . . is that I'm going to be your boss, and I don't breathe. Maybe later I can tell you more. Would you *like* that?"

"Yes," said the Governor, seeming to grow calmer. "That . . . and also to be untied from this chair."

"All things in due time," the Tycoon answered. "All things in due time."

THE REPORTER

Jessica arrived back at the arena later that afternoon. Having texted George something to the effect of her interviews with local voters taking longer than expected, she took her time milling through the convention hallways. They were more crowded now. Media representatives from all across the world were arriving, as were convention delegates and staff. Jessica made a beeline for the section of the convention housing the worst of the conference rooms—the ones holding TruthTeller and its ilk.

Jessica found the doorway she wanted and stepped furtively through. There were now perhaps ten people from different outlets inside the dingy room—chatting, milling about, and typing on laptops. Jessica looked them over. After only a few seconds, someone cried: "Found her!"

Jessica glanced up to see a very large man with half a powdered doughnut hanging out of his mouth. His eyes were wide, and he was pointing as if he had seen a ghost. Nearby, a bald man with cheap tattoos spun around with an almost-violent intensity. He also pointed, as if confirming the spectral sighting.

"Jessica Smith," he whispered. "That's her."

A couple of other people in the conference room also looked, not understanding what the fuss was about. It was starting to be embarrassing.

Jessica looked around for Tim, but couldn't find him. Then he stepped through a side door that linked their humble confines to an adjacent media room. He was carrying three coffees in a cardboard holder.

Tim looked at Ryan and Dan, and said: "What are you guys on about?"

Then he saw Jessica and almost dropped his coffees.

"Jessica!" he called. "Are you all right? What happened to you? We were just about to call the cops."

He set the coffees on a table occupied by two college bloggers—who both said "Hey!" in protest—and hurried over.

"Are you hurt at all?" Tim asked. "You saw what they did to my neck brace."

"I'm fine," she said. "It's a long story, but I'm okay. I came here looking for you, actually. Is there someplace we can go and talk? Some things have happened that I need to tell you about."

"Absolutely," Tim said. "There's an empty conference room just down the corridor."

They filed out into the hallway. Jessica noticed that Ryan and Dan had followed. She was on the point of saying something, when Tim whispered: "They know. They're the only ones."

This made Jessica uneasy, but she decided she'd have to roll with it.

Down the hall, they found a conference room that was indeed empty save for a couple of cleaning staff vacuuming the carpet and disinterestedly arranging chairs. They ducked inside. The noise of the industrial-sized vacuum cleaner helped to hide their voices.

"First of all, have you written anything, yet?" Jessica asked. "Published it, I mean. There's nothing on your website?"

"No," Tim said. "*These two* wanted to run something right away, of course. But I realized we needed to work on the bigger story. What *is* the bigger story, by the way? What happened to you?"

"This is some spy versus spy shit," Jessica said. "You know how cops pose as hitmen to catch people trying to bump off their spouses? That guy Francis was posing as the Knights of Romero so he could find people looking for the Knights of Romero . . . and kill them. That gun he had in his belt? That was for us."

"Who were those people who hauled you into their SUV?" Tim asked.

"They were the real Knights," Jessica said, and she began to tell Tim (and Ryan and Dan) the rest of the story. She left out no detail.

"This is amazing," Tim said as Jessica finished.

The arena staff finished vacuuming the room and stacking the chairs. The workers exited, leaving the four members of the media to speak more openly. Jessica sat down in one of the empty chairs.

"This is potentially connected to so many things!" Ryan interjected excitedly. "The Bilderberg Group. The Knights Templar. And what's George Soros's position on zombies? He's *got* to have one."

"As corrupt as most politicians are, maybe having a zombie in charge of things wouldn't be so bad," mused Dan. "At least he'd be predictable. Slow, but predictable."

"So what do we do with this information?" Tim asked. "What *can* we do?"

Jessica stood up again and carefully surveyed the empty conference room for any sign of a crack in the cheap, mobile divider wall that might allow someone to listen in.

"If a major-party candidate is a zombie, we need to prove it," Jessica said. "We're going to need a lot of evidence, and it will have to be really solid. I almost . . . I almost wish this wasn't happening."

Jessica suddenly looked a bit ill. Her face fell, and her shoulders slumped forward. Tim hadn't seen Jessica in a couple of years, but he'd *never* seen her like this. She genuinely looked as though she might cry.

"Hey," he said, mustering the bravery to provide some comforting hoverhand just above her shoulder. "You've been through a lot. Most people would have a full-on breakdown if they were kidnapped in a shootout like that. Don't push yourself."

"It's not that," Jessica said between sniffles. "It's the story itself."

"It's okay," Tim assured her. "This isn't a bad thing. It's the scoop of a lifetime! When I was telling the guys about this before, we were all saying how big this is going to be. We'll win awards."

Jessica gave Tim an annoyed glance.

"Maybe this is the part of J-school you dropped out for," she said. "But the bigger the claim, the more proof you need. The more evidence. Do you realize what we have to do now? A photo's not going to cut it. We'll need more. A lot more. TruthTeller can run whatever it wants. And if you get something wrong, your readers are quick to forget and forgive. If someone threatens to sue you, you claim it was all satire any-way—and that you weren't really doing journalism. You were playing a character. But *I am doing journalism!* Papers like the one I work for have reputations that go back 150 years. We fact check it when somebody says the sun came up today. And you know why? Because when we're wrong—and we *have* been wrong—countries go to war. People die. *Really big shit* happens. On top of all of that, I am brand-fucking-new. It'd be one thing if I was a senior editor with gray hair and 30 years of experience. But this time last year, I was reporting on what local bars were opening and which galleries had art shows."

"Plenty of young reporters have broken big stories," Dan barked.

Dan's loud voice jarred Tim so much that he actually touched Jessica's bare shoulder for a moment. Appearing aghast and terrified, Tim quickly shrank away. Jessica hardly noticed.

"We're going to need evidence solid enough to convince one of the biggest news outlets in the world to risk its reputa-tion," she said. "And I just . . . I don't know if I know how to do that."

"It's okay," Tim said reassuringly. "Between the two of us, I'm pretty sure we can work something out."

Jessica was unsure what Tim meant by this. Was he just saying whatever he thought she might like to hear? But no. When she looked at him, something in his expression seemed genuine.

"What do you mean?" she asked.

"We can do a two-pronged approach," he said. "I've thought about it, and I think it will work! Look, the candi-date and his party hate your outlet, but they love mine—not necessarily because we support him, but because we ask the hard questions about his opponent—about *her*—that you in the mainstream media *won't* ask."

"That's because your questions are nonsense taken from internet memes," she found herself replying automatically.

Ryan and Dan both bristled, but managed to stay silent.

"Be that as it may," Tim quickly continued, "his side is going to be looking for support from us. How the hell do you think an outfit like ours got passes to this convention? It's because they know they can count on us for flattering pieces. With you, they expect a poisoned dagger to be hidden behind each line you write. But with *us*, they certainly don't expect questions they'll have to think carefully about. Questions that might reveal something. And that's where we'll get them. When they're not thinking."

Jessica's head seemed to clear. Tim was making sense.

"So you're *really* ready to do this?" Jessica asked. "Remember, once they realize what you're up to, you're going to get shunned by the campaign. You're going to risk sacrificing all the access you've built. Can *I* trust *you* to do that?"

Tim looked genuinely hurt. Now that Jessica looked, the whole TruthTeller staff did.

"What you can trust, is that we all care about the truth," Tim said. "What you can trust, is that we give a damn. It's never been any other way. If we seem like we're harder on *her*—and not so hard on *him*—it's because she lets on like she never has anything to hide. Which is nonsense. Which is bullshit. With *him,* you know what he's done. He's not smart enough to do anything too evil—just run-of-the-mill stuff— and he's certainly not smart enough to cover it up. But with her . . . Let's just say there's room to wonder. *That's* why we're hard on her. If I'm being honest, yes, I still think she's a smart criminal who is connected to globalists and hiding a bunch of things. It's just that it looks now as if *he* might be a smart criminal too. Or at least smarter than he lets on."

Jessica nodded. She would have never believed that the first big risk of her career would involve utterly trusting a group of conspiracy theory neckbeards to be fair and balanced, but now it seemed she would be doing exactly that. She tried to steel herself. Something told her the great wheel was about to go into motion. When and where it would stop was anybody's guess.

THE FAKE NEWSMAN

As Ryan and Dan looked on, Tim leaned back in his chair and dialed Tom Ellerman. Jessica looked on too. They waited while it rang.

Tom Ellerman was officially an assistant deputy communications manager for the Tycoon's campaign. He was about Tim's age, was from Southern Illinois, and had begun his career working in a senator's D.C. office. He had joined the campaign only in recent months, as part of Jay McNelis's team.

Whatever Tom Ellerman's official duties might have been listed as on his LinkedIn page, his real job was to deal with entities like TruthTeller. The fringes. The bottom of the barrel.

"Hello?" Ellerman's voice came back after the fourth ring.

Tim waited a moment to make sure it wasn't voicemail. Ellerman's demeanor and tone were so restrained that even in spontaneous moments he sounded pre-recorded.

"Tom, it's Tim Fife . . . with TruthTeller?"

"Yes, go ahead," Ellerman said.

"Look, we're at the convention, and just trying to get our stories lined up for the week," Tim began.

"We're going to release the speakers scheduled very soon, but I can't give you any previews if that's what this is about," the communications professional said. "I mean . . . *maybe* I can tell you that fans of 1980's sitcoms will not be disappointed by one of our surprise mid-week speakers. But then . . . I've already said too much."

"Uh, that's real exciting," Tim said. "It's actually not about that."

"How are the doughnuts?" Ellerman asked. "I was told we should have you guys well-stocked with doughnuts and coffee."

"The doughnuts are great," Tim said. "Really, top notch."

"Then what else can I do for you at the moment?" Ellerman said.

"It's about your boss, actually . . ." Tim said.

"What about him?" Ellerman replied. "He's travelling at the moment. And the future president is with the future vice president in Florida."

"Yeah, so we're kind of thinking it'd be neat to do a piece about how *he's* the real story . . . your boss, that is. Sort of the story *behind* the story. The candidates have been done to death. Your boss hasn't. We'd like to do a profile. Maybe snag a couple of minutes with him early this week?"

"You want to interview Jay?" Ellerman said, sounding surprised.

He had put no emphasis on the word "you," but Tim knew it was there.

Outlets like TruthTeller were expected to gratefully reproduce press releases from the campaign practically verbatim and call it a day. The only favor they could count on someone like Tom Ellerman granting was to issue an official "no comment" on one of the more outrageous accusations against the Tycoon's opponent. Asking for an interview with senior staff was not something TruthTeller did. Jay McNelis went on Sunday political shows, attended million-dollar fundraisers, and he did interviews with outlets that had audiences stretching into the hundreds of thousands or millions. Without being explicit, Eller was asking Tim why he suddenly thought he got to wear the "big boy" pants.

Tim had to make the case that his pants had changed.

"See, this week we're going to be doing a special series on gun violence," Tim began. "Specifically, on the potential for gun violence in and around the convention. I think you know how concerned some people are about security, with so many passionate supporters of open carry in the area."

"The campaign has issued repeated statements on there being no higher priority than the safety of the citizens and attendees during the convention," Ellerman replied. "I can resend those emails if you need. The Cleveland Police have assured us that—"

"Sorry to interrupt you, but I'm not talking about that," Tim said. "I don't know if you heard about the shooting at Kidd's Bar this morning? The place out in the suburbs? It was maybe random gun violence, maybe gang related, maybe something else. Anyhow, I'd like to talk to Jay McNelis about that. You can tell him I was *personally present.*"

There was a very long pause.

"You want to talk about a *shooting at a bar* with the person in charge of this campaign . . . during the most important week of the campaign?" Ellerman replied.

It sounded to Tim that Ellerman might be close to hanging up.

"All I can tell you is I think this will be important to Jay," Tim continued. "I'm just asking you to pass along the request."

There was another very long pause. For a moment, Tim thought Ellerman actually might *have* ended the call. Then he heard the man breathing. Tim's request was so bold and so strange that the communications pro was afraid he might be missing something. Either that, or wondering if Tim Fife had just plain gone crazy.

"Yeah, okay . . ." Ellerman managed absently.

Tim's eyes widened, and a smile rose to his lips.

"Is that a yes?" Tim asked gently.

"Uh-huh," Ellerman confirmed. "I'll pass on the request. If Jay wants to do it, I'll let you know."

"That's great, Tom. Thanks so much."

Tim ended the call. He looked up at the group and pumped his fist.

"What just happened?" asked Dan, running his tattooed hands over his bald head in confusion.

"Let me explain," said Tim. "The way things went down behind that bar this morning was a surprise to everybody involved. It was a fuck up for all sides. Nothing went to plan. The operatives who posed as the Knights of Romero—who lured us to the meeting with Francis—they have to be confused as hell right now. What happened to me? What happened to Jessica? How much do we know? And I'm sure that the candidate's status as a zombie—and the force protecting him—is kept to a pretty tight circle. The first thing I want to find out is if Jay McNelis is in that circle. Does his whole campaign know? Do his closest handlers?"

Jessica nodded as though this made sense.

"If McNelis is in the inner circle, he probably got briefed on what went down this morning," Jessica said.

"No probably about it," Tim said. "He'll know for sure."

"And then he calls you right back," Jessica said.

"Uh huh," said Tim. "Or he sends someone to wack us in our sleep tonight."

Dan glanced around nervously.

"I'm kidding, Dan," Tim clarified. "At least I think I am."

"And if he *doesn't* know what's going on . . . ?" Jessica said.

"Then nothing," said Tim. "He doesn't bother to call us back, and he wonders why the hell we're bothering him about a shooting in a bar parking lot. But in either case, we'll know what he knows."

At that moment, Jessica's phone buzzed. The three men looked on as she took it out of her purse and brought it up to her face.

"It's not the campaign," she said. "It's a text from my boss. He's wondering where I am. I guess I need to get back to him for a while. I'll keep in touch if anything else happens. Let's circle back tonight sometime?"

"Yeah, that sounds good," Tim said. "I . . . I'm glad you're all right, Jessica. I was really worried."

"Thanks Tim," she said with a smile. "I'm glad you're okay too. When you went face down like that. Ouch!"

As Tim watched, Jessica collected her things and made her way back out into the convention center hallway. There she merged with the steadily swelling flow of reporters and dele-gates, and was soon out of view.

THE TYCOON

Time was short.

The Tycoon and the Governor both understood the need to return to their campaign obligations sooner rather than later. The world would come knocking. Or at least Jay McNelis.

But there was *always* time for a meal.

Accordingly, the Tycoon and the Governor (now freed from his restraints) sat together in the Tycoon's private, pri-vate dining room. There were many private dining rooms, but this was the extra-private one. Double private. The one that very few staff at the club even knew existed. (The Tycoon had long despised the title-inflation that seemed to beset the places and institutions that strived to cater to the upper classes. Exec-utive lounges were filled with persons who were definitely *not* executives. First class cabins contained passengers who were not first class people. V.I.P. areas were always bluffing when it came to the "I" part. And, most assuredly, private rooms had a way of being accessible to just about anybody. Hence, his private, private spaces on the property. If it took using the same word twice to get the idea across, the Tycoon was happy to do it.)

The walls of the private, private dining room were gold. As were the chairs. As was the molding that ran around the doorframe (which was, itself, also gold). The only thing that was not gilded was the dark dining table which ran the entire length of the room. There were only two place settings at the moment. One for the Tycoon, and the other for the Governor. They had been seated at opposite ends, a comically large distance apart.

The Governor looked down the table and smiled politely.

The Tycoon had been told that it was be politically undesirable to replace a vice presidential choice after the convention. But he trusted his advisors about as far as he could throw them. If the Governor proved resistant, the Tycoon was willing to replace him with extreme prejudice. A part of him kind of hoped that that would happen. The man looked delicious.

One of the golden doors opened and an attendant entered carrying a silver tray covered with a cloche. He placed it in front of the Governor and removed the top. Revealed beneath was a filet cooked to perfection, and sides of potatoes and creamed spinach.

"This looks wonderful . . . but I may not have much appetite," the Governor said. "What I saw before—you in that water tank—it's got me feeling a bit at odds."

The Tycoon shrugged to say the Governor could eat or not, as he pleased.

"Are you going to have something?" the Governor asked. "I hope this isn't all for me."

"It's not," the Tycoon said.

The Governor forced himself to take up his knife and fork, and explore the meat that had been set before him.

The attendant walked to where the Tycoon was seated.

"We have several choices tonight, sir," the man said. "Though I'd like to recommend the wealthy Midwestern tourist. Young and lean. Vacationing alone. We can bring him in lightly sedated or—"

"No," the Tycoon said. "Please bring it as-is. This will be a learning experience for my friend, the Governor. I'd like everything to be as fresh as possible."

"Very good," the attendant said, and departed swiftly.

The Tycoon looked back down the table. His expression was stern and he did not smile. The Governor took a small bite of steak and chewed nervously.

"Do you know why I selected you as my running mate?" the Tycoon asked. "I don't mean the bullshit that McNelis talks about; how we 'counterbalance' one another, and so forth. Do you know the *real* reason?"

The Governor shook his head as he carefully chewed.

"When my advisors brought me the profiles of all the different candidates, you went to the top of the pile for one reason," the Tycoon said. "Now . . . there were some pretty prestigious people in those dossiers. Retired four-star generals. Fortune 500 CEOs. Senators. Yet you stood out above all of them—*all of them!*—for one reason alone. And that reason was your strong commitment to personal freedom."

The Governor, still anxious, smiled and nodded. Forced himself to spear a fingerling potato.

"You've made the Hoosier State a fine example of so many things," the Tycoon went on. "But your commitment to personal freedom stood you head and shoulders above the others. I mean . . . if I own a bakery in Muncie and I don't want to bake a cake for a gay wedding, I should be *free* to not do that. That's what you said. That's what you pushed for. And to your credit, Governor, I don't think your detractors realized that the door swings both ways. I should also be free to refuse cakes for weddings that *aren't* gay. I can refuse to bake cakes for straight weddings. Or for weddings entirely. What if

I don't like weddings at all? What if I don't like cake? What if I want to serve up *something else* entirely? Should I be charged as a bigot if that's the case? I think you'll agree, the notion's ridiculous."

The Governor chewed potato and nodded cautiously.

"You were selected because, when it comes to people's faith—and what faith dictates they should do, or *not do*—you said 'Hands off!' You said the government should stay out of that sphere entirely. That is why you are my running mate. That is why you are sitting here tonight in the private, private dining room."

The golden door opened, and the attendant reappeared once more. He set before the Tycoon a chef's knife roll, carefully unfurling it to reveal a gleaming set of blades. He also set before the Tycoon several implements that looked more at home in a carpenter's workshop than in a kitchen. There were mallets, hammers, and battery-powered saws—all polished to a gleam. When these items were satisfactorily arrayed, the attendant reached into his pocket and produced a white cloth square. The Tycoon stood and pushed away his chair. The attendant unfolded the cloth into a large apron which he placed over the Tycoon's suit, tying it tightly in the back.

The Governor said nothing. The attendant once more removed himself from the room.

"Personal freedom!" the Tycoon boomed. "The idea that the beliefs and practices of others should be allowed, not forbidden. That America is great because, here, you can do what you want, right? *Be* what you want. In the days ahead, our nation will have a choice to make. Do we want a country where people are regulated and restrained, or one where they are free?"

The Governor was, at core, a canny man. Though he nodded along at the Tycoon's words, something in the depths of his conscience told him that there was going to be a catch.

At that moment, the golden door to the private, private dining room opened yet again.

The Tycoon smiled.

"*Speaking* of people who are restrained . . ." he said through a wide grin.

The sight that came through the doorway seemed very strange to the Governor. His mouth hung open and his steak knife fell entirely from his hand, clattering against the marble floor. What entered the room reminded the Governor of footage of prisoners being held at Guantanamo Bay. The attendant pulled a man by a rope tied around his hands. The man wore a paper jumpsuit, emblazoned with the Tycoon's logo. He was blindfolded, and hearing protectors had been placed over his ears to render him deaf.

The man looked young and terrified. He was weeping a bit, and his nose ran steadily. He took the short, careful half-steps of the blinded. He muttered as the attendant urged him on.

"Please . . ." the man whined. "My parents have money. I'm from Kenilworth. Do you know what that means? It means they can pay you a lot."

The Tycoon glanced at the Governor and grinned.

The Governor had gone white as a sheet, and was eyeing the gold door on the far side of the dining room, opposite the Tycoon. Fight-or-flight had set in. The man wanted to bolt. He rose to his feet.

"Don't even *think about it!*" the Tycoon barked. "If you do that, it is over for you."

The Governor hesitated.

"Leave now, and it ends. All of it. You can go back home and finish up your term, then be president of Purdue University for a while, then die in obscurity. Is *that* what you want? Governor, at this moment, your place in history stands on the edge of a knife."

As if to emphasize his point, the Tycoon selected a ten-inch chef's knife from the collection and swung it like a sword.

With what was clearly great effort, the Governor forced himself to take his seat. An involuntary tic began to appear in his left cheek. He looked like a man trying his best not to scream or vomit. It seemed likely that he might do both.

"That's better," said the Tycoon. "I need you to sit and watch, because I need you to know what I am all about. I need you to understand my culture of freedom. See what *I* need to be free to pursue."

With that, the Tycoon swung the knife. Few things in the Tycoon's life had ever required him to develop acumen or skill. The negative consequences of, say, not studying hard or not practicing diligently were limited by the massive empire he would (and did) inherit from his father. As a consequence, the Tycoon only developed skill in things he really and truly loved. To hold his attention, an activity needed to bring him real joy. And one thing that did that was feasting on the still-thinking brains of the living. Thus, to that project, the Tycoon had mustered a devotion and skill almost never seen in those cursed with massive inheritances.

The Governor realized many things as he watched the Tycoon working away with the blade. Chief among them was the fact that he was watching a master. The sight unfolding before him was murder, not doubt. Butchery. The kind of thing he had seen while making campaign stops at farms and slaughterhouses. That could not be denied.

At the same time, it was a masterpiece. There was and could be no other word for it. The skill with which the Tycoon ended the tourist from Kenilworth's life and deftly separated the head from the still-flailing body. The practiced motions that then carefully set the severed head on the table before him, like a chef working with a priceless truffle. The movement of the spike and the chef's mallet that cracked the tourist's skull with a few sure, strong strokes (the way a practiced islander might open a coconut). The delicate, measured work that cleared the bone fragments and opened the forehead to reveal the mushy pink prize within.

It was many things. Many the Governor did not like to watch (or even think about). But it was also a masterpiece.

To leave no doubt that this was a show of skill, the Tycoon finished by turning the severed, split head around so that it faced the Governor. This gave the prospective vice president an excellent view of his handiwork. The Governor understood that he was meant to look, and tried to widen his eyes. He succeeded, but the tic in his cheek became even more intense.

The Tycoon smiled, evidently pleased with himself. He grinned as he might for the cameras at the dedication of a new building with his name on it. Then he fell upon his prey.

The Governor was shocked all over again.

It was not the cannibalism that so unnerved the Governor. Rather, it was the speed of the transition from human to . . . something else. The five-star chef was shoveling down his own immaculate creation like a man who'd been starved for days. Even werewolves had transition periods, the Governor thought to himself. One moment they were normal men.

Then they sort of fell on the ground, rolled around howling, and grew hair and fangs. *Then* they began their nocturnal prowl as their newly animal-selves. But this had been instantaneous. One moment the man had been preparing his kill with practiced mastery, and now he was frantically forcing his mouth into the hole he'd bored in the skull. He was gobbling up the brains as if nothing else in the world existed, as if he'd forgotten himself entirely. He looked (and acted) like a yokel at a pie-eating contest. He had lost all control.

While in this state of abandon, the Tycoon uttered moaning noises that normal humans did not make. Mostly they were long nonsense syllables, but every once in a while something came out that sounded an awfully lot like "Braaaaaaaaaains."

When it seemed the Tycoon was completely lost in his reveries—and his line of sight blocked by the dislodged bits of skull—the Governor allowed himself a single shudder. He had never shuddered so hard in his life. Not from cold or terror. Not from anything.

After what seemed an interminable length of time to the Governor, the Tycoon appeared to finish his repast. His frantic gobbling slowed. The moaning ceased. He lifted himself away from the bloody, open head. He also seemed to *remember* himself. Humanity—or some semblance of it—flowed back into the Tycoon. The animal madness drained away.

The Tycoon stared down at the empty cranium and licked his lips meditatively. Then he gripped it by what remained of the scalp and held it aloft. Like Hamlet with Yorick, he inspected it carefully for any trace of brain he might have missed. He dangled the skull over the table and smacked it several times, like someone trying to get the last bit of ketchup from the bottom of the bottle. Yet no further brains were to be had. Accepting this with a kind of grim resignation, the Tycoon tossed the head away as though it were an empty beer can. It fell onto the large and expanding pool of blood already spreading across the marble floor.

As if on cue, the attendant arrived with with a wet vac and several plastic bags. The cleanup phase began.

The Tycoon slumped into his chair. He looked hard at the Governor's spastically twitching cheek, and absently wiped his mouth with his apron.

"Questions?" he said, raising his eyebrows.

The Governor made a small sputtering noise, but did not precisely speak.

The Tycoon looked down his nose at the man.

"Z-z-z-z-z-" the Governor sputtered more.

The Tycoon made circles with his hand to say "You're almost there . . ."

"Zombie!" the Governor cried, as if in great catharsis. "Zombie! Zombie! You are a zombie!"

The Tycoon smiled and leaned back in his chair. The attendant turned on one of the electric cleaning machines, so they were forced to raise their voices over it.

"Yes," the Tycoon shouted. "And you are one of very few people alive today who know that. Most of those are not even 'alive' in the real sense. They are also like me."

"Who?" said the Governor. "Who else?"

"Not the guy who washes your car or drycleans your suits," the Tycoon said. "Ours is an excusive club. We don't admit just anyone. We are leaders of men—though not, technically speaking, 'men' ourselves. We are those who were already great, and aspire to something even greater. And with one bite or one scratch, I could make you one of us."

The cleaning machine finished. The Governor looked, once more, as though he might run out the door.

"But I have no plans to do that," the Tycoon said quickly. "I do not believe it will be necessary. Yet it is important to me that you and I . . . *understand each other*. I value your commitment to personal freedom. Now you understand the way in which my kind require to be free. That's all we want. All any American wants. The freedom to be yourself. To do what you want to do without interference from the government."

"What about that man?" said the Governor, pointing to the headless body being hastily bundled in plastic. "What did *he* want?"

The Tycoon was surprised by this temerity. The Hoosier *would* press a few points after all. Very well.

"That man—whoever he was—also did exactly what he wanted to do," said the Tycoon. "He wanted to come to Florida and carouse on the beach and spend his father's money. So he did. And I wanted to eat his brains. So I did. I really don't see that any contradiction is involved. We were both free and unencumbered by the government. All is as it should be."

"You can pick up drifters and eat them to your heart's content already," said the Governor. "You don't need to be leader of the free world to do that."

The Tycoon tented his fingers thoughtfully.

"Zombies want brains . . . but we don't *only* want brains," he said. "We want *more brains*. There are enough of us now—in enough powerful places—that we've decided to do something about it. We have some big plans for this country. Big league, believe me. We want to do something really special. Really outstanding. It's gonna be really huge, and nobody's ever going to forget it."

The Tycoon had begun to speak in the generalities he used when publicly describing one of his real estate developments. The Governor noticed this. His mind searched for any way it could possibly bode well.

But the Tycoon only smiled back at him. The Governor realized he would get no answer this day. He might never get one at all.

The Tycoon had not had to properly explain himself in many years. Certainly, he did not feel the need to explain himself to so low a personage as the future vice president of the United States.

As the Governor sat quietly, the attendant moved away the body and wiped up the blood and brains that had spattered onto the table. The attendant excelled at his work. He had clearly done this many times before, and would probably do it many times again. He worked swiftly, and by the time he was finished, it was as though the murderous deed had never happened at all. Were it not for the cruor stains running down the Tycoon's face, someone chancing to join them in this golden dining room might have found nothing amiss.

The Governor was nearly able to convince himself that that was the case.

Nearly.

THE REPORTER

"Bob Hogson?"

"Yes," George said.

"Wants to talk to *me*?"

George hesitated.

"He was told he had a choice between the two of us, and he picked you," George eventually answered. "So be flattered, but just a little."

Jessica allowed herself to be.

Bob Hogson was a former governor of Arkansas who had run for president several times, never advancing beyond the primaries. He had been bested yet again in this most recent contest, and now seemed to be angling for a spot in the Tycoon's future administration.

As conservative as he was porcine, Hogson had hesitated initially to endorse his former rival. Some of the Tycoon's attacks had been decidedly below board in Hogson's book. And the Tycoon's flair for bestowing cruel nicknames also did not fly with him. But—at least in recent weeks—Hogson seemed to have noticed something else. Probably, it was that the Tycoon's tactics worked. As much as he liked a rack of ribs or a side of bacon, Hogson liked being on a winning team. All the Tycoon's trespasses had lately been forgiven. Hogson now gave every appearance of wanting to be the man's new evangelist.

"And that's later this evening?" she asked.

"Right," George said. "The candidates are apparently flying back from Florida. Hogson's as good as we're going to get for tonight. Are you feeling up to it?"

"Oh definitely," said Jessica. "Yeah."

"Look," George said. "I can tell you're a little frazzled from your interviews this morning being duds. I just have one thing to say. Don't worry about it! You're not the first reporter who told her boss—or his boss—they had a line on something great and then spent the day talking to a bunch of yokels who gave them nothing. It happens to all of us. Put it out of your mind and move on. There's a whole bunch of convention left to cover. Got it?"

He smiled reassuringly.

"I've got it," Jessica said. "Thanks for being understanding, George."

"No worries," he said. "But be as tough as you can tonight with Hogson. Hit him hard on the flip flop. That is, why's he prepared to endorse now? How can he do that after everything they said about each other during the primary? If I were you, I'd spend the next few hours watching tapes of the primary debates. Be ready to throw his own words back at him. Not too aggressively. Just here and there. Oh, and ask Hogson about his rock band at the start of things. That's my advice. He loves to talk about his band."

"All right," Jessica said. "That sounds good."

Leaving George in the media den, Jessica returned to her hotel room for the first time since her abduction that morning. It already seemed a world away. Unreal. She half expected to collapse involuntarily as she closed the door behind her and latched it. But she realized she did *not* feel faint or overcome. Quite the opposite. She was galvanized. Doing what she felt she had been born to do.

She sat on her bed, opened her laptop, and stared into a flood of emails that she knew she would not answer. Not at the moment. Besides, the Knights had her phone number. They were not going to be sending her anything by email.

Seeing nothing even worth opening, Jessica began to pull up videos of the last primary debate before Hogson had dropped out. It was a murderer's row of (mostly) white (mostly) men in late middle age, standing uncomfortably behind wooden podiums, trying hard to smile. Poured into their suits. Squinting under the hot lights as their makeup congealed and mixed with sweat. Bereft of the helpers and lackeys who usually surrounded them. Trying hard to remember their talking points.

These were the men asking for permission to run the world.

The Tycoon's nickname for Hogson—during the primaries, at least—had been "The Crisco Kid." It was an older reference, but the Tycoon's supporters did not seem to care. Soon they were chanting it at rallies, putting it on t-shirts, and making memes in which Hogson wore a cowboy hat and carried cans of shortening in holsters. Hogson, like most of the other candidates, had not really responded in kind. He admonished the Tycoon for "taking the low road" whenever the nicknames were brought up, but this hardly seemed to help Hogson's case with the voters.

Jessica cued the recording to the sections featuring Hogson. There were far too many candidates at this debate—eight in all—to have any kind of meaningful exchanges. The best most could hope to do was say something memorable that might get turned into a sound bite the next day. By this point in the primary, it was clear that Hogson would be dropping out soon. This made him not worth attacking or even responding to. He was given very few chances to speak, and when he did it was like he was talking into a vacuum. The others simply waited for him to finish before moving on to the real business at hand.

Jessica fast forwarded, backed up, and took notes. In the entire ninety-minute debate, Hogson gave only three answers. All told, he spoke for less than five minutes. His first response concerned the need to get tough with North Korea, and then somehow wended its way to Christian missionary organizations that had been trying to do humanitarian work in that country. His second response was very brief and heartily approved of reducing taxes on job creators. In his third and final response— Hogson's only real interesting moment of the night—he took a couple of minutes to disagree with the Tycoon on the need for a southern border wall. The Tycoon had just finished explaining how it would keep out bad hombres who were stealing American jobs. Most of the candidates nodded along, but Hogson shook his head no. When asked by the moderators if he'd like to give a further response, Hogson spoke at length about the need to pursue openness with America's neighbors. He said that curbing illegal immigration was important, but that erecting permanent border walls around America was not the best way to achieve it. He asked the audience to imagine what Jesus might have done in such a situation.

A final turn involving a pious thought experiment was typical for Hogson, so nothing really seemed out of place in this response. But then something. Something at the very end of his answer made Jessica sit up and take notice. She backed up the recording at watched again.

As Hogson spoke, the camera sometimes cut to the other candidates. The Tycoon, when he was shown, seemed only mildly annoyed with Hogson. Until, that was, he got to the border wall. Here, the Tycoon seemed to exude a hardly contained fury. The man positively seethed. Hogson seemed not to notice it until the very end of his response. Then Hogson looked down the row of podiums and saw something that made him dissemble.

After spending a full minute reminding the audience of Jesus's encouragements to help those in need, Hogson sputtered to a finish line: "Although the need to keep America safe is, um, foremost. All the candidates here have their hearts in the right place. All these men and women care deeply about keeping America safe. We all agree that, however we do it, safety is the most important thing. Thank you."

Hogson looked as though he had seen a ghost, but during the final part of his answer the camera had lingered only on him. Whatever he had glimpsed had not been shown.

Jessica got online and sifted through web clips from the debate, looking for alternate camera angles. It didn't take long for her to find what she was looking for. A political web forum had leaked amateur cellphone video taken from the audience. Probably shot by one of the Tycoon's loyal supporters, it lingered exclusively on his face during Hogson's answer. Jessica watched, riveted.

As The Crisco Kid made an ecclesiastical case against the wall, the Tycoon grew annoyed and then downright angry. As Hogson hit his stride on his answer—right where the televised feed cut to a close up—this web video stayed on the Tycoon. After a few moments more of glowering and grimacing, the Tycoon stopped his gesticulations entirely. Then he simply leaned forward, over the front of his podium, turned straight to Hogson, and gnashed his teeth.

He performed the action only once, but there was no mistaking it. A gnash. A gnash, and nothing else. And Hogson had seen it. Directly afterward, Hogson had begun his retreat from his position on the wall.

Hogson's answer was not remarked upon by any of the other candidates. Afterward, the Tycoon seemed to return to his typical self. (He rolled his eyes, cut people off, and made comments about the size of his hands—but there was no further gnashing of teeth in anyone's direction.) Jessica watched the post-debate analysis by the television news crew. The gnashing was never mentioned. Hogson was only mentioned once, and that was to note that he was expected to drop out of the race later that week.

Jessica closed her computer and thought.

Chomping teeth was not typical debate behavior. But what made Jessica really pause was Hogson's reaction. The man appeared to show actual fear.

If you thought the Tycoon was just an expressive blowhard with no self control, an aggressive flash of his pearly-whites would hardly be notable. If anything, you would hope it made him look stupid. It might get used against him in an animated internet video.

But if you thought the Tycoon was an undead monster who could literally eat your family?

In that case, a well-timed gnash might send another message entirely.

Jessica began to realize that her interview with Bob Hogson could hold more potential than she had first suspected. She opened her laptop back up and began researching the relationship between Hogson and the Tycoon. If she had only one chance to ask the man questions, she was going to be ready.

A few hours later, Jessica found herself waiting inside a small media room for Bob Hogson to arrive. Her laptop was open, and her digital recorder was already in the center of the table. Hogson ran late. When he did arrive, he did not apologize for or even acknowledge his tardiness. Hogson wore a plaid shirt with suspenders. Buttons had been pinned to the suspenders.

Most were political buttons supporting the Tycoon, but one said "Bass Players Do It Deeper." Jessica shuddered inwardly.

"Miss Jessica Smith," Hogson said in a voice mellifluous with southern charm.

Jessica offered her hand but immediately regretted it when Hogson appeared to consider kissing it. In the end, much to her relief, he merely gave it a polite shake.

"Thank you for taking the time to speak with us," Jessica said. "If you'd like to have a seat, we can begin."

"Of course," said Hogson, squeezing into one of the media room chairs. "And may I say thank *you* for doing this interview. Your friend George seems to have it out for me. That is to say, the things he's written about me in the past haven't seemed fair. I hope you'll be more evenhanded. You see, I'm here to express my support for our party's candidate, and demonstrate the unity we're all feeling right now. I hope that will come across in your article."

Jessica smiled politely to say it might be possible.

Jessica began by noting that Hogson had been particularly hard on the Tycoon in his comments during the primaries, especially when it came to his tendency to belittle and use nicknames.

Hogson smiled patiently, then responded: "Yes. I understand you have to bring that up. It was the primaries. This is politics. That's how it works. He said some things, I said some things, but at the end of the day we are on the same team. I'm here for the good of the party, and I'm excited to talk about what we can do for America."

"Right, so, speaking of your party, the pundits aren't giving your side much of a chance to win right now," Jessica said.

"Do you think anything that happens at this convention is going to change that?"

"In sports-casting, they say: 'There's a reason we play the games,'" Hogson replied. "Well, there's a reason we hold the elections. You never know what's going to happen. Opinions change all the time, and polls can be wrong."

"You think that all the polls that show your candidate with almost no chance of winning are wrong?" Jessica interjected.

"I said what I said," Hogson replied, a little annoyed but not quite defensive. "Polls *can* be wrong. That's objectively true. And when the American public learns a little more about our party during the convention this week—and sees all that we want to do for America—you're going to have some serious adjustment to whatever polls you're seeing now. I guarantee that."

Jessica nodded and—even though her recorder was capturing every word—took notes on her laptop. Hogson seemed to be working on autopilot, which was just what she'd hoped for. Her questions had been the ones he would have anticipated. She needed him feeling comfortable, sensing nothing amiss.

With this in mind, she continued.

"So you've talked a lot—here, and in other interviews I've seen—about how bygones are bygones. How everything that was said in the primaries was water under the bridge. If that's the case, I wonder if you would tell me about the traits of your party's presumptive nominee that you admire."

Hogson smiled.

"Oh, Jessica," he began. "I don't think you've got enough tape in your recorder for me to do that."

"Actually, it's digital," she said.

"Then simply for the sake of time I'll give you the short version," Hogson said. "I think he is a man who will keep America safe. He is a man who will put America first. A man who cares deeply for his family. He won't get bogged down in political correctness. He rejects the false song of globalism. He will make America great again. Maybe greater than it's ever been."

"Mmm," Jessica said, nodding. "Yes. And how do you feel he's handled the scandals so far?"

"I don't think there have been any scandals," Hogson said icily. "I can't think of one real, true scandal. But if you'd like to tell me what piece of slander you're referring to, maybe I can respond to it."

"I'm referring to *several* things," Jessica said. "There are the statements he has made about women. The fact that he's had multiple wives, all of whom are still living. There's the history of the property management companies he owns pursuing a policy of not renting to certain racial groups. The allegations of cannibal behavior. The close connections to the Russian president."

It took a moment for this litany to register with Hogson. A creeping grimace overtook his face. His eyes scanned the corners of the room. He seemed equal parts furious . . . and concerned that he had not heard her right.

"Excuse me. *What* did you just say?"

"The Russian president," Jessica clarified, as though nothing were out of the ordinary. "Rides around shirtless on a horse? Acts like a czar?"

"Before that," Hogson said intensely. "What did you just say *before that*?"

"The, uh, cannibalism allegations?" Jessica said, pretending to scroll through notes on her laptop. "You know, the claims that he likes to take a bite out of people every now and again? There have been some blurry photos, too. They seem to show him eating body parts. The Obamas' dog is on record as having bitten a White House guest, but we've never had a president actually bite someone personally. Though I guess it's not entirely without precedent, if you look globally. Idi Amin liked to take bites of people. And the current president of Equatorial Guinea has eaten some of his opponents, allegedly."

Jessica raised her eyebrows to ask if he cared to comment.

Hogson, for a moment, looked as though he might lose control. That he might slap her, storm out of the interview, or both. But then Jessica saw him glance down at the device on the desk. And then at the camera on the back of her laptop which—for all he knew—might also be recording. (You could never be too careful these days!) Hogson was a veteran politician who knew better than to lose his cool. He was also a man who still wanted things. Power for himself. Appointed office, if he could not have the elected kind. He was likely to secure a place for himself within the Tycoon's administration if he played his cards right, and knew it.

And so Jessica looked on as he endeavored to do so.

"This really is disappointing to hear," Hogson remarked in tones that said Jessica was a star pupil who had just been caught cheating. "I expect these kinds of questions from other news outlets. It's such a shame that I'm hearing something like that from a newspaper of your pedigree, which claims not to be biased. I thought giving you this interview was the right decision. I see now that I was wrong. I'm very disappointed, Jessica. And before you ask, yes, I will have to tell your supervisors about this. Not a great start to a career, young lady. Not at all."

And with that, Hogson rose from his seat.

Jessica, instinctively, rose too. Instead of shaking (or kissing) her hand, Hogson shook his head back and forth, and silently left the media room. As he passed through the doorway, he mumbled something under his breath about the questions being "outrageous."

Jessica watched him depart. Then she shut the door to the small interview room, sat down in her chair, and took a very deep breath.

It was happening. This was real.

The flash of recognition had been there. The fury and the astonishment too. Nobody reacted like that unless something hit home.

If Jessica had asked Hogson to respond to new rumors that the Tycoon had two heads, Hogson would have been confused as to how she could have brought up something so demonstrably false. Then he would have laughed it off, and that would have been the end of it. But instead, she had seen fury in his eyes. Fury, and something else. Something like terror. Jessica thought again of the Tycoon's toothy threat during the debate. It was as though he were warning Hogson very directly that if he kept it up, he (and perhaps those he loved) might get eaten.

Jessica took out her phone and texted Tim two words: "Hogson knows."

Then she waited.

THE FAKE NEWSMAN

Tim's phone buzzed, but he did not look at it immediately. He was too riveted by the one-line email message he'd just received from Tom Ellerman:

Jay says when can you meet

"Fuuuck," said Ryan, chewing on something cream-filled and looking over Tim's shoulder. "Jay McNelis took you seriously!"

"Dammit man," Tim said. "What did I tell you about reading over my shoulder? But yes, it sure looks that way."

"So that means he knows," Dan stated more than asked.

"It sure makes me liable to think he might," said Tim.

"Fuuuuuck," Ryan said again. "This is crazy."

"Hey, you want to watch your language?" Tim said. "The Christian Bloggers Alliance is just two tables over, and they really don't like it when. . . . fuuuuuck."

"But now you're . . . now you're . . ." Ryan tried to object between bites.

"Shut up a second, Ryan," Dan admonished. "What is it now?"

"Jessica says that Hogson knows too," Tim said, keeping his voice low enough that the Christian bloggers might not hear. "This is crazy."

"Bob Hogson?" Ryan said.

Tim nodded.

"About the thing that happened to you behind the bar today?" Ryan asked.

"I don't know if she means about that or about the nominee or what. I need to connect with Jessica and find out more. But Jesus, this is all happening so fast. *Jesus.*"

There was a deliberate throat clearing from two tables away. Tim lowered his voice further.

"I almost can't believe this," Tim said.

"What are we going to do next?" Ryan asked.

"I'm thinking," said Tim. "We've got to be very careful."

Dan sat down in the chair closest to Tim. He pulled himself even closer. The light from the fixture above reflected off of his shiny bald head.

"Before we do anything, I have something I want to run by you," Dan said intensely.

"Um, okay," Tim replied.

"Have you considered the possibility that this could be a false flag?" Dan said seriously.

Ryan listened in, chewing thoughtfully.

"A false flag?" said Tim. "Planted by who? Why?"

Dan rolled his eyes as if to say Tim was missing the point. But Tim did not see what other point there could be.

"Maybe some people would see an advantage to being perceived as a member of the walking dead," Dan said.

"Waaaaaait," Ryan interjected. "You're saying that maybe *he*—the nominee—is *not* a zombie, but he wants people to *think* he is?"

"There are a lot of things intersecting here," Dan continued. "I'm just trying to look at this from every angle. Could be we are playing right into somebody's hands."

"Just when I thought this couldn't get more confusing," said Ryan.

"Or maybe his political opponents," Dan theorized. "The other party. What if they started this rumor? It'll be so juicy, so difficult to ignore, that then we'll spend all our time looking at him instead of looking at *her*."

"That kind of makes sense, I guess," said Ryan. "She does have that email server thing."

"I don't know," Tim said, shaking his head. "We can't think like that. We've got to follow the evidence and go where the leads take us."

"Then answer me this," Dan said aggressively. "What are you working toward, eh? What are you trying to prove with these leads, with this evidence?"

"If a major party candidate is a zombie, then people have the right to know that," Tim said. "That's what I'm working toward."

"So, proof?" Dan asked.

Tim nodded.

"What would that even look like?" asked Dan.

Here, Ryan decided he could be helpful.

"Ooh, you could ask him if he wants to eat somebody . . . and if he says yes? Boom! You've got him. At least, probably you do. Maybe he could say he was kidding though. I bet that's what he *would* do . . . now that I think about it. Never mind."

"We don't have to know exactly what is going on—or exactly who is a zombie—to report that a cover-up is happening," Tim said. "That might be enough to start with. A stepping-stone on the way to establishing he's a zombie. The history of journalism is full of cases like that. First you get proof of the cover-up, and *then* you can get proof of what is being covered up."

"But there's not been any talk of a cover-up so far," Ryan pointed out.

Tim nodded thoughtfully.

"I have an idea," he said. "I think we should talk to Jessica again."

"About what?" Ryan said. "Tell us."

"Well, if Hogson reports back—to someone like McNelis, say—that the mainstream media is asking about zombies, then Jessica's sort of broken the seal already," Tim said. "And maybe I have too, asking McNelis about the shooting. My idea is—and this kind of picks up from what Dan was saying before—what if we weren't asking about certain politicians being zombies because we were looking to out them. What if we were asking because we wanted to help them keep the secrets? Maybe we can position ourselves as even more useful than we already are."

Ryan narrowed his eyes.

"So we say, 'We know you're a zombie . . . and we're *down* with that? We think it's good'?"

Tim nodded.

"You know it could work," Tim said confidently.

Ryan and Dan did. TruthTeller wasn't the largest or most influential outlet perceived to be on the Tycoon's side, but it had always been a good soldier. Always fallen in line. That could mean something now. Tim reasoned that if details did emerge that characterized the Tycoon as somehow "zombish," a trusted ally like TruthTeller could surely cast those traits in a positive light. They had already done it in other areas. The Tycoon was not poorly-spoken and habitually wrong, he was "folksy" and "genuine" and "talked like a real American." He was no sinister objectifier of women, merely a relatable chum who engaged in "locker room talk" and said out loud what most men were thinking anyway. He was no upper-class twit with inherited wealth, rather he was "an entrepreneurial job creator." (And when his projects went south? He wasn't an incompetent bankrupt; he was a good American availing himself of the laws and protections due him.)

If TruthTeller could recast *these things* so handily and effectively—turning negatives into positives at every turn— then a little zombification should be no problem at all.

Tim knew they had the skills, and that the Tycoon's team understood this acutely.

In order to learn more about the Tycoon's status as a zombie, they might need only to offer their services.

"What?" Dan wanted to know. "Why are you smiling like that?"

"Because I'm starting to feel like we can do this," Tim said. "Like maybe we're the best positioned to pull it off. I sort of can't believe it."

But believe it, Tim had to. They all did.

The next morning Tim met Jessica for breakfast at the horrible buffet in the hotel lobby restaurant. They met early, as soon as the place opened. Reporters rose early, but Tim thought they'd still be safe from most prying eyes. He knew that this might be the last time it would be safe for them to be seen together. For the moment, they could still play it off as J-school chums reconnecting over eggs and toast.

The arena and surrounding hotels were becoming more crowded now. The convention would start properly the following day. A carnival atmosphere pervaded. Not a first-rate carnival, but maybe a second- or third-circuit one—the kind that usually played county fairs and high school fundraisers. There were unlicensed vendors of every sort on the streets outside, selling unauthorized and copyright-infringing political t-shirts, stickers, and hats. Ahh, the ubiquitous red hats. They were flooding in, and showed no signs of stopping. It seemed that every other man—and a few of the women too—sported a red cap in addition to his trademark khaki pants and blue blazer. There were also rabble rousers of every sort. Protestors and rock bands. It all had the feeling of the night before a battle. And maybe, in a way, it was. Tim and Jessica had never experienced anything quite like it.

"I've scheduled a chat with McNelis for later this morning," Tim whispered over a pair of pre-fab eggs benedict, extra hollandaise.

"So your plan is we play both sides?" Jessica said.

"Correct," Tim said. "Pincer formation. You'll come out aggressively on the zombie stuff. I'll make like my team is ready to defend his side against it. I, um, may have to attack you personally—depending on how this goes."

Jessica turned her head to the side and wrinkled her nose.

"In the early stages, I mean," he clarified. "To gain their trust. In the end, we're on the same team. It's just that nobody can know."

Jessica nodded thoughtfully, then appeared to hesitate.

"What?" Tim said. "You look like something's wrong with your food."

Jessica shook her head.

"My food's fine," she said. "It's just . . . You don't think there's any chance that we're wrong about some part of this, do you?"

"Wrong?" said Tim. "We wondered that last night. Dan brought up how it could be a false flag. But after all we've seen? The shootout. The Knights of Romero. The way Hogson and McNelis have reacted . . ."

"Yeah, I know," Jessica said absently. "It's just that if this keeps up, I may be breaking this story as a freelancer."

"What do you mean?" asked Tim.

"After he stormed out of the interview, Hogson called my boss and gave him an earful. As far as I can tell, Hogson only characterized me as combative, and partisan. Said that I was 'way out of line.' That's enough to get me in trouble. But he *didn't* say that I had brought up cannibalism or zombies. I think that's good. I think Hogson is hoping I'm some kind of rogue agent that needs to be taught a lesson."

"You kind of are," Tim said.

"Stop," she replied with a smile. "Anyway, I think his call to George would have been different if he thought George had put me up to it. Hogson thinks I acted alone."

"Was George pissed at you?" asked Tim.

"Kind of, yeah," Jessica said. "I have the sense that he'll probably give me a mulligan because I'm new, but I feel like I just used it. I also said I struck out with human interest stories when I was really getting kidnapped yesterday, so . . . Let's just say the paper is probably not super-happy with me right now."

"So George didn't ask to listen to your recording?" Tim asked.

"No," Jessica replied. "If he does, I'm just going to say I already deleted it. But whatever happens next, I'm on thin ice."

Tim nodded to say he understood.

"So what's next for you?" Jessica asked.

"I'm going to try to make some overtures with McNelis when we meet," Tim said. "Anything he gives me, I'll turn around and share with you. Hopefully you can find a way to use it on offense."

"Okay," Jessica said. "I was up half the night scanning broadcast tapes of the debates, looking for anybody else who might have reacted like Hogson did. I haven't found anything definitive, but I'm going to keep looking. And meanwhile, I have to churn out some stories for George too."

"Sounds good," Tim said. "Keep your eyes open. You never know when you're going to see something or hear something that ends up being useful. But you don't need me to tell you that. By the way, did you turn off your phone before you came here, and leave your smart watch in your hotel room?"

Jessica nodded. She had.

"I think that's how we're going to have to play it from here on out," Tim continued. "Just assume we're being watched and tracked. Our emails will probably be monitored too."

"How should we get in touch with one another?" Jessica asked.

"We should try to meet in person when we can," Tim said. "You need to find me, drop by the TruthTeller booth. You can trust Ryan and Dan if you need to leave a message with them. If nobody's around, leave me a note with the name of the bar we used to drink at on 110th Street written on the outside of the envelope. Or use something else only you and I know about."

"Okay," Jessica said. "This is so crazy."

"Yes," Tim said ominously as he finished off his eggs. "It certainly is something."

After breakfast, Tim showered, thought about shaving, and then put on his finest pair of jean shorts. He consulted a map of the conference center until he found Entrance C1-AA, which was where Tom Ellerman had said McNelis would be. Tim sniffed his armpit and decided his shirt was probably okay for another day. Then he grabbed his laptop bag and headed out.

His hotel was connected to the convention arena by an umbilical walkway. Tim hurried across it, not wanting to make McNelis wait. Tim could feel himself sweating from anxiety and too much coffee and the general strain of walking faster than a slow amble. He forbid himself from thinking about what he was preparing to do, and what the implications might be. There was no going back now, only forward.

A few paces into the arena it became clear that going forward would mean contending with an enormous crowd of people. To think, the convention did not properly get underway for another twenty-four hours, and already it was like this! The hallways were filled with staffers and reporters and early conventioneers—in addition to other persons whose functions were a total mystery to Tim. Yet they all wore expressions that said that they were supposed to be there. That, and their lanyards, seemed to be enough.

Cruising at near his top speed, Tim made his way down these crowded hallways until he located the forbidding double doors that would lead to Entrance C1-AA. As near as he had been able to tell, this entrance was a loading area from which equipment (or people) might gain quick in-out access to the convention floor. Tim wondered if it was where the speakers would arrive and depart when things were in full swing.

Tim pushed through the heavy doors and found a utilitarian metal staircase beyond. It went down to another set of doors. The lighting inside was stark and utilitarian. There was a man in a grey suit standing with his back to this second set of doors. He wore sunglasses and gave just enough of a grin to tell Tim that he had found the right place.

Tim huffed and puffed down the metal stairs, and passed through the doorway. Beyond he found a loading dock with a segmented garage door that had been raised. A large black town car was parked at the entrance to the dock. In the second that it took Tim to gawk at the vehicle, a back door opened and a familiar voice—familiar to those who covered political campaigns, at least—called out.

"Mr. Fife?" it said.

Tim smiled and awkwardly saluted with his laptop bag.

The town car door opened wider. There, in all his ruddy glory, was that patron saint of spin and broken blood vessels known as Jay McNelis. Tim nodded hello several times like a supplicant approaching a king.

"Get in," McNelis said. "It's such a nice day, I thought we'd go for a drive."

It was not a nice day. It was overcast and muggy.

"Sure thing," said Tim, hoisting himself into the seat beside McNelis. Tim slid his bag to his feet and crossed his hands across his chest, trying to make himself as small as possible. The back seat was designed for three people, but he and McNelis filled it up completely.

The driver—another nondescript anonymous man in sunglasses and a suit—slowly pulled away from the convention arena. Apparently he had whatever clearance was needed, because McNelis seemed comfortable speaking in front of him.

"So, a kerfuffle broke out in a suburban bar?" McNelis said. "Shame to hear it. And you were in the vicinity? What are the chances? I hope you're not any the worse for wear."

"Well my neck brace . . ." Tim began, then stopped himself. "But no, I'm fine. More than fine, actually. That's what I wanted to talk to you about."

McNelis raised an eyebrow.

"You want to talk about how you're more than fine?" asked the campaign manager.

Tim nodded.

"See, the things I heard and saw in the back of that bar revealed some things to me," Tim said. "Some incredible things. Some exciting things."

"Go on," McNelis said after a very long pause.

Tim wondered if the driver was waiting for a code word from McNelis, at which point he would spin around and hit him twice in the chest with a silenced 9mm.

Despite mounting terror, Tim kept talking.

"I just want you and your team to know . . . that we're on board," Tim said.

He swallowed hard and waited for the hitman's bullet. No gunshot came, silenced or otherwise. Instead, McNelis only smiled disingenuously and blinked. It was impossible to gauge the meaning of this reaction. (The man's cratered moon-face was so deformed as to make his expression inscrutable half of the time. Tim began to wonder if he knew this, and intentionally used it to his advantage.)

Eventually, McNelis said: "What do you mean, 'on board'? What are you on board *with*?"

Tim breathed a sign of relief. He was not dead yet. Now it was time to wheedle.

"All I'm saying is that we at TruthTeller see a lot of advantages to a presidential candidate having unique qualities that might make him stronger, braver, and more special than his opponents," Tim said carefully. "You know . . . A president who couldn't be assassinated through traditional means—except maybe with a headshot—would be a good thing. A boost to national security. Having the toughest leader in the world? Who *wouldn't* want that?"

McNelis said nothing. It was a heavy kind of nothing, pregnant with possibility.

"Or a president who never needed to rest?" Tim continued. "Think of the advantages there. No more 'Do we wake the president?' when something happens at three a.m. The president will *always* be up. How is that not a positive? How does that not make our nation safer and more secure?"

McNelis looked hard at Tim with his scotch-soaked eyes, but again stayed silent.

"And what about implications for things like the estate tax?" said Tim. "We know that that money's already been taxed once—and that taxation is theft, anyway—but if certain Americans, like maybe very prominent ones like the president, aren't going to be leaving an estate because they aren't going to be 'leaving' at all, then TruthTeller would be excited to tell the story of how that changes *everything* on the issue. Makes a good case for getting rid of that tax entirely."

Then, the remarkable thing.

Almost imperceptibly, McNelis nodded. (For an instant, Tim worried it might have only been the jostling of the town car. But no. It was real. A definite nod.)

"And anyone who criticized a candidate with these new, exciting enhancements . . . ?" Tim continued excitedly. "Well, they would be bigoted, wouldn't they? A strong word, yes, but the correct one in this case! They would be discriminating against someone's innate orientations and inborn proclivities. By God, the other side would be hypocrites if they said a single word against it. I can't wait to make the memes, let me tell you!"

McNelis sat back in the plush leather seat of the town car and thought. The car had now moved away from the convention area, and drove silently across a great truss bridge that crossed the Cuyahoga. A pair of strange stone sentinels attached to pylons looked on as the vehicle passed. For a moment, Tim Fife and Jay McNelis were as still as the statues.

Then McNelis spoke.

"It is good to know that we have your support in any eventuality. Campaigns are strange things. Just when you think you know what's going to happen, things go haywire. Scandals appear. Most of them break up like waves against a rocky cliff, but now and then something tidal does occur. It warms the cockles of my heart, Tim, to know that if fantastic rumors do begin to circulate . . ."

Here, Tim opened his mouth to pledge further undying support, but McNelis silenced him.

"*If* rumors circulate, you will be there to help us," McNelis continued sternly. "*If.* But at present, there is no pressing need to create excitement where none yet exists. Do you understand?"

"I . . . I do, absolutely," said Tim.

"And you will wait to hear from me before you print a single article or you craft a single political cartoon," McNelis said. "Do you understand."

"Yes," Tim said anxiously. "One-hundred percent. I just wanted to meet now because I respect you so much, and I wanted to tell you face-to-face that you have TruthTeller's support. No matter what."

McNelis gave Tim a squint from the side of his eye. The meaning was clear. A master bullshit artist was wondering if he was being bullshitted. Tim stayed very still and tried to look earnest. His head suddenly felt very heavy. For a moment, he worried he might pass out.

Then McNelis turned off the high beams and directed his gaze back out the window.

"All right," McNelis called to the driver. "You can take us back to the convention, Steve."

The town car performed a dramatic U-turn into oncoming traffic. The driver steered as though quite confident he was above the law. Tim was jostled back and forth.

Tim looked over at McNelis, but the man was already working on his laptop and a cell phone had appeared between his neck and ear. Tim realized the campaign manager was done with him. There would be no small talk.

The car pulled not to Entrance C1-AA, but to a side street a block away from the arena. It took Tim a moment to realize why the car had stopped. McNelis appeared to be listening to a conference call now. The driver signaled to Tim that he could exit.

"Oh," Tim said. "Thanks."

He opened the door and turned one last time to McNelis.

"Thank you," he said with mock enthusiasm, and flashed a thumbs up.

McNelis regarded him as though he were an insect, and turned his attention back to his call.

Tim walked down a street filled with mounted police, vendors, and protestors. The town car sped away. A moment later, it was out of sight. For a moment, Tim felt nothing. Then, gradually, he began to lose himself in the din of people around him. He was lost enough to let the mask fall from his face. And he smiled. A great and knowing smile.

He had done it.

McNelis had said very little, and neither man had used the z-word, but it was enough. Tim felt his veins fill with the electric lava of hope.

He had never been so excited or so possessed. He knew that he was among those making history.

The walk back to the TruthTeller conference table in the second-rate media room was a blur. Tim felt as though he were walking on air instead of concrete and cheap casino-style carpeting. He hardly noticed the crowds of people he pushed past.

Tim found Ryan and Dan waiting. Their faces were filled with anticipation. Tim sat down and they huddled close.

"McNelis didn't say it, but he didn't have to," Tim told them. "I think this is real, and I think he just confirmed it. Also . . . I think maybe they were taking me somewhere to bump me off if I said the wrong thing, but I didn't, so I'm still here."

"Holy cats," said Ryan. "Bump you off? Like in the movies?"

Dan just grinned.

"So, um, there's something we should tell *you*," Ryan said. "Something happened while you were gone. And if all *this* weren't going on, it would be the big thing we'd be all excited about. But as things stand, I guess it feels a bit like an afterthought."

"What?" Tim said. "What is it."

Dan took over.

"All our most reliable sources are reporting an unexpected meeting of the Uneeda Society. Like, we think it's happening tonight. Based on where the private jets are headed, we think it will be somewhere in the American Southwest."

This certainly *was* unexpected, thought Tim. And it would definitely have been the biggest news of its kind . . . on any *other* day.

The Uneeda Society was one of the international organizations of powerful globalist elites monitored most closely by TruthTeller. It was always mentioned in the same breath as the Bilderberg Group, Bohemian Grove, and the Trilateral Commission. Yet of all of them, it was probably the least known. Its membership was reckoned to be the smallest, clocking in somewhere between fifty and one hundred members. It was also one of the newest. Bilderberg could trace its origins back to the 1950s, the Trilateral Commission to the 1970s, and Bohemian Grove all the way back to the 1800s. The Uneeda Society, in sharp contrast, had seemed to come into existence sometime during the 1990s. The origins of the group—and even its founding principles—were rather murky. But several of the most prominent leaders in finance, politics, and the arts were said to be members. And that, Tim suddenly recalled, included the Tycoon.

"*He's* a member, isn't he?" Tim said to his TruthTeller colleagues. "I mean, he's *supposed* to be, right?"

"That's right," said Dan. "And the campaign just announced that while the future vice president left Florida to return to the convention, the future president would not have his schedule made available until sometime the following day."

"Yeah," Ryan chimed in. "They want people to believe he's still relaxing at his club."

"Huh," Tim said. "Dan, you're more of an expert on the secret societies than I am, but doesn't Uneeda usually meet . . ."

"Once a year, in Kentucky," Dan said. "That's right."

"So what are they doing now?" Tim said. "What are they doing in . . . in . . ."

"We're hearing from contacts that there's a sharp increase today in private plane traffic at the Tucson International

Airport," Ryan added. "Though it's all being kept out of the logs. If we didn't have so many air traffic controllers who read TruthTeller, we'd never have known."

"Okay," Tim said, running his fingers through his hair. "Wow."

"We've got to run something," Dan said. "This is the biggest secret society scoop since the Bilderberg food poisoning in Davos."

"I agree," Tim said. "But let's leave names out of it for the moment. At least names of politicians. Take an angle that's hard on the artsy types instead. A bunch of A-list Hollywood actors and wife-swapping Nobel laureates meeting to decide there are now 37 genders. That sort of thing."

"Can do," Dan said excitedly.

"But also, keep your ears open for what's really going down," Tim quickly added. "An unscheduled Uneeda meeting right before the convention? It *can't* not be connected. Something's going on."

The TruthTeller reporters rubbed their (often multiple) chins and considered what mysterious conspirings might be afoot in the distant deserts of the Southwest. Then they sprang into action and began to type.

THE TYCOON

The door to the Tycoon's jet opened slowly. The warm desert air blew inside.

The Tycoon almost never traveled in airplanes that were not owned by him and bore his name emblazoned across the side. For this trip, however, an exception had been made. An anonymous unmarked craft had been chartered. The Tycoon would normally have been annoyed to travel without all the familiar amenities he enjoyed on his personal craft, but at the moment they hardly registered. There was simply too much on his mind.

The Tycoon had travelled alone. He sat by himself in the cavernous interior of the jet, waiting for the door to finish lowering. He had brought nothing with him. No luggage. No computer. Not even his phone. (The urge to Tweet could be overwhelming, and he did not trust himself not to accidently betray his current whereabouts.)

When the walkway was finally in place, the Tycoon exited the aircraft and strode directly to the car. Limousines were conspicuous. Uneeda members learned to make do in the passenger seats of sedans with tinted windows, and with drivers dressed to look like local residents. The man in the Arizona Cardinals cap gave the Tycoon a perfunctory nod as he climbed inside. Then they pulled away from the airport and into the sandy reaches beyond.

The Tycoon drummed his fingers on the door of the car and assured himself that all would be well. He would make his case. Of course he would. They had come this far. They would not ask him to pull out now. It was a nearly done thing.

Somewhere in the foothills of Mt. Lemmon, the sedan turned down a side road appearing to be reserved for government vehicles accessing a remote ranger station high in the hills. Turning down a further unpaved side road, the car began a precarious climb into the pine-covered mountains above the city. The sedan's engine strained and sputtered. Eventually, the Tycoon noticed another unremarkable American car making the same trek along the road ahead.

Moments later, another moved into position to the Tycoon's rear.

In minutes, the Tycoon's car reached the secluded luxury hunting lodge nestled high atop the hills. Private security had formed a tight perimeter around the building. Other men with automatic weapons and trained security dogs patrolled in the distance. The rocky escarpment in front of the lodge had been turned into a parking lot where fifty or so vehicles had already been left. The cars and SUVs were unremarkable and certainly not high-end. This gave the lodge the appearance of a working-class restaurant on a busy Saturday night. Yet when one looked closer at the men and women slowly filing inside, it was clear that these were not farm or factory workers enjoying a day off. These were titans of industry. The world's most powerful leaders. And those who had influenced art and culture for decades, and would influence it for years to come.

Yet even among this most-exclusive company, the Tycoon was the one who turned heads. As his car pulled to the door of the lodge and he stepped outside, the reaction from the onlookers was electric. Heads turned. Fingers pointed. Whispers rippled through the warm mountain air. The Tycoon tried his best to treat it like any other campaign stop. He grinned and gave a cursory wave, then ducked inside the venue.

The lodge—usually a Spartan, dusty place—had been fitted for the meeting with no expenses spared. Armenian and Turkish carpets covered the floors. The windows had been cleaned. The heads of dead animals that regularly festooned the walls had been moved into storage. The center of the lodge had been converted unto a meeting room where about a hundred people could sit comfortably. At the front was a small mobile stage with a single lectern.

The members of the Uneeda Society chatted with one another, grimly and softly. Yet all conversation shushed when the Tycoon stepped into the room. As he made his way to the lectern, the Tycoon stopped to perfunctorily shake hands and accept congratulations from several society members. Here, a tech startup whiz-kid worth billions of dollars (in stock at least). There, the aging Hollywood director who had essentially defined the 1980's. After that, one of the world's most powerful CEOs. The Tycoon negotiated all of them as quickly as he could, but it still took several minutes. By the time he had actually reached the podium, the last of the society members had filed inside the lodge. Unseen assistants closed the door and shuttered the windows. Their group was now quite alone. The Tycoon cleared his throat. The gathering was so intimate, no microphone was necessary to amplify his voice. The members of the society took their seats.

"Ladies and gentlemen of the Uneeda Society," the Tycoon said. "A little over a year ago, I addressed this body to put forth an idea that, I believed, could change our organization forever. I outlined a plan to take bold new steps toward creating a world where we could live openly, securely, and without sacrificing the positions of power we have made it our lives' work to obtain. Not everyone liked my plan. I understand that there were concerns. I understand that many of you *still* have concerns. That's why I promised that when everything about my presidential run was finally settled, and all loose ends had been secured, I would convene an emergency meeting and personally provide an update. So here I am."

The Tycoon smiled. Unlike the enthusiastic cornfed audiences at his rallies, this room of billionaires delivered no automatic showers of applause. Instead of cheers and hollers, the Tycoon was greeted by a hundred intense stares.

"And I have good news," he said, trying to keep things positive. "The best news, actually."

"What?" someone shouted. "Your running mate decided to join us?"

The Tycoon stared in the direction from where the voice had come. The room was dark and it was hard to tell who had spoken.

"That was never going to be necessary," the Tycoon said. "He's not that sort of man, anyway. At least I don't think he is. But he *is* a man who can know a thing and keep his mouth shut about it. He has shown me that in a bigly way."

"There are already *too many* who know!" someone else called.

"This makes me very uncomfortable!" said another.

"You're taking more unnecessary risks!" cried another still.

"*There is no reward without risk*!" the Tycoon snapped. "You all know that. All of you are here because you are risk takers. Doers. Empire builders. I say again, there is no reward without risk. And what a reward it will be. Imagine the world we can build together after I am president. A world where we are free to walk in sunlight as our true selves. A world where no one will dare to criticize us because we are different. A world where our *diversity* is accepted. With the Governor of Indiana fully on our side, we are going to be unstoppable. And after what happens in Cleveland this week, there will be no room to doubt it."

The CEO of Europe's largest oil company looked left and right, then around the rest of the room. Really? Was nobody else going to say anything about it? *Really?* Fine, then. He would have to do it.

"There are reports that the Knights of Romero have resurfaced," this CEO said loudly. "In Cleveland. As recently as two days ago. This is despite our use of leading technology and expenditure of virtually unlimited resources to eradicate them. Still, they persist. If our best efforts are unable to eliminate a small splinter group of radicals, then what assurances can you give us that information integrity can be maintained until your administration is installed in Washington D.C.?"

A round of murmurs broke out. The Knights of Romero were reckoned as having been defeated "for real, this time" on several previous occasions. They had an irritating habit of popping back up after they'd seemingly been put down for good. (A bit like a zombie, the Tycoon privately considered.)

The Tycoon nodded to say he understood the serious nature of the CEO's concern.

"I am aware of the . . . incident," the Tycoon said. "And I can assure you that steps are being taken to ensure that no further surprises occur."

The CEO stood and expressed exasperation. (He did so in his own language, which the Tycoon could not understand. This annoyed the Tycoon, because he did not like feeling left out.) Another round of murmurs came. Their tone seemed to indicate that the Tycoon's answer had not been sufficient.

The Tycoon realized more drastic measures might be needed.

"Listen, everyone . . . everyone," the Tycoon said, raising and lowering his flattened palms in an attempt to quiet his audience. "The Knights are not going to stand in our way. Are you kidding me? They're pipsqueaks. Runts. A bunch of losers and amateurs. We're literally the most powerful people in the world. They are . . . nothing."

"You know the dangers of overconfidence!" someone else shouted.

"I do, believe me," replied the Tycoon. "I know it in a very big way."

Yet the murmurs rose. The most elite zombies were, not coincidentally, among the most cautious. They might not yet rule the world literally. They might not be able to walk openly as their true selves. But what they had was still pretty goddamn good, and they knew it.

Some of the society members stood, as if they might soon depart.

The Tycoon had a decision to make. Something that had been turning over in his mind for months. Really, he knew that he ought to discuss such an announcement with McNelis first, but there was no time. This was a moment that called for brave, decisive action. Wasn't that precisely what U.S. Presidents were supposed to do? Act decisively? That sounded right to the Tycoon.

"Which is why . . ." he said, now raising his hand over his head to quiet the din. "Which is why—if necessary—I am prepared to execute Initiative X. You heard me. Initiative X. I'll do it. Just me."

The room hushed. There was a clattering sound as a cane fell from a wizened hand, and a high-pitched tinkling as a monocle literally popped from a socket. You could have heard a pin drop.

An elderly zombie seated near the front—by day, he was president of an Ivy League university—croaked: "You are saying that you . . ."

"Will assume all of the risk, while sharing any reward," the Tycoon said. "But I am willing to do it. For the good of all of us. *If it comes to it,* you understand. My operatives tell me that everything is still very much going to plan. We're not sure what happened earlier in the week was even the Knights. It could have been impostors, imitators, cosplayers. I don't *anticipate* having to use Initiative X, but I'm telling you that if it comes to it, I am ready."

A stunned silence pervaded. The Tycoon could see the Uneeda Society members trying to make up their minds. They looked at one another. They looked at him. They whispered. Then they began to shrug and to nod.

The Tycoon realized that he had done it. For the moment at least, he had saved the day.

THE REPORTER

Jessica spent the balance of the convention's opening trying to get back into the good graces of her boss. She filed several pieces in quick succession about the impact of the conventioneers on the Cleveland economy, the role of Gen Y'ers in the election, and the potential for violence breaking out. She interviewed and wrote. Wrote and interviewed. She filed stories that George hadn't even asked for, just to show that she was working hard.

Her heart, however, was elsewhere.

As the convention speakers were—eventually— announced, she studied each one for signs of zombification. The old general. Had he been bitten by a member of the undead while serving in foreign lands? The New Jersey governor. Did an outsize taste for human flesh explain his girth? The ageless 1980's sitcom actor? Had his long absence from the limelight been due to an extended zombification process? (And what *was* that process? Jessica still had so many questions. There were resources on the web that claimed to reveal the secrets of the walking dead, but so much of what Jessica found did not comport with what the Knights of Romero had told her. That zombies had become their own sort of secret society. That they had learned to blend in. Jessica second-guessed every speaker, worrying she had missed some telltale sign of membership in the legion of the dead.)

At the end of the first day of the convention, Jessica stepped outside for a rare smoke break. She had told herself she would curtail the habit completely many times before—or at least move to vaping—but the bracing knowledge that the next leader of the free world might be a zombie seemed to override the impulse for self improvement. There was a large smoking area on the side of the arena. Jessica joined perhaps a hundred others in lighting up and milling about idly.

Jessica's head swam. She could not remember feeling so exhausted and unnerved, yet so galvanized at the same time. Some part of her wished desperately to curl up with an electric blanket and a bottled of schnapps for the next 24-48 hours. Blueberry schnapps. Definitely blueberry.

Jessica hardly noticed when a small figure concealed in a baggy pink sweatshirt eased up beside her.

"Got a light?" a voice said.

Immediately, Jessica snapped back to the present. Blankets and schnapps were suddenly light years away. The voice was familiar. It was the bald member of the Knights of Romero. The one they had called Trish.

"Don't look," Trish said as Jessica leaned over, all agog. "Just light my smoke and keep looking straight ahead."

Jessica tried to do so.

"I've been wondering if I should get in touch with you," Jessica whispered. "I found out that Bob Hogson knows. He let it slip in an interview. More or less."

"At the moment, Hogson is small potatoes," Trish said. "Listen to me carefully. Tomorrow something's going to happen during the convention. Something *very important.* You know how there's a slot in the evening schedule where it just says 'An Address'?"

Jessica did. But everyone knew that the Tycoon was expected to use it to make a "surprise" appearance and welcome attendees to the convention. Just a little hello before his big speech on the final night. It was the worst kept secret in town.

"We've got something planned," Trish continued.

"*Okaaay,*" Jessica said, still staring straight ahead. "What do you need from me?"

Trish did not turn, but Jessica felt something small and plastic being pressed into her hand.

"Take this," Trish said. "It's a drive."

"What's on it?" asked Jessica.

"You'll see that tomorrow night," Trish said. "The whole country will see, if our plan goes off . . . which I think it will."

"You think it will?" said Jessica. "What if it doesn't?"

"That's what that drive is for," Trish said. "If nothing happens tomorrow night during his speech—if it all goes off just like you'd expect it to—then it means we've failed. And I want you to open the drive and look at what's on it. You'll know what to do from there. But you have to make us a promise."

"What?" said Jessica.

"You have to promise you won't look at what's on there beforehand," Trish said. "And we'll know if you do. The moment that drive is plugged into a computer—*any* computer—we'll know."

"Okay," Jessica said. "But . . . tell me what's going on."

"I can't do that," Trish said. "There are too many potential leaks already. Too many places where there might be holes in our armor. We can't afford another person knowing. Even a good-intentioned one. It should be enough for you to understand that after tomorrow night, if things go right, the world is going to be a different place."

Jessica did not know how to respond, and so only stood and smoked her cigarette. Normally, when people said things like that to reporters, they were not well mentally. But something gave Jessica the feeling that Trish was not insane, and not bluffing or in need of psychological help. The thumb drive felt heavy in Jessica's hand. She tucked it into her suit pocket. When she looked back at Trish, she saw the woman in the pink hoodie disappearing into the crowd. Jessica opened her mouth, but could not think of anything to say. Soon, Trish was lost entirely in the throng.

Minutes later, Jessica strode into the second-rate conference room that housed TruthTeller. There she found Tim, Ryan, and Dan hunkering down for a working dinner. Pizza. They were already on their second pie.

Only Dan noticed her approach. He lowered his slice of pizza and began to point.

"You three," Jessica said. "Meeting. Now."

Tim looked up in stunned surprise. Ryan made a choking noise and spat out a half-chewed crust. Dan continued to point.

"But I thought . . ." Tim began to protest.

"This is too important to worry about being seen together," Jessica said. "There's a bar across the street at Bolivar and Seventh. Meet me there in ten minutes."

She hesitated for a moment, then added: "And bring a laptop."

The bar had gone all-in for the conventioneers. American flags adorned every surface. Drink prices had been doubled. It was packed and rowdy, but the reporters still managed to find a booth together in one of the corners. All of them had turned off their phones.

"We were actually going to get in touch with *you*," Tim said, easing himself into the booth beside her. "We think the Uneeda Society met last night. I don't have any source information on what was discussed yet, but it can't be a coincidence that it's the week of the convention."

"Then it may be that we're here about the same thing," Jessica said. "One of the Knights of Romero just took me aside and gave me this."

Jessica held up the nondescript thumb drive.

"She said that something is supposed to happen tomorrow night when the candidate drops in to do his little teaser," Jessica continued. "Apparently, if that thing doesn't happen—the thing the Knights are planning—I'm supposed to look at this drive."

The TruthTeller trio exchanged a glance.

"Or . . . we could just look at it now," Ryan said, adjusting his backside in the small, crowded booth.

"She said not to . . . and that if I do, they'll know," Jessica replied. "Is that right? Can they do that?"

Ryan and Tim looked at Dan.

"Theoretically, yes," Dan said. "That's Ed Snowden-level shit, but it's possible to do. You put a drive into a computer, it can send a signal back to home base confirming as much."

"We could buy a new computer that can't connect to the internet," suggested Ryan. "Or, like, break the internet part of the computer, right?"

"Yeah," Jessica said skeptically. "We *could* do that. We could also wait and see what happens tomorrow night."

"What *is* going to happen?" Tim asked. "You're the one who actually spent time with the Knights. Did they tell you anything? Drop hints?"

Jessica shook her head. The table was silent for a moment as the harried, overworked waitress arrived with a tray and set four watery domestics before them. She regarded the quartet skeptically. They were not attired like wealthy conventioneers who might leave exorbitant tips. The waitress decided to cut her losses and move on.

"What could it be, really?" Jessica said. "They're not going to assassinate him, after all."

"That's right," said Dan, as if speaking from some expertise. "Onstage at a political convention would be about the hardest place to do that. You'd definitely want to catch him when he was in transit. Just explode his whole motorcade. Wouldn't be that hard to do, even. Believe me."

After an awkward pause, Tim added: "And also, that doesn't serve their purposes. My understanding is that the

Knights aim to prevent the rise of zombies. Killing a presidential candidate, presumed to be human, doesn't do that. So I can really only think of one thing."

Tim looked up into Jessica's eyes. She understood that they both saw it.

"They have to . . . unmask him somehow," Jessica said quietly. "They have to show him for what he is. And they have to do it before the party can formally nominate him."

Tim nodded back.

"Yes," he said. "I just can't see how they'll do that."

"Neither can I," Jessica said.

They all looked again at the small, nondescript drive in Jessica's hand.

"It's not going to be the picture of him eating the hand," Tim said. "It needs to be something more."

"Right," Jessica said. "But what?"

Suddenly, Ryan—who had already finished his beer and waved at the waitress for another—stopped cold. He set down his empty glass and put his palms flat on the booth's wooden table. His eyes were flitting back and forth very quickly.

"What?" Tim shouted at his TruthTeller colleague. "*Ryyyyyyyyan* . . . ? What are you thinking of?"

"It's . . ." Ryan sputtered. "It was just such a minor thing. I didn't even think to mention it before. And then I guess I forgot about it."

"*What*?" both Tim and Dan said at the same time.

"Jeez, relax," Ryan said. "It's just that I got a note from one of my regular tipsters a few hours ago that John Gitelman's office just got broken into. They didn't want to file a police report, but he—my tipster—attached some pictures from the scene that looked real. Apparently some hard-copy files got rooted through, but nothing seemed stolen."

Dr. John Gitelman was the Tycoon's personal physician. He had made news earlier in the election cycle by penning a much-ridiculed letter suggesting that the Tycoon was the healthiest man ever to run for President of the United States. This had been his lone brush with national fame. The notorious letter had now been mostly forgotten in favor if fresher, meatier news items.

"Why does anybody care about his doctor?" Dan asked, finishing his beer. "Are they still trying to find out of his hair is real?"

"I never thought about that, but it makes sense," Jessica said. "If you're a zombie you don't have a heartbeat and brainwaves. And yeah, your hair probably doesn't grow anymore either. But the public wants to think you're healthy and normal, and going to live another four-to-eight years. So you'd need a doctor's collusion."

"Yeah," said Tim. "His doctor would *have* to know."

Jessica said: "Would a doctor actually keep a file somewhere that says his patient is a walking dead man?"

Yet again, they all glanced at the drive in her hand.

It seemed to Jessica that a medical record would not be conclusive, but it would certainly be a start.

"What else did your contact say, Ryan?" Tim asked.

"That was pretty much everything," Ryan replied with a shrug. "I'll forward you his email with the pictures of the busted-up office. That is, if I can even still find it."

"Do that," Jessica said. "I don't think we can know too much."

"What are we supposed to do at this point?" asked Ryan.

"What *can* we do?" Tim responded. "A thing is going to happen tomorrow night. Our jobs are to report on it better than anybody else."

Tim turned to Jessica.

"The only other thing I can think of is that we—you and I, Jessica—have to decide how much *we* want to be a part of the story," he continued. "You need to think about if you want to include the conversations you had with the Knights. If you decide you *do* want to include those details, you're probably going to need to be able to show a bunch of fact checkers that it actually happened. I'm happy to be a reference for my part of it, if you need."

"Yeah," Jessica said absently. "To be honest, I'm trying not to think about that part of it. It feels like a giant black wave that's going to crash over me, and then . . . I don't know what. Everything I did this week is going to get picked apart. I'll be faulted by somebody, somewhere, no matter what. Every decision I made will be criticized. It just feels like. Ugh. To be totally honest, it makes me want to move back home with my parents and not be a journalist anymore."

Ryan looked around the table. Then he said: "We could probably get you a job at TruthTeller, if you wanted."

Jessica did not respond.

Tim shook his head.

"What?" said Ryan. "We probably *could*."

"No . . . it's . . . that's okay," Jessica said, putting the thumb drive in her bag and preparing to stand. "I don't think there's anything else I can do at this point. Anyway, if I'm gone much longer George will miss me. I should get back to it."

"If nothing happens tomorrow night . . ." Tim said, rising to let Jessica out of the booth.

"I'll see if you're available when I look at the drive," she told him.

"Oh, we'll be available," added Ryan. "You can be sure of that."

"Okay," Jessica said. "Thanks."

She walked out of the crowded tavern and back into the warm summer night. She felt as though all the pieces of a puzzle had been presented to her, but she could not yet see how they fit together. She could not form them into any coherent shape, no matter how she rotated them mentally. She felt frustrated and increasingly inadequate.

She allowed herself to hope that, overnight, the solution might come to her.

THE FAKE NEWSMAN

Tim Fife was alone. He was sitting in a theater with hundreds of empty velvet seats, but he was alone. The walls were draped in blackout curtains, and the stage before him was also curtained-over. It was hard to see much. It was very dark and very quiet. He did not know precisely where he was or how he had gotten there.

Then a rousing noise jarred him. It was patriotic music, played through an unseen speaker system. The curtains hiding the stage did not move, but suddenly the illuminated Seal of the President of the United States was projected onto them amidst the tremendous fanfare. Then the seal faded. The heavy curtains gradually rose to reveal a screen. On the screen were animated reenactments of important scenes in American history. The Inauguration of George Washington. Lincoln delivering the Gettysburg Address. Kennedy asking not what his country could do for you, but what you could do for his country.

And all at once a rush of emotions swept over Tim, and he realized not only where he was but *when* he was.

He was ten years old. At an amusement park in Florida. *The* amusement park in Florida. In the Hall of Presidents. Something told him his parents and his younger brother Ralph—not to mention other park visitors—ought to be present. But for whatever reason, they had stepped away for the moment, leaving him alone inside the enormous theater.

His parents had assured him that everyone loved the Hall, and that he would too. Yet the idea of stiff, jerky animatronics of long-dead leaders filled him with ambivalence. It seemed such a thing could not fail to be strange and unnatural. Tim's curiosity overrode any doubts or hesitations, however, and he stayed in his seat. Tim watched the glowing wonders pass before his eyes. He surrendered to the spirit of the program. He leaned back into his plush red seat and relaxed. And that was when all of it seemed to go wrong.

The next image projected on the screens showed American soldiers huddled together at Valley Forge. While George Washington consulted with his officers, a group of enlisted men clustered together in a corner of the frame. The soldiers huddled close around a small campfire. Their faces were grim. Atop the licking flames, they seemed to be cooking a shoe. Tim had heard that things at Valley Forge had got that dire. But now that he looked closer, it seemed that a foot had been left *inside* of the shoe. Was *that* also how it had been? Before he could see any more, the image faded to black.

Further images of Washington followed, but all of them seemed to contain new details Tim had never before noticed. In a familiar-seeming portrait, the first president's chin and riding gloves were spattered with a thin patina of blood. As he crossed the Delaware, his crowded boat was piled high with human body parts. And a scene of him retiring to Mt. Vernon after serving two terms appeared to show a prosperous house and farmstead . . . where walking dead with outstretched arms littered the horizon like scarecrows in a field.

The presentation then skipped to a series of images concerning Andrew Jackson. Here, he fought bravely in the Battle of New Orleans—not just stabbing a British soldier with his sword, but biting him in the neck and releasing a frothy geyser of blood. In the next image, Jackson survived an assassination attempt. Sequential art showed him beating the attacker with his cane after the would-be killer's gun misfired, then licking the end of the cane with great satisfaction.

The images shifted again, this time to FDR. In the first portrait, he reassured America during World War II with avuncular fireside chats. Subsequent photographs showed the seated president carefully reading into a microphone, while other shots showed hardscrabble American families listening intently to their radios. Only by chance did Tim notice the jar of human toes set alongside FDR's ashtray and water glass.

Then more. Other images of other presidents. They came so quickly that Tim could hardly keep track. White haired Whigs holding human fingers in their mouths as though they were cigars. Twenty-first century presidents giving speeches in tailored suits with twin pins on their lapels; one pin, an American flag—the other, a pink human brain.

Tim's uneasiness began to spiral into all-out alarum. He looked frantically around the darkened theater for a friendly green EXIT sign, but saw none. There appeared to be no exits at all. He resolved that he would stand up and find one, even if it meant feeling his way along the edges of the auditorium's darkened rear walls. Yet he found that his body could not stand, no matter how firmly he willed it to.

Tim could only look on in horror as, then, the screens began to retract up, revealing what he had always known would come next. Forty-three animatronic figures standing on a series of raised platforms. At first, they were only silhouettes against a softly glowing backdrop. But then the footlights at the front of the stage began to come up. (Tim wished he could do anything to stop them—to diminish their glow—but he was powerless even to look away.) The rising lights revealed an orgy of blood. Most of the presidents familiar to Tim—if not from television news clips then from history textbooks—were covered in blood spatter. The blood was a mix of old and knew. Some presidents wore garments that showed months of crusted red stains. Others positively glistened, as if coming fresh from a kill. A few of the presidents were still actively eating, raising and lowering various limbs to their mouths while taking jerky, robotic bites. The automatons pretended to masticate, grinning through permanently ruby teeth. FDR had been rendered in his wheelchair. He wore a bib and held a knife and fork. Before him had been placed a small end table, and upon that rested a full human brain. The robotic FDR lifted his cutlery every few moments, appearing to cut at the brain like a man carving off a piece of filet. The robot then brought the empty fork up to its mouth and appeared to eat. Once, it even paused to wipe its mouth.

Tim slowly turned his head from left to right, doing a slow pan, trying to take it all in—absolutely everything that was happening on the enormous, horizontal stage. He would have rather not looked at all, but something compelled him. Something held him fast.

The floor of the stage was full of thick red liquid. It pooled at the front of the stage. It threatened to flow down into the first row.

Then, as Tim looked on, a narrator began to speak.

"The spirit of America is incarnate in a profoundly simple idea," said the hauntingly familiar basso voice. "That from among men like these, we should choose our own leaders. That our hopes were their hopes. That our desires were their desires. Our appetites, their appetites."

Suddenly, Tim began to feel a bit sick to his stomach. What was the narrator implying?

But no. He realized that it was not nausea he felt. Not disgust. At least not completely. It was also . . . peckishness. Hunger. Something about the sight before him had put Tim in the mood for a snack. His stomach grumbled.

"Ladies and gentlemen," the narrator said, "I present to you the presidents of the United States."

The disembodied voice began naming presidents. A spotlight shone on each as his name was called. When thus acknowledged, the president paused from his feasting and nodded to the audience.

Tim's stomach growled again. He looked down and saw a popcorn bucket sitting in his lap. Tim rarely took in any kind of show without popcorn. Yet as he reached down into the extra-large tub and began to bring his hand up to his face, Tim realized that it was not popcorn resting warm and fragrant between his legs (though it had precisely the feel and consistency). Rather, it was ground meat and bones. Human meat and bones.

As he glanced down at the warm handful, a human eye (mangled by the grinder, but still essentially intact) glanced back.

It was only then that he started to scream.

Tim Fife awoke in time to reach the toilet before vomiting up what remained of his pizza. He reclined beside the basin when he had finished, and pressed his face against the cool tile floor. He breathed quite hard, as if he had just very gently exercised.

"What the fuck was that?" he wheezed as he looked up into the white bathroom ceiling.

Then he threw up again.

When he had recovered from this second bout, Tim chanced to look at the digital clock set into the bathroom mirror. Somehow, it was already seven in the morning. Tim rinsed out his mouth and flushed the toilet. It was possible, just possible, that one of the most consequential days in American history was about to begin. He showered, dressed, and did his best to prepare himself for it.

The morning passed with interminable slowness. Tim checked his phone and email constantly for anything that might be salient. Lunch came and went, and Jessica still had not been in touch.

"Are you okay?" Ryan asked as they lounged nervously around their conference table. "Your face looks white. Like, whiter than usual. Extra-white. And you didn't even have seconds at lunch."

"I had a bad dream last night," Tim said. "Let's leave it at that. It made me lose my appetite."

"Oh," Ryan said with a shudder, as though this were an especially heinous outcome.

The second day of the convention-proper would not really begin until 5:30pm. This was not to say that there was not activity in the convention hall or on the stage. Bands played. Civic, charitable, and religious groups made presentations and proclamations. Local Cleveland business leaders delivered remarks.

The Tycoon's "surprise" cameo—which everyone knew was coming—would occur at about seven p.m. After welcoming the conventioneers, he would introduce his adult daughter, who would be the evening's keynote speaker. He was scheduled to be onstage for no more than five minutes. Tim could think of no other five-minute period that had ever occupied his mind so intensively.

TruthTeller did not have access to the best press areas inside of the arena, but Dan had taken it upon himself to do some scouting and networking. He inveigled three seats near the top of the arena in the back. It was in an empty section where there were no conventioneers. The seats were very high up. It might have been far from the stage, but they would have a very clear line of sight.

As the day crept on, Tim attempted to prepare pre-emptive stories he could run the moment that the mysterious event happened . . . whatever it might be. With Google and Facebook (and, as most TruthTeller readers insisted, the NSA) logging his keystrokes, this made Tim more than a little nervous. Accordingly, he wrote several scenarios and tried to spread the sensationalism around. The Tycoon assassinated. The Tycoon revealed to be a zombie. The Tycoon revealed to be a zombie and *then* assassinated. The Tycoon *surviving* an assassination. The Tycoon eating someone's brain on live television. The ejection of protestors who held signs and shouted slogans insisting that a major party nominee was actually a member of the walking dead. The Tycoon delivering absolutely normal remarks and then introducing his daughter, with nothing unusual in the slightest happening.

Of all the briefs he wrote, it was this final scenario that might have disturbed Tim the most. What *if* nothing happened? He and Jessica were so very ready for something massive and world-changing to occur. But what if nothing came at all? What if, instead, they had to see what was on that thumb drive?

By five in the afternoon, all three TruthTeller staff members were in their seats high above the convention floor. They were alone in this area of the arena. They listened as a no-name cover band provided music. The audience, only half paying attention, clapped politely when they remembered to, but mostly just talked among themselves.

Dan produced three sets of binoculars and passed two others out to his comrades.

"I don't know if I can sit here until seven," Ryan objected. "I'll have to pee. I had too much Mountain Dew."

"Then sit on the end of the row," Tim said, moving to the aisle so that Ryan could switch seats with him.

Thus rearranged, they peered through their binoculars at the area immediately surrounding the stage. There were conventioneers, staffers, and omnipresent security. Nothing looked out of place.

"Would you recognize any of the Knights if you saw them again?" Ryan asked, binoculars scanning.

"Honestly, I don't think so," Tim said. "I only saw them for a moment, and they were shooting at me. At least I thought they were."

"Where's Jessica?" Ryan asked.

"I don't know where she's going to be watching from, or if she's even in the arena," Tim said.

"Oh," said Ryan, lowering his binoculars. "So if nothing happens tonight?"

"We'll find her, or she'll find us," Tim replied. "Then we'll look at the drive."

Dan was still gazing intently at the stage.

"It's so locked down, it's ridiculous," he said. "I don't know what the Knights think they're going to do. You tried to take one step on that stage, ten guys would swarm you."

"Yeah," said Tim, taking another look. "I guess we'll just have to wait and watch."

Wait they did.

After half an hour, the TV cameras began carrying the convention live, coast-to-coast. The proceedings kicked into high gear. Relatively speaking. The convention was called to order by the committee chair, colors were presented by a military guard, and Cleveland religious officials led in the Pledge of Allegiance and an opening invocation. Then the speakers began. The star of a duck-hunting reality show. The former Governor of Texas. A retired Navy SEAL. A couple of congressmen.

The speeches hit on all of the Tycoon's favorite themes, each speaker drawing on his own personal story to arrive at the same conclusions. A border wall was needed. The current healthcare system was broken. America had lost its way.

The TruthTeller staff looked on anxiously. The hour was getting late. Tim saw nothing out of the ordinary. He looked at his watch repeatedly. Ryan got up from his seat and went to the bathroom three times.

Then, finally, the former Mayor of New York City took the stage. His remarks would be predictable and brief, and then the Tycoon would make his cameo appearance.

Tim opened his laptop and scrolled through his inbox. There were no last-minute messages from Jessica. No tips having to do with the Tycoon's appearance, or anything concerning the Knights of Romero.

Tim noticed Ryan and Dan were looking at him.

"Nothing," he said.

His colleagues nodded. The former mayor wrapped up his talk.

And then everything changed forever.

The lights inside the arena darkened (not completely, but considerably more than one expected at a political event). Strains of Queen's "We Are the Champions" were piped in. Then a blinding set of footlights came on, right at the base of the stage. A large white screen had been draped behind the podium, and now it was illuminated. As the expectant crowd looked on, a familiar-looking figure stepped into view. Though the lights meant they could see only his silhouette, the crowd roared their lungs out. The Tycoon stepped to his mark and stood there, obviously basking in the applause that seemed as though it might swell forever.

It was only because they were seated so far in the rear of the arena that Tim noticed a corresponding flickering—or something—against the latticework of metal walkways set against the arena's ceiling. Somewhere up there, metal parts were shifting. Something was moving, as if animatronic parts were rearranging themselves.

Tim elbowed Ryan in the flesh that covered his ribs, and pointed. Then he glanced over to Dan.

"Already saw it," Dan said, training his binoculars up into the darkness above.

Meanwhile, the footlights on the stage came down just enough to reveal the Tycoon. He wore a dark suit and a bright blue necktie. He smiled from ear to ear. The overhead lights in the arena were slowly raised. A montage of patriotic photographs was projected on the screen behind the Tycoon.

Dan stayed focused on the anomaly happening up above them.

"Drones," Dan said. "And they look military-grade."

Tim craned his neck back toward the dark latticework. In the gradually increasing illumination, he saw it too. Or rather, saw *them*. It looked like five or six drones, small and black, hovering against different parts of the scaffolding. Trying, probably, to remain unseen.

"Did you hear anything about drones being used in his presentation tonight?" Tim asked.

"No," Ryan said.

"No way," Dan added. "I got quite a bit of inside info from the technical guys working the AV tonight. There's a lot of bells and whistles in this thing, but drones ain't one of them."

"Some of them look like they have cameras," Ryan said, peering through his own binoculars.

"Let's *hope* those are cameras," Dan said ominously.

Ryan looked horrorstruck.

"You don't mean that they're . . ." he said, aghast.

"Some kind of weapon?" said Dan. "We wouldn't be any kind of newsmen if we counted *out* that possibility."

Tim spoke up.

"They don't all have cameras . . . or guns," he said. "A couple of them have things hanging from the bottom. Clusters. They look like fancy speakers you get installed in a car."

Now Dan and Ryan saw this too, but none of them knew what to make of it. The Queen song was lowered completely. The Tycoon stepped behind the microphone and began to speak.

"Thank you, everybody," the Tycoon said. "I love you. I love you. We're gonna win, and we're gonna win bigly. We're gonna win *so* bigly. Thank you very much."

The crowd loved it. The applause rose again. They clamored for more.

Meanwhile, the drones moved out. Gliding slowly and silently, they crept across the top of the arena, high above the action, lost in the metal beams and walkways. Maintaining formation, they inched forward until they were nearly above the candidate. Only then did they begin, every so slowly, to descend.

"Must be controlled by computer," Dan said, as though he admired the artistry of the flying. "That coordination is *ridiculous*."

"Ry, are you filming this?" Tim asked.

"Oh yeah," Ryan said, shifting his position to reveal the handheld camera at his side. "Not sure what I'm capturing though. It's so dim up there."

"Keep on it," Tim said.

As the trio watched, two of the drones—the camera kind—broke formation and descended to the very edge of the manufactured shadow that encircled the stage. They stayed just out of the light. They were something almost nobody would notice. (And if anybody *did* notice them, they looked like precisely the kind of thing that was *supposed* to be there.)

The Tycoon finished his "thank yous" and prepared to read from the twin teleprompters that framed him. At the same time, the patriotic images behind him began to dim.

But something happened. Something the TruthTeller staff caught immediately, but most people in the arena did not. As the official images faded to black, others—similarly rendered and lit—seamlessly took their place. And the two drones that hovered at the edge of the shadow began, very subtly, to glow.

"Projectors!" Ryan said. "Holy cats."

Tim saw that indeed they were.

As the Tycoon waited for the last of the applause to die down, the drones began to shine new images on the screen behind the candidate. These were not still images, but rather recorded video. The projection showed a scene that looked very much like the interior of the conference rooms located throughout the arena.

In the conference room was a table (definitely the same kind of cheap plastic folding table that every group at the convention had been issued). On the table was a square device not much larger than someone's fingertip. It was black, and had a small red light on the top. If it had not been displayed as the focal point of the shot, one might have missed it entirely.

"Is that another thumb drive?" Ryan asked.

Tim shook his head wordlessly to say he didn't know. He looked through his binoculars, riveted.

The camera pulled back to reveal two people standing on the far side of the table, facing the camera. One appeared to be male, and the other female. Both wore business suits, and had lanyards around their necks containing all-access convention passes. However, the camera stopped just short of revealing their faces.

Back at the podium, the Tycoon began the short speech that would introduce his daughter. The audience acted as though nothing were amiss. Perhaps the screen behind the Tycoon would show his daughter walking from backstage out to the podium. Perhaps this visual was intentional.

As Tim looked on, one of the headless figures—the male—reached out and grasped the small black box. He brought it up to the camera, and placed it in the pocket of his jacket. As he did, a red light on the box began to blink, and a noise could be heard reverberating across the arena. It did not drown out the Tycoon, but there was no missing it. Tim realized it was being played by the speaker-bearing drones above. The sound was unmistakable.

Tha-thump. Tha-thump. Tha-thump.

The Tycoon seemed to notice that some kind of audio feedback was occurring. He glanced down at the monitors at his feet, but did not stop speaking.

After just a moment, the male figure in the video took the box out of his jacket pocket and placed it back upon the table. The red light ceased. As did the familiar noise.

"Oh my God," Tim said, lowering his binoculars to glance at Dan and Ryan. "It's a heart monitor."

Dan and Ryan looked at one another to ask if that could be right. Then all three men turned their gazes back to the screen behind the candidate.

As they watched, the female figure in the suit picked up the small device and put it in a pocket on her hip. Almost instantly, audio of her heartbeat began to play across the arena—slightly faster than the male version.

By this time, the technical crew running the show had begun to realize that something was amiss. Tim noticed them raising and lowering the Tycoon's audio slightly, perhaps searching for the source of the problem.

After a few moments, the woman in the video took the monitor out of her pocket and placed it back on the table. The background *tha-thump* abruptly stopped. Then the camera began to move. Someone had picked it up and was holding it at about shoulder-height. At the same time, a third person walked into the shot and picked up the device. It was a young woman with a nearly shaved head. She wore a business suit and kept her face positioned away from the camera. As she held the device, the beating of a human heart could once again be heard reverberating.

At the podium, they were still looking for the source of the malfunction. The Tycoon reached out and touched the microphone before him, bringing it closer to his face.

Back on the screen, the young woman opened a door and left the small conference room, stepping out into the hallway. It was crowded with people and covered with American flags. Everyone wore lanyards.

"That's today," Ryan announced. "That's here, and that's earlier today."

"Are you sure?" Tim asked, his eyes still buried in his binoculars.

"The people she's walking past . . ." Ryan said. "Those are people I saw earlier, in the same clothes. I've got a near-photographic memory for those things. It's one of the reasons

TruthTeller hired me, remember? It made my UFO sightings so reliable."

Tim did not remember this, but saw no reason to say it. Instead, he remained glued to the video. The young woman walked through the hallways of the arena. It was not clear where she was headed or what she was doing. Many in the arena audience might have thought it was the Tycoon's daughter, heading to the backstage area to deliver her speech. (Perhaps she had recently changed her hairstyle.)

The woman in the video turned down a side corridor and approached an alcove covered by a curtain. A guard who might have been Secret Service stood beside it. As the guard looked on, she held up her lanyard. He studied it closely, nodded, and waved her through. The camera then lowered for a moment, and displayed only two pairs of men's shoes. The cameraman was likewise verifying his clearance with security. All must have been in order, because a moment later the camera was raised and passed through the curtain.

Now it showed a backstage area, possibly behind the stage. Equipment cases stacked against the walls. Men dressed in black and wearing headsets studied a wall of monitors. The camera once again found the woman with the short hair. She was striding purposefully past the technical crew toward a group of people huddled at a table. It was easy to tell, even from a distance, that one of them was the Tycoon.

"Holy fuck," Tim said. "It's him."

"And there's McNelis beside him," added Dan. "The whole goon squad."

"That's the necktie he's got on right now," Ryan observed. "See, this *is* today."

As the Tycoon came into view, a new wave of alarm seemed to ripple through the technical staff. Men in black clothing and headsets—some, the same men who had been shown onscreen moments before—began peeking out behind curtains and gathering at the edges of the stage. They pointed at the screen, up at the drones, and then, angrily, at one another.

"They don't know what's happening," Tim said out loud. "This is amazing."

Back onstage, the screen showed the woman with the short hair sidling up to the Tycoon's inner circle. Now the woman reached into her purse and produced something. A book. It was the Tycoon's latest. On the cover, he glowered sternly to show his dissatisfaction with the direction the country was headed. As the person holding the camera paused a few steps away, the woman with the short hair approached the Tycoon and waited just outside his inner circle. The palaver concluded and the men stood. The young woman pressed forward. She proffered the book—and also a pen—in the Tycoon's direction.

The Tycoon continued speaking with McNelis, but gripped the book and pen. As soon as he did, the video froze. Tim suddenly realized this was the first time the broadcast had ceased to be a contiguous, unaltered shot. As the video stopped, a large red circle was superimposed on the candidate's hip, indicating the viewer should focus his or her attention. Then the video started up again.

The woman in the video watched the Tycoon sign the book. As she did, she jostled herself against him slightly. (The Tycoon seemed not to notice. [Or, if he did, to have liked it.] His smile remained constant throughout.) As she jostled, the woman's free hand appeared to place something into the candidate's pocket.

Then the video stopped again, rewound, and zoomed in on the red circle. It was clear that a transfer had been made. The small black heart monitoring device had been slipped into the Tycoon's pocket.

Then the video started up again. The smiling Tycoon signed the book with quick flourish, and returned both the book and pen to the young woman. Then he and his entire entourage walked out of shot.

Immediately after the transfer of the device was made, the audio ceased entirely. The steady, soft *tha-thumps* that had echoed across the arena were no more. The implication was clear. The heart monitor had grown quiet because it no longer had anything *to* monitor.

The screen showing the Tycoon departing with his entourage slowly faded to black. The projector drones stopped projecting. They rose back up to the scaffolding that ran along the arena roof. Soon they had disappeared against it.

Down on the stage, the Tycoon continued. He probably assumed that whatever audio malfunction had transpired had now been corrected. The technical staff that had massed by the edges of the stage seemed to be calming. They still pointed and frowned and rubbed their chins, but the strange interruption—whatever it had been—now appeared to have passed. Secret Service men and women paced the edges like predators, clearly alert to the fact that an irregularity had occurred.

For a quick moment, Tim lowered his binoculars.

"Did you guys fucking see that?" Tim asked.

"Saw it, and recorded it," Ryan replied, indicating his camera.

"Do you think this will be enough?" Tim said. "It's weird . . . but it just looked like an AV malfunction. Are people going to understand the point of it? I mean . . . *we* see what they're going for here, but *we're* looking for it."

Dan lowered his own binoculars and shook his head doubtfully.

"Yeah, I don't know," he said. "There'll be a lot of room to say it was CGI or faked or something. The major TV networks haven't cut in over his speech to say anything's amiss."

Dan held up his laptop on which four network feeds played simultaneously. The focus on the Tycoon was tight. Viewers at home might have not even seen the disruptive video.

Tim turned his attention back to the podium. The Tycoon appeared to be wrapping up.

"I'm just telling the truth when I say I'm a winner who has experience at winning," the Tycoon was saying. "The people who work for me, they know it. My rivals know it. But there's another group of people who know it—my family. Which is why I'm so excited to be able to introduce the next speaker for this evening. She is a former jewelry designer and model. She is a business leader, and she is a champion of women's rights all over the globe in a very big way. I'm talking, of course, about my daughter."

The crowed applauded and cheered as a photograph of the Tycoon's oldest daughter came up on the screen behind him. The success of this projection seemed to relax the technical staff even further. Whatever had gone wrong, now the good guys were back in control.

Then it happened.

As the Tycoon began reading off a further list of his daughter's accomplishments, something started to beep.

Beep. Beep. Beep.

It was a loud, mechanical beeping, and it was coming from the Tycoon himself.

He stopped speaking. As the audience waited, he inspected the microphone and podium to see if he could locate the source. He patted his pockets and produced his cell phone. Verifying that he'd indeed switched it off—as, no doubt, Jay McNelis had instructed him to do a number of times—the Tycoon further patted himself down, looking for whatever was making the sound.

He seemed to find it in his pocket. He reached in and brought out a small black box. The very same box that had been featured in the video moments before. The heart monitor. The light on it was flashing, and it was beeping loudly.

Yet it was not beeping to sound the cadence of the candidate (or anyone's) pulse, Tim realized. Rather, it was beeping to say "Here I am."

As the Tycoon held aloft the strange beeping box—turning it over in his hand, trying to make sense of it—a Secret Service agent rushed out onto the stage. He grabbed the device from the Tycoon's hand, flung it to the ground, and then flung himself on top of it. A moment later, two other agents rushed on after him. They grabbed the surprised Tycoon and bundled him off, stage right. The convention floor erupted into alarm and chaos. The arena lights went up. Law enforcement sprang into the aisles. More Secret Service encircled the edges of the stage. A voice on the arena loudspeaker asked the convention-eer to remain in their seats and to remain calm.

Only one noise was audible above this din. It came from drones hiding in the arena rafters. It was not a mechanical beeping. Instead, it was the beating of a human heart. It beat fast. So very fast. It was powered by the adrenaline coursing through the body of the Secret Service agent who doubtless believed he had fallen on some sort of explosive device.

Tha-thump-Tha-thump-Tha-thump!

More personnel arrived. The Secret Service agent holding the heart monitor was helped to his feet, and he—along with the device—was taken away. The audience clucked in confusion. Cell phones were out capturing everything from every possible point of view.

Yet after a few moments, the heartbeat audio ceased. Perhaps the device had been smashed or thrown in a bombproof box. Police and Secret Service began to clear the stage. Technicians checked the microphones and muttered to one another. Eventually they left the stage too.

Finally, improbably, the stage was cleared.

Moments later, the Tycoon reemerged. He walked to the microphone. No great extemporaneous speaker, what he lacked in nuance and skill he made up for in enthusiasm.

"Didn't I tell you this would be the most exciting convention ever?" he asked.

The worried audience, needing some stress relief, cheered wildly.

"Okay, I'm told we had a technical problem," the Tycoon continued. "We had a technical problem and it concerned my security. The Secret Service. They're always so concerned about me. It's like they don't know what a tough guy I am. Like a beeper is going to hurt me? I'm really tough! Seriously, I am. People who know me, know that. I'm a tough guy!"

The audience applauded wildly, and broke into chants of U.S.A.-U.S.A.-U.S.A.!

"Anyhow," the Tycoon continued, "it really annoys me that my security just did that, because I wasn't finished telling you about my wonderful daughter. Where was I? Okay. Here we go again. She is an entrepreneur who has created jobs in the fashion industry . . ."

The Tycoon continued and the audience settled down. When he had finished the introduction, his daughter strolled onstage. The two embraced—it lingered perhaps a bit too long, but this could be forgiven considering the security scare. Then the Tycoon walked off and she took the podium, launching into a speech about her father's forthcoming initiatives for women in the workplace. All seemed disturbingly normal once more.

Only a few attendees inside the arena—a number that included the entire staff of TruthTeller—noticed the technical staff rushing across the roof scaffolding to recover the drones.

THE TYCOON

"I really appreciate you taking the time to sit down with us today," she began. "People have so many questions about what happened last night."

The Tycoon nodded froggishly to show his general understanding of this idea.

"Of course," the Tycoon said. "People are curious. I'd be curious if I saw something like that. But I'll tell you something. It made for great television. And believe me, I know great television."

Diane Laughlin nodded and smiled enthusiastically from her chair opposite the Tycoon. Diane was the Tycoon's favorite newscaster from his favorite network. When McNelis had insisted that they schedule something to nip any gossip in the bud, the Tycoon said he would do it if they could get Diane. McNelis had made it happen. Now McNelis watched from the corner of the suite as the Tycoon grinned opposite her in the glare of the portable television lights.

"First of all, are you feeling all right after last night?" Diane asked. "The voters are going to wonder about that. If elected, you'd be oldest person ever to assume the presidency."

"Look, I don't assume anything," the Tycoon said, misunderstanding her. "I can tell you *for a fact* that my health is fine. Doctor Gitelman, my doctor, he's one of the best doctors in New York. You've seen what he had to say about my health. The healthiest president ever."

"Right, right," said Diane. "Though some questioned if he meant the healthiest *for your age*. After all, President Kennedy was only in his forties when he became president, so—"

"Excuse me," the Tycoon said sternly. "He said I would be the healthiest president ever. And that's a doctor talking. A *doctor*."

Diane Laughlin smiled politely and consulted her notes.

"In the papers this morning, some people are saying the incident last night raises questions about how your campaign is handling security," she said.

"Okay, two things," the Tycoon replied. "Firstly, people are right to be concerned about security. We have people coming into this country—nobody knows why they're here. Our borders are not secure. There are ways for bad people to come here and do bad things. I get attention because I'm the only candidate talking about it. I'm definitely the only candidate who is going to *do* something about it. Secondly, what happened last night was— I'm told—one of the technical people had placed something in my pocket in the course of getting me mic'ed. It was a technical thing. Something to do with sound. It malfunctioned, and that was the noise we all heard. The Secret Service took it and destroyed it—which is, I guess, what they do with such things—and that was the end of it. The guy who screwed up and put that thing in my pocket? Is he fired? You better believe it!"

Diane Laughlin nodded sympathetically.

"Okay, right," she said. "And it might sound a little bit silly, but I have to ask about the video that was projected behind you. The network cameras caught some of it, and then there was a complete version leaked onto YouTube earlier today. I know you and your staff have watched it. Anyhow, there is a general theory that the intent of the video was to imply that the device in the video was a heart monitor, and that it stopped working when it was placed it your pocket."

"Look," the Tycoon said. "I've been called heartless before. Don't think I haven't. People have been calling me that for over forty years. Other names too. Far, far worse things. Things I can't even say on television. When you're powerful and successful you make enemies that are jealous of your constant winning. So, am I surprised that one of my detractors pulled a stunt to say that I'm heartless? Not really. But trust me, I've heard it all before."

"Um, yes," the news anchor said cautiously. "But the point seems to be that they—whoever made this video—are trying to make the point that you literally don't have a heart. That you're not in possession of a pulse."

"A new low for fake news," said the Tycoon. "Very sad. I can't believe that anybody could believe it."

"So if I took your pulse right now . . ." Diane Laughlin said with a grin.

"You would feel my heart beating just like with anybody else," the Tycoon replied.

The Tycoon paused. A rare smile came across his lips. He looked to Jay McNelis who nodded. Now was the time.

"As you know, I hate fake news so much," the Tycoon continued. "Any time you give me a chance, I will go against it. I will prove it wrong. I can't believe we did this, but we actually brought a . . . whaddayacallit . . . stethoscope in. Here, James, can you bring it over."

While the Tycoon and the newsreader waited, McNelis produced a stethoscope from his jacket pocket. He walked into shot and showed it to the camera. Then, before Diane could protest—or even react—McNelis was placing the plastic earpieces into her ears.

"Thank you, James," the Tycoon said. "Now put the end of that thing right against my shirt, Diane. Go ahead. Tell the people what you hear."

Diane shrugged and smiled. She was game. She put the stethoscope bell up against the Tycoon's chest.

"Now what do you hear?" he asked. "Tell all the people at home."

"I hear your heart beating," she replied, sitting back and taking the earpieces from her ears.

"There, you see?" said the Tycoon. "I can't believe we had to do that. It just goes to show what a crazy world we live in. The other side knows they can't beat me on the issues, so they waste their time and money to set up wild conspiracies and fake news about me. I'm glad we could clear this up."

McNelis reappeared and took the stethoscope from Diane.

"So turning back to the convention," she said. "Your running mate, the Governor of Indiana, speaks tonight. Do you think his message is going to bring Americans' attention back to the issues at hand?"

"I do," the Tycoon said. "As you know, I think the Governor is a tremendous fella. Just tremendous. He's made Indiana a success story. He's shown what we can do for the entire country. Take my word for it. There will be no more distractions. Everything else is going to go smoothly. And when I speak the next night, it will be a tremendous end to an already tremendous convention. So tremendous, people won't even believe it."

The Tycoon removed the lavalier microphone and gave Diane Laughlin a cursory handshake. McNelis walked Diane and her crew down the hallway to the elevator. Moments later, he was back in the suite.

McNelis had cleared out all of the regular staffers who usually clustered around during their morning meetings (hovering attentively and nervously like stuntmen waiting to be punched in an action film). This lack of administrative support meant that McNelis really wanted to talk today. That was good. That was what the Tycoon wanted too.

The Tycoon stretched himself out on the sofa. McNelis took a more vertical position at a nearby desk chair. He turned on the suite's wall-sized television, and tuned to the Tycoon's favorite network, where the just-concluded interview would shortly air.

"Well, what do we do now?" the Tycoon asked.

McNelis, who seemed confident, answered: "I think we've just done it. I think we've deflected and deflated. In the minds of the voters, this wasn't anything other than a stupid prank."

The Tycoon nodded seriously. He had recovered from his apoplectic fits of the prior evening. Now he was all coiled tension. He realized that their reaction to this unscheduled interruption was absolutely key. Everything might hang in the balance.

"This was their knockout punch," McNelis continued. "Imagine how much trouble it must have been for them to coordinate this. Set it all up. Get those drones inside. This was supposed to leave you unconscious on the canvas, but it looks to me like you're still standing."

The Tycoon smiled. He liked the idea that he was tough and resilient, and could survive an enemy's worst hay-maker.

"Think about it, what else do they have left?" McNelis said. "If they had other ammo, they would have used it. Anybody who believed their insinuations is going to get written off as fake news. I really do think we're in the clear."

"That was a nice touch with the stethoscope," the Tycoon said. "Worked like a charm."

"Thanks," said McNelis.

"Incidentally," said the Tycoon, "how did you . . ."

"One of our tech people rigged it up," McNelis said. "Wasn't cheap to get it done overnight, but you get what you pay for."

"It was worth every penny," the Tycoon asserted. "A stethoscope is going to become a symbol of our movement. The political cartoons will have me as a doctor here to heal America. You'll see."

"If this didn't stop you, sir, nothing's going to," McNelis said.

"What about the Uneeda members?" the Tycoon asked. "Be honest."

McNelis shrugged to say it was a small matter.

"We got some calls saying they were concerned, of course. But I assured them we're handling it. When your interview airs, they'll see it's been handled."

"Excellent," the Tycoon said.

McNelis began to scroll through his phone. It seemed as though something had just occurred to him.

"Oh," he said. "There is one other thing."

The Tycoon raised a hairy blond eyebrow.

"Nothing to worry about," said McNelis. "It's the Governor. Apparently he'd like to meet with you this afternoon, before he gives his speech."

"Why?" the Tycoon said grouchily. He had better things to do.

"Doesn't say," McNelis replied. "Maybe he just wants a pep talk from you. Maybe he thinks it's traditional for the presidential and vice presidential candidates to commune before a big speech."

"Sentimentalist nonsense," said the Tycoon. "But fine. We'll get it over with as quick as we can. I know . . . Have someone put together a list of inspiring quotes that presidents have told vice presidents. I'll quote some horseshit that feels historic to him, and we'll be on our way."

"Of course, sir," McNelis said.

The Tycoon reclined even further on the couch and closed his eyes.

He did not "sleep" in the traditional sense, yet the Tycoon found it pleasant, on occasion, to clear his mind and limit his interactions with others. Often, this was most effectively accomplished through the simulacra of a nap.

McNelis took the hint and moved off to a different part of the suite to work.

The Tycoon felt like a general who had just survived the enemy onslaught. Or maybe that wasn't quite it. It was more like he'd seen the enemy's superweapon, and it was a big ol' dud. It felt to the Tycoon like he would not be stopped. Could not be stopped. At this rate, Initiative X would not be necessary.

McNelis had done a good job. After he was president, the Tycoon would reward him. A seat on the National Security Council, say. (For whatever reason, McNelis was in that small fraction of the Tycoon's inner circle who *did not* desire zombihood for himself one day.) Nobody was perfect, though. McNelis could have something else.

The Tycoon allowed his mind to wander. As zombies did not need to breathe, he did not focus on his own respiration to relax, but instead on the low hum of the air conditioner in the next room. The Tycoon felt pleased and confident. Everything was going to plan.

Sooner than he expected, the afternoon had rolled around. McNelis stood in the doorway and cleared his throat.

"Got some Grade A sentimental hokum," McNelis said proudly, dangling a dossier in his hand. "Starts with Washington's advice to Adams and goes from there."

"Great!" the Tycoon said, rising to his feet and smoothing down the front of his jacket. "I'll only need one or two. And if I misremember the words a little, it'll just seem more authentic that way. More real."

"Of course it does," McNelis agreed.

The Tycoon looked at his wristwatch. (It was from his own brand's signature collection. It was flimsy and made in China, but few of his customers knew or cared.)

"I was out for a while," the Tycoon said. "Everything is going to plan downstairs at the convention today?"

McNelis nodded.

"Yes. I've been watching the coverage, too. Your interview did the trick. No surprises. No hiccups. People loved the stethoscope."

"Tremendous," said the Tycoon. "Then I suppose we should get this over with."

They prepared to depart. The Tycoon snatched the dossier from McNelis's hand as he walked past. Moments later, they were in the elevator, heading down one floor to where the Governor and his staff were encamped. The Tycoon hastily read the words of Washington, Jefferson, and Madison assembled for him. Then he closed the folder and pushed it back at McNelis.

"I can't make sense of this," he said.

"Their language is archaic, of course," McNelis told him. "It's two hundred years old."

"How important can it be if I can't understand it?" the Tycoon said.

McNelis nodded to say that there must be some deep truth to this observation.

"I'll just wing it," the Tycoon told him. "A thousand dollars says he'll never know the difference."

Moments later the elevator arrived and the Tycoon and McNelis stepped off. A few feet away was the Governor's suite. A member of the Secret Service stood outside the door and nodded at the Tycoon. McNelis knocked and one of the Governor's staffers answered.

"Right this way," the staffer said, and conducted the two men into the spacious rooms beyond.

Immediately, the Tycoon saw that it was crowded. *Too* crowded. An extra ten or twelve people. That was the first thing that raised the Tycoon's hackles. The second thing was that the assemblage looked far too devout for its own good. Some of the men in the room wore traditional garb of some sort, and long orthodox beards. Others looked like the Governor. In addition to the gold crosses on their chests, they had cheery dispositions, meticulous shaves, and short haircuts that bespoke early bedtimes and a profound disinclination to question authority. There was a nun, too. An honest-to-God nun in a habit!

In the center of them all was the Governor. He had a look on his face like a kid caught with his hand in the cookie jar. He smiled sheepishly as the Tycoon approached.

"Before you get mad, I just want you to know one thing," the Governor said, raising a finger. "I want you to know that this is *exactly* what it looks like! We're living in moments of great spiritual awakening. And after what you showed me in Florida—and no, these good people don't know all the . . . particular details—I realized that your soul was in need of saving, friend! To that end, I've flown up my special team. This is the group that helped me organize that religious freedom bill we passed down in Indiana. These are the best of the best, and they're passionate about making this country the best that it can be. They're also passionate about helping you to see the light!"

The Tycoon found it difficult to hide his slowly-building sneer.

"I know you're not the most regular churchgoer," said the Governor. "That doesn't matter. Everybody needs a good come-to-Jesus every now and again. Or come to Yahweh. Or even Allah. Or whatever you like. The point is that you get there."

The Governor extended his hand.

"I'd like to offer you our fellowship," he said. "I believe that you can have a transformation here today. That you can mend your ways. Not only that you *can*, but you *must* before you assume our nation's highest office. The good book shows us that no man is beyond redemption. Tell me, will you pray with us?"

The assembled clergy looked on expectantly. The Tycoon realized that the Governor was serious.

Stark-raving serious.

The Tycoon let out an unnecessary sigh.

"Okay," the Tycoon said. "Fine. Let's pray."

The Governor grinned his televangelist grin.

"You have no idea how happy I am to hear you say that," he told the Tycoon. "No idea at all."

They prayed. In tongues and traditions that were wholly unfamiliar to the Tycoon. In shouts and in mumbles. In spoken words and in song. Now and then, something in the prayers might seem vaguely familiar to the Tycoon. He had heard it in a poem, or seen it on a television show. Other times, the utterances seemed utterly alien and strange. But whenever the religious officials around him clasped their hands together, the Tycoon clasped his own with all his might. When they bowed their heads, he bowed as low as he could. When they affected expressions of great contrition, the Tycoon tried to feel as sorry as he possibly could for all the things that he had done.

Great, gold-embossed books were brought out. Some were ancient and dusty, while others looked newer than the ministers' haircuts. Whatever their states, they were cracked open and read aloud from. Sometimes they were passed to the Tycoon. As much as he disliked the written word, the Tycoon cleared his throat and read in a clear voice whenever prompted. He read as though he loved what he was reading. As though his life depended on it.

It went on for the better part of an hour. The enthusiasm of the religious assembled around the Tycoon showed no sign of waning. This was probably the highlight of their year, he thought to himself. They were imbued with limitless energy. In mounting horror, the Tycoon realized that—after nearly an hour—they were just getting started.

But *he* could not stand much more of it. He certainly could not bear to keep it up until the future Vice President left to give his speech. (And in a larger sense, the Tycoon became concerned about what precedent this might set. This ambush by the Governor was not appropriate. In the subsequent years, would the Vice President feel himself free to convene a prayer gathering whenever he deemed the Tycoon's actions or demeanor insufficiently pious? The hubris! The very *idea*! No. It would not do.)

The more the Tycoon thought about it, it seemed that drastic action must be taken.

"Hallelujah!" the Tycoon cried, interrupting a reading from the Kabbalah. "I am bigly saved! Bigly, bigly saved, I assure you. I don't think anybody has ever been so saved!"

"Hallelujah!" several members of the assemblage cried.

"Yes, hallelujah!" the Tycoon continued. "And I want to thank all of you for taking the time out of your busy schedules—and all the important work you do—to facilitate this incredible, spectacular thing that has happened here today. You've changed me so deeply. I renounce my former ways!

But listen . . . We all know the Governor is really the one I should be thanking the most."

The Governor gave an "aw shucks" grin.

"No, I'm serious," said the Tycoon. "In fact, I wonder if you could leave us for a moment. Yes, I'd like to be alone with the Governor. I think that he and I should pray together, just us. This is a very special moment for a future president and vice president . . . God willing, of course. I'd like to impart some special words that I believe George Washington once said to John Adams . . ."

The Tycoon looked up earnestly at the assembled religious officials, to the Governor's staffers, and to McNelis.

Then he gave McNelis a quick wink. The man nodded as though he understood perfectly.

The Governor, for his part, was beaming, delighted to have saved a soul.

"Yes, let's give the next president and vice president some private time together," McNelis said. He helped to usher everyone else out of the room. The doors were closed from without, leaving the Tycoon and the Governor alone in the drawing room of the suite.

Surprising the Governor, the Tycoon fell to his knees and clasped his hands.

"Please, pray with me," the Tycoon said.

The Governor enthusiastically knelt beside him on the carpet.

Both men closed their eyes. The only sound was the Governor's breathing. The Tycoon put a hand on the back of the Governor's neck and pulled him close.

"I want you to know how much all of this means to me," the Tycoon said. "Your taking this step shows me that you're a man of conviction. You wouldn't do all this if you didn't care. So I want to show you that I care too. I really do."

The Tycoon held the Governor tightly now. Too tightly. So tightly that his hand vibrated. For a moment, the Governor seemed to accept that this enthusiasm was the result of a religious conversion. But then the Tycoon's manicured fingernails began to dig deep into the Governor's neck. The Governor's eyes opened and he blinked uncomfortably.

"Watch the scratches, friend," he said through a nervous smile. "I've got to give a big speech in a few hours."

"I am aware of our timeline," said the Tycoon. "I am also aware that a scratch *tends* to get the job done . . . but a bite is *always* a sure thing."

Before the Governor could react, the Tycoon pulled him close, pulled down on his white dress shirt, and bit him—hard—on the nape of the neck.

The confused Governor tried to surrender himself to it, like a kitten being carried by the scruff. But the pain became too much. The Governor tore himself away, and the Tycoon was left with a small piece of flesh stuck between his teeth.

"What?!" the Governor said in confusion. "What are you doing?"

He reached back, gingerly touched his neck, winced, and brought his hand up to his face. His fingers were covered in blood.

"What have you . . . ?" the Governor said in bewilderment.

"So sorry about that," the Tycoon replied, spitting the flesh onto the carpet. "An old fraternity tradition, from business school. It's a show of respect. You should be bigly flattered."

"Wait . . ." said the Governor, a hard truth dawning on him. "Did you just . . . ? Am I . . . ?"

"Here, let's pray some more," the Tycoon said. He stayed on his knees and clasped his hands. (One eye was shut, but one was watching the Governor. The Governor looked around the room anxiously.)

"I think I should get this looked at," he said, again and again dabbing the back of his neck and bringing his bloody fingers to his face.

"The only medicine we need is the healing power of prayer," the Tycoon said.

Secretly, he realized something more was required. As drops of blood began to fleck the carpeting around them, the Tycoon reached into his pocket and depressed a button on his phone. The one that automatically summoned McNelis.

Moments later, the Tycoon heard McNelis assuring the religious officials he would only be a moment, creeping into the room, and shutting the door.

"Jay," the Tycoon said, rising to his feet. "The Governor is undergoing a conversion of his own."

McNelis nodded and smiled. A few steps away, the man from Indiana was turning white. He had become unsteady. His eyes looked big as dinner plates.

The Tycoon said: "Let's wrap that bite with a bandage so . . . I was going to say 'So it doesn't get infected' but by the pallor of your skin, I'd say it's already too late."

"I feel sick," the Governor said. "I think I might throw up. What is going on?"

"Oh, I think you know," the Tycoon replied.

McNelis went to the bathroom and returned with a set of towels. With surprising strength, he ripped them into thin strips and tied them around the Governor's neck to staunch the flow of blood. Meanwhile, the Governor's legs gave out and he collapsed onto a couch.

"My speech . . ." the Governor mumbled. "I need to call my chief of staff."

The Governor managed to reach into his pocket and come out with his phone.

"*I'll* take that," McNelis said, snatching it from him.

"My . . ." the Governor protested, his disorientation and sickness increasing.

"Don't worry, you'll get your phone back," the Tycoon said. "You'll also be fine to deliver your speech tonight. More than fine. Something tells me it's going to be one of the best speeches you've ever made."

"What are you . . . ?"

But the Governor could not finish. He collapsed onto the couch and grew quiet and still. The color continued to drain from his face. McNelis placed a wad of towels under his head. Then he looked over at the Tycoon.

"Cutting this one a little close, boss."

"It'll be fine," the Tycoon said confidently, glancing at his watch. "How long does it usually take? An hour? Ninety minutes? We'll be fine."

"Time-wise, sure," said McNelis, rubbing his chin. "But I'm thinking more of the shock to the system. If he's 'off' tonight, people are going to notice. Especially after what happened to you yesterday."

"Jay, he forced my hand on this!" the Tycoon said. "He really did. I didn't have a choice, did I? Prayer sessions?

Conversions? Repentance? There isn't room for that kind of thing in this organization. I tried to let him take the other route. I showed him what I was and invited him to make his peace with it. But no. That wasn't enough. Now he has to take the consequences. Besides, I think it's better this way. Now we know for sure that he's on the team."

McNelis shrugged to say there was no use in second-guessing it. The die had been cast.

"What do you want to do about . . . ?" McNelis asked, gesturing to the group waiting outside.

"We need to give it some time, obviously," the Tycoon said. "Can you take them on a tour of the arena or something? Distract them?"

"I can," McNelis said. "They'll have questions, though. You two were a bit loud just now."

"Tell them we were speaking in tongues," the Tycoon said. "Tell them anything you like. Hell, I don't care. Just make sure they stay occupied."

"Aye aye," McNelis said, and gave a little salute. The Tycoon frowned in a way that told him to knock off the hijinks. This was serious business.

McNelis let his expression take on a grimmer aspect, and sauntered back to where the religious officials waited. The Tycoon sat down on the couch beside the Governor. He looked down at his white haired running mate intently.

"My goodness," the Tycoon said to the unconscious, unmoving body. "You *have* been a bit of trouble, haven't you? Well that's all behind us now. Your new life starts tonight. We're going to be in perfect harmony—you and I—from this point forward. Isn't that nice?"

The Tycoon leaned back on the couch. Even though he could not sleep—would never again sleep—he allowed himself, once more, to close his eyes.

THE REPORTER

"**W**hat is wrong with people?"

That, it seemed, was the only question to ask.

Jessica had posed the query at the hotel bar next to Tim. (The other members of the TruthTeller staff had not been able to pull themselves away from their work.) Both Jessica and Tim had been awake most of the night, following up on developments and churning out copy. Jessica had had only two swallows of her sixteen-ounce Guinness, but was already feeling lightheaded.

"I mean, people saw everything," she continued, looking into the murky brown of her drink like a seer staring into a crystal ball. "They saw a heart monitor get planted on a major-party candidate, *during that party's convention.* They saw that it showed he had no pulse. And . . . ? And everybody just thinks it was a joke. They think it was a way of calling his policies 'heartless.' I can't believe it. Then there's what was on the thumb drive. His goddam medical records . . . which show there is nothing to record. That his body doesn't, shouldn't function. And my bosses won't even consider running those— nobody is running those—because they can't be verified. What more do people want?!"

Tim sighed in solidarity and stared into his own drink.

"That stunt this morning with the stethoscope was good," he said. "Of course, it wasn't a controlled environment, and the stethoscope wasn't provided by the journalist—but still. Good television. Makes it look like he's not afraid of anything."

Tim took a sip and asked: "You've heard nothing else from the Knights?"

Jessica shook her head.

"Total radio silence," she said. "I think this was their one, big push. All their efforts had to have gone into it. Think about it. Building those drones? Getting those passes to access the backstage area? Doing it all so fast?"

"Yeah, it was a lot," Tim said. "A lot of money and favors got spent. No question."

"I just feel like . . . I feel like I can't just give up and go home," Jessica said. "I met the Knights. They're real people. One of their members died right in front of us. I can't pretend like I don't know what's going on here. At the same time, if what happened yesterday didn't do it? I mean, what am I going to do? I don't even have any proof that I met the Knights. Except for you."

Jessica took another swallow of Guinness.

"What did Deep Throat tell Woodward and Bernstein?" Tim said, struggling to recall. "Follow the money? Right?"

Jessica glanced askance at him and wrinkled her nose.

"That never really happened," she said. "They just added it in the movie version of *All the President's Men.* You might have known that if you'd actually finished J-school."

Tim decided not to take this dig too personally. Jessica was in a foul mood and did not mean anything by it, he assured himself.

"Well, with most people, you *could* say 'follow the money' because money's what people want," Tim opined. "But what do you do with a zombie? Follow the brains?"

"If money can get you brains, then I'd *still* say follow the money," Jessica said dourly.

"What does he still want at this point?" Tim asked. "He's a billionaire tycoon who lives at the top of a golden tower. And he's a member of the living dead, which means he gets to live forever. What is left for him? Why run for president and risk it all?"

"There is no explanation," Jessica said between sips. "People who run for president have something wrong with them. Look at any field of presidential candidates and you're going to find something from the DSM-5 for each one. Narcissists. The power-mad. People with delusions of grandeur. People who think they're sent by God to carry out a holy mission. Xenophobes looking to keep unwashed hordes at bay. Psychopaths who'll do or say *anything* to get something. There's literally no understanding these people."

"Maybe," Tim said evenly. "But rich and powerful people still want to stay rich and powerful. What do the billionaires in groups like Bilderberg or Uneeda want?"

Jessica went to take another drink but stopped when her Guinness glass was halfway to her lips. Something had just occurred to her. She set her glass back down.

"Speaking of Uneeda, what happened with that? They met right before he spoke. We thought maybe it was because he was speaking, and . . . What?"

Tim shook his head to say he had not pieced it together yet.

"Our sources couldn't get us intel from inside," he said.

"Do you think they *know* about him?" she asked.

"It's possible," Tim said.

"What if Uneeda members don't just *know* about him, but they're also like him? Also zombies?"

Tim considered this.

"Now that you mention it, it makes a lot of sense. I've heard crazier things, at least. The Uneeda membership are prominent people who tend to gradually fall out of the public eye. Now and then, a press release will come out saying one of them died at 101, but they haven't been seen for years and the funeral's always closed casket."

Gears continued to turn inside of Jessica's head.

"Are there any other members of the Uneeda society here at the convention?" she asked. "Besides the candidate, I mean."

"I don't think so," Tim said, taking out his phone. "But lemme check. I've heard rumors that Hogson has petitioned to join. That would also make his reaction make sense during the debate. Maybe when he snarled, it wasn't a threat to bite him, but instead to . . . not bite him."

Tim sent a text and set his phone down on the bar. A few moments later, the phone vibrated and he picked it back up.

"Dan says there's one," he announced. "Cornelius Van Bergen. Old money from Albany. Descended from the first Dutch settlers. Ancestors were in timber way back in the day, and then in so many things people kind of lost track. Cornelius is very old now, but they say he doesn't look a day over 95."

Tim's phone vibrated again.

"Dan also says he's a guest of the delegation from New York. Doesn't have any scheduled appearances, but he's supposed to be around for part of the week. That's all he can find for the moment."

Jessica remained very still.

"What?" Tim said. "What are you thinking?"

"If we can't follow the money, maybe we should follow the brains," Jessica said, finishing her drink.

"What does that mean?" Tim asked.

"I feel like we should try to talk to Van Bergen and see if we can get something from him," she said. "Depending on what the Uneeda Society actually is, he could know something more. Or *be* something more. That's the story here. What does a zombie want? What does this candidate want? If we can figure that out, maybe we can show people something that will *make* them believe the truth. We can find something that won't be dispelled by TV anchors fiddling with stethoscopes."

"Yeah, like maybe zombies aren't all identical," Tim said. "In terms of their personalities, I mean. Maybe there's a way he would talk to us."

Jessica thought for a moment more.

"That . . . you could have something there," she said, signaling to the barman that she would take another pour. "Maybe there are other zombies who don't want one of their kind to be president. Like, they're happy with what they have. They're rich and can live in mansions and have brains delivered by a butler on a silver tray—and that's enough. Maybe they also think that it's crazy to want to go for the presidency."

Jessica thanked the barman and accepted her new drink.

"So you want to find a dissenting voice?" Tim asked.

"I dunno," Jessica said, taking a sip. "Or maybe we can pry them apart some other way. If there's zombie solidarity, we could try to break it. Make this guy Van Bergen wonder if he's heard wrong. Do *something* that gets him to talk."

"I just don't see—" Tim began.

"Look, do you have a better idea right now?" Jessica asked. "I spent half the night writing stories making it very fucking clear how this candidate could be a zombie, and what that projector-drone stunt was supposed to show. My own paper told me it was too extreme to run. Too wild. You saw my article after they were through with it. It's like I was reporting on a projector malfunction, instead of, I don't know, reporting that good evidence was provided that a major party candidate is a zombie."

Tim silently shook his head, picked up his phone, and sent another text. A moment later it was answered.

"Dan says he'll make some calls and get a line on Van Bergen's whereabouts," Tim said.

"Okay," Jessica said. "When Dan finds him, I think I should be the one to make the approach."

"What do you mean?" Tim said.

"Are you going to make me say it, Tim?" she replied. "You work for TruthTeller. I don't think that's a name that's going to open the kind of doors to get to someone like Cornelius Van Bergen."

"You're forgetting that I met with McNelis, and he thinks we're basically part of the campaign at this point," Tim said, a bit defensively. "I would say we have some of the best access of any news outlet here."

Jessica finished her second drink and pantomimed for a third.

"Maybe we can work together," Jessica said. "*That's* what they won't be expecting. Good cop, bad cop."

"I . . . I'm not sure that makes sense," Tim said. "Do you usually drink this much?"

Jessica waved off his concerns.

"I feel more clearheaded than I've felt in days," she replied. "We should do this more often."

Tim seemed to think for a moment.

"Actually, I think I see how this could work," he said.

"Right? Let's do shots to celebrate."

"You need to *stop drinking now*," Tim said, sliding her Guinness away from her.

"Don't infan . . . infantizz . . . infantilz . . ."

"Infantilize you?"

"Yes. It's misogynistic. Men have been doing it to women for years."

"Yes, but I literally can't follow you when you're drunk. Back in J-school, you always got confusing when you'd had more than three drinks."

"What? *Fine.*"

"Now . . . you're thinking of going in as the bad cop, right?" Tim said.

"Yes, obviously," Jessica replied.

"So what if we do it like this?" Tim said. "You send a few feelers out to his staff, but shit they're sure to ignore. Be cagy about what you want. They won't initially respond because they don't like your outlet. Then, I use my access to make contact. It'll be confirmed that TruthTeller is down with the campaign, on the right side, yeah? I'm touching base because there's an emergency. A fire we need to put out."

Tim looked at Jessica, signaling that now she could take the baton and run with it.

"So you tell them that I've got a bee in my bonnet because someone told me something-something Uneeda zombies," she said. "Like, I've heard that their candidate is going to make them a protected minority group when he's president . . . or something. But you . . . you thought you better mention it because McNelis told you he wasn't even going to float that the government was *aware* of the undead until after the first hundred days. And he was going to wait until his second term to fully reveal the truth about the Uneeda Society."

"Yes!" said Tim. "Only I can't get in touch with McNelis or his people for some reason—because he's busy; because it's the third night of the convention—and I'm worried you're going to do something rash. You've heard that he, Van Bergen, is in Uneeda, so you're going to try to get him to give a confirmation. You've got this idea that your story should run on the last night of the convention. So I need . . . I need to tell him to keep to the party line. The Uneeda line. Whatever."

"Right," said Jessica. "And then his staff will see the junk queries I sent. They'll confirm I've been trying to get in touch."

"Yes!" said Tim. "But I tell him that I'm going to handle everything . . . but that's after I've gotten him to confirm what we need confirmed. On tape. Maybe on camera. It will already be too late for him. And then we take *that* up the ladder. Or just take it public. Make them have to deny it. Often, that's the best approach. Make it so they all have to lie about it. So it really comes back and decimates him when it gets proven true."

"That would . . ." Jessica said. "That would work, I think."

Jessica looked into Tim's eyes for a moment, feeling stunned.

"Okay," she said, pushing back from the bar. "Then I'm off to send Cornelius Van Bergen some emails."

THE FAKE NEWSMAN

Tim Fife stood outside the door to the arena suite and waited. A security guard in a dark suit and darker (somehow) sunglasses blocked his path. The guard remained motionless, his expression unreadable. He waited for the voice in his earpiece to come back with a response. Yea or nay.

Inside the suite sat Cornelius Van Bergen, who had not chosen to join the New York delegates on the convention floor.

Tim had let the guard know that he was with TruthTeller, shown his press pass, and said he needed to speak to Van Bergen on a matter of utmost importance. Said he was expected. That'd he'd already been in touch.

When it was clear from the man's expression that this would not be enough, Tim had also managed to include the words "Jay McNelis" and "Uneeda Society" in his pleas. Those had been the magic words. The guard had spoken into a receiver in his coat, and then told Tim to wait.

Tim looked at the door, smiling politely.

Inside, his guts roiled.

It had taken Dan's sources—whoever or whatever they were, Tim still did not know—several hours to locate Van Bergen's precise location. This delay had given Jessica time to leave plenty of inquiries with his people, but it also cut things close. The festivities taking place on the stage had almost reached their culmination. The Governor of Indiana would take the podium shortly.

"Okay."

Tim looked back up into the face of the imposing guard, whose face still seemed like stone.

"Excuse me?" Tim said. "Did you just say something?"

The guard looked Tim up and down, smiled like a snarling dog, and nodded.

"Did you . . . Did you say—"

"I said okay," the guard replied.

"Oh!" Tim said, greatly relieved. "I'll just step inside then. If . . . If that's all right."

He took a step forward. Then another. Even as he did so, it seemed to Tim that something was off. That only some strange misunderstanding accounted for the guard's failing to perform an ornate martial arts throat-punch on the chubby reporter, sending him to the floor, gasping for breath and dazed. Even as Tim passed through the doorway and walked inside the suite, he still half-expected the blow to come. The man exuded a capacity for great violence. (When the door shut behind him, Tim's first thought was of how he must pass this sentry again on the way out.)

Beyond the gatekeeper was an arena suite arrayed in the way arena suites so often were. There was a kitchenette and several serving islands where chicken wings, sausages, and burgers had been presented in large metal trays. There were also plates of fruit, and coolers stocked with soda and beer. And none of it had been touched. Absolutely none of it. There was a "wrongness" to it that quickly settled over Tim. This food was days old. The ice in the coolers had melted. The Sterno burners underneath the trays had burned out.

More detail than this was difficult for Tim to ascertain because of another unusual quality of the suite. The lights had been dimmed to a positively inconvenient degree. Enough to make it hard to get around. At first, Tim thought perhaps this had been done to emphasize the images on the three wall-mounted televisions carrying coverage of the convention below. But the figures in the room—there only seemed to be three of them—were not seated anywhere near the televisions.

Rather, they were clustered together in a dark corner, near the edge of where the suite opened up to the arena-proper. They were eerily, perfectly still.

Tim approached. Despite his substantial carriage, the suite was carpeted and his footsteps made no noise. At a loss for what to do, Tim cleared his throat.

Still the three figures did not move. Still there was no response. The speaker at the convention below was a middle-aged woman (the head of a faith-based charitable organization, as Tim understood it) with a very soft voice. Tim cleared his voice a second time. Still the trio kept their backs to him. Tim found it inconceivable that they did not detect his presence. He drew even closer.

Suddenly, the figure in the center turned its head.

Tim had seen some startling things before. Anyone who worked on a website that operated in "uncensored" realms "too extreme" for the mainstream saw his share of wild and disturbing subject matter via his inbox. But *this* face . . . It was a Halloween mask. It was a special effect. It seemed not merely too old, but too *exaggerated* to possibly be real.

The ears and nose had grown enormous. The pair of warts on the left cheek were large as thumbs. The brow wrinkles were so deep and heavy that the top of his forehead seemed to droop down as though trying to reach the eyes. The pate was bald—nothing so bad there—but the bad toupee covering it gave the man a further strange and hideous aspect. He looked like some kind of gargoyle attempting to pass as human for the day.

Tim made an involuntary noise that was very short and very high-pitched.

"Young man, if you have something to say, I exhort you to say it!" the horrible masque intoned.

Tim was shocked into silence for a moment, but only a moment.

"Mister Van Bergen?" he asked hopefully.

The grotesque thing nodded. The two figures surrounding it also turned and looked. They were thin, nondescript men in late middle age (though they seemed positively youthful next to Van Bergen)—possibly his handlers or assistants, possibly something else. They narrowed their eyes and exchanged a quick glance. Who was this interloper, and how did he deserve to be here if he didn't even recognize Cornelius Van Bergen on sight?

"I mean . . . Mister Van Bergen," Tim quickly asserted rather than asked. "It has come to my attention that a certain East Coast news outlet has been trying to substantiate a particular set of facts regarding the next president's plans for . . . members of the Uneeda Society and their ilk."

The horrible old man turned his attention back to the convention floor. He waved the ancient gnarled claw that was his hand in a dismissive circular motion, to say that his associates could handle this one.

"You are referring to the queries from . . . ?" one of the men said leadingly.

Tim realized this was a test.

"From Jessica Smith," Tim said. "As I expressed to Jay McNelis previously, if my outlet, TruthTeller, can help the campaign in any way, of course we'd want to. I may be able to reach out to Jessica and convince her to change the story or pull it entirely. She comes from a rich family, so she's not subject to a lot of the normal inducements. But she and I have a connection. You can verify that. I think I can get her to come around."

One of the mysterious men looked back and forth between Tim and an image of Jessica he had pulled up on his phone.

Whatever the TruthTeller reporter might mean, a connection of a romantic nature was probably not what he was getting at.

"Why have you come here, really?" one of the two men said, putting his phone away. "What do you need from Mr. Van Bergen?"

"Well first of all . . . he hasn't responded to Jessica?" Tim asked.

"*Of course* not," one of the men hissed. His tone asked "What kind of operation do you think this is?"

"Right," Tim said carefully. "But because she's singled out Mr. Van Bergen, we need to be careful. After all, he's the only other member of the Uneeda Society at the convention, and the only member of the walking dead not standing for election. I haven't been able to raise Jay McNelis to ask how we should handle it, so obviously I wanted to check with you. I want to err on the side of safety and discretion. You know."

There. He had done it. Tim had just mentioned Uneeda, the walking dead, and knowledge and complicity on the part of Jay McNelis. And the three recording devices secreted upon his body had captured all of it. The hidden camera in the bridge of his eyeglasses had it on video that was being instantaneously uploaded to the cloud.

The only question was what would come next.

"This is not an emergency, and this is not worth Mr. Van Bergen's valuable time," one of the mysterious men said firmly.

Okay, Tim thought to himself. That was a start. They hadn't said "What the hell do you mean by the walking dead? Get out of this suite immediately!"

But Tim needed more.

"Right," Tim said. "It's just that Mr. McNelis was able to apprise me of how . . . how . . . let's say *nuanced* the rollout of the full platform is going to be. The positioning of the undead policy elements is going to be a very careful thing, he says. I just want to ensure TruthTeller comports with that positioning. Maybe I shut my friend Jessica down completely, get her to kill the story, sure. Or *maybe* the best approach is to give her something that will lay the groundwork for what's to come . . . in a way that connects with the objectives of the campaign? Oh, and the Uneeda Society, of course."

Would that do it? Would they give him anything more?

For a moment, it seemed they would not. One of the men actually turned back around to watch the convention speaker, as if to signal that this matter was closed. The other man considered it for a moment, then shook his head. Yet just as he opened his mouth to say something dismissive, another voice spoke.

"Boy," it said. "Come and sit by me for a moment."

Tim realized the speaker was Cornelius Van Bergen.

His twin handlers looked at one another in surprise.

"Move, you two," Van Bergen croaked. "He is a wide young man. You will have to make some space."

Tim swallowed hard.

Van Bergen wanted Tim to side beside him. He could think of nothing more fortuitous to his investigation. And nothing— nothing in the moment, at least—that sounded more abhorrent than being physically close to such a creature. Van Bergen rotated his horrible neck nearly 180 degrees. His eyes were cloudy but his gaze nonetheless piercing. He smiled to reveal prominent canines, ancient and yellowed beyond all reckoning.

Tim summoned his courage and forced himself to advance. The twin assistants glowered as they scooted over. Tim pushed past and gingerly seated himself next to Van Bergen.

Tim did not know if he had ever been this close to a zombie. It aroused his curiosity as well as his abject disgust. How long had Van Bergen been a member of the walking dead? Had he been bitten late in life and preserved in advanced age, or had he been bitten as a younger man? And did the signs of age on his face arise from something other than passing human years? Was he supernaturally aged? Did zombies deteriorate in some other way, not yet understood outside their own circles?

He could imagine Van Bergen as one of the original Dutch patroons, settling New York before the British. He could also imagine him as a twentieth century industrialist who had come to zombihood in retirement. Who knew what to believe?

The only thing Tim understood for certain—as he chummily sidled up next to the creature—was that the thing invoked disgust and fear as deep as he had ever known. It was no longer a mystery to Tim why people ran screaming from the walking dead.

"Young man," Van Bergen said, looking down at the convention speaker below. "You're not the first person who was ever been keen to do a favor for the Uneeda Society. Not many look to help us without an eye to their own membership. Jay McNelis is the only exception to that rule I know. Something is deeply wrong with that man."

Tim nodded and hoped Van Bergen would not look him in the face again. It was easier when the man's ancient, milky eyes were turned away.

"Those two vultures over there?" the zombie continued, staring hard at his handlers. "They want it. They're in line. A whole lot of people are. Too many, it seems to me. And how about yourself?"

Tim thought carefully about how to respond.

"I would be lying if I said I'd never thought about it," Tim answered. "I mean, who wouldn't be tempted? Living forever. Getting to spend your time pursuing the one thing in the world that you *know* can bring you happiness and pleasure? That sounds like magic to me."

Van Bergen smiled. A grim and horrible smile to be sure, but still a smile.

"Perhaps it is magic of a sort," he said. "But it may not be around much longer."

Tim smiled politely, wondering to what the man might be referring.

"As you already know, there are those in our membership who have decided to wager it all—everything we undead have carefully built for ourselves—out of a desire for even more," Van Bergen continued.

The zombie gestured to the podium below where the speaker prepared to introduce the Governor of Indiana.

"What did you think all of this was?" he continued. "I'll tell you, young man. It's a bid for more. Some years it's the oil companies. Other years, the defense contractors. Well, this year it was our turn."

"That's got to be exciting though, right?" Tim asked innocently.

Van Bergen smiled again.

"That's one way of putting it," the zombie said. "The undead are making themselves vulnerable like never before. That is true."

Suddenly, there was a great roar from the audience below. Music began to play. The tired conventioneers stood. The Governor of Indiana had been introduced. Now, in just a moment, he would take the stage.

Tim felt this would be the ideal time to depart. He had what he needed. In spades. He could not wait to connect with Jessica, and with his TruthTeller colleagues, and decide upon the best way to break the story.

"Well, I'm sure you'll want to watch the Governor," Tim said, easing out of his seat. "I believe I've taken enough of your time."

Yet as he stood, Tim was stopped abruptly by something that felt like the stiff branch of an old tree pressing hard against his shoulder.

Tim looked over and saw he was in the ancient zombie's grasp.

"What is your hurry, young man?" Van Bergen asked.

"Oh," Tim said hesitantly. "Nothing, really. I just assumed you'd like your privacy."

Van Bergen leaned in close. Tim immediately wished that he had not. Van Bergen no longer smelled human. There was a "thinginess" about him now. He was no longer a "who" but an "it." Zombies like the Tycoon doubtless concealed this aspect beneath makeup, cologne, mouthwash—and who knew what else. Van Bergen, it seemed, did not feel the need for these pretenses. He presented himself just as what he was. And that was a thing which was quite horrible indeed.

"Between you and me, I get sick of those two buzzards," Van Bergen said, glancing down at his assistants. "Why don't you stay and watch the next speech with me? I could use the fresh blood around."

Tim visibly blanched.

"Ah, I don't mean that you are on the menu," Van Bergen said, flashing his terrifying yellow chompers. "Only that your company would be appreciated. And this matter with your reporter friend . . . It sounds as though it will sort itself out, no?"

Tim wondered if perhaps he really ought to stay. If Van Bergen sensed anything amiss, it would be easy for him to call for the large security guard at the door. And besides, the footage and audio recordings he'd captured so far were safe in the cloud. In other words, he had what he'd come for. If the mission required he spend a few moments more with this unpleasant fossil, Tim would grit his teeth and do it.

"Sure," Tim said, shrinking back into his seat. "I'll stay. Bet it'll be a stemwinder of a speech! The, uh, Governor of Indiana's an incredible man. Brings a lot of balance to the ticket."

The applause below became deafening as the Governor took the podium.

"Done wonders for his home state, he has," Tim prattled on, raising his voice over the din. "I can't want to hear what he says. In fact—"

At that point, Tim stopped talking because he could tell that something was wrong. Beside him, Van Bergen had frozen. And not in a typical, zombie sort of a way. The old man looked aghast. Moments before, Tim would not have deemed this physically possible, but the expression somehow made Van Bergen's features even more unpleasant.

"Son of a *bitch*," Van Bergen said slowly. "He has the look!"

"What?" Tim said, wondering if he had misheard the elderly zombie above the din.

"See how he stands!" Van Bergen shouted. "That is the pose of the recently converted. See how he hesitates a moment too long before changing his facial expressions. See the awkwardness of his wave! Of his smile! See the fresh thirst in his eyes!"

Tim stared at the Governor, and wished he'd brought along his binoculars. The Governor *did* seem to be standing stiffly and waving awkwardly . . . but also, he was just a stiff, awkward guy. To Tim, nothing on display necessarily signaled more than an ill-fitting suit and natural nervousness arising from giving the biggest speech of your life.

Tim pointed this out, but Van Bergen remained unmoved.

"Don't you think I can tell one of my own?" the ancient Dutchman barked. "This was not in the plan . . . This was never . . ."

Van Bergen seemed to forget that Tim was present. He called over to his assistants.

"Get me McNelis, quick!"

The two quickly drew their cell phones like guns and began tapping madly.

"He's not picking up," one of them said. "I'll keep trying."

"Do you realize what this means?" Van Bergen asked Tim.

Tim looked back and forth and shook his head.

"Now . . ." Van Bergen said ominously. "Now everything is going to change."

THE TYCOON

The Tycoon sat in an improvised lounge in the backstage area and watched the bank of monitors. They had been arranged so that he could see the Governor on every camera feed.

"I think he looks good," the Tycoon said chummily to McNelis.

His eyes flitted over, daring the man to disagree.

"Considering what he's been through in the last six hours," McNelis said carefully. "I guess I'd agree."

"Harumph," responded the Tycoon. "He looks fine. More than fine. He looks great, and he's going to *do* great precisely because he's one of us now."

McNelis did not immediately comment.

"He *is* going to do great," the Tycoon asserted.

McNelis sighed.

"Is there a record of a member of your order ever engaging in public speaking within twenty-four hours of a conversion?" he asked casually.

The Tycoon seethed.

"You know there isn't," he replied. "But if there was, I'm sure the record would say that his speaking was bigly improved."

McNelis raised his forehead and shrugged in a way that said this scenario was not *technically* impossible. Then he and the Tycoon returned their attention to the bank of screens. While they watched, the Governor finished his opening thank-yous, announced that he was there to accept the nomination (to more applause), and launched right in to the meat-and-po-tatoes of his speech.

"You know," the Governor began, in a dry, halting voice. "I never thought I would be the one standing here tonight. I thought for sure I'd by watching this convention back at home with all my friends and family in the Hoosier State. But life has a way of surprising you. And just a few short days ago I found myself in New York City meeting with the man who beat a score of primary opponents, won state-after-state-after-state, and then captured the nomination."

The Tycoon smiled. The Governor was speaking carefully and slowly, but he was pulling it off. So this was fine. This was all going to be fine.

"I stood there and accepted my place on the ticket from this colorful, charismatic, exciting man," the Governor continued. "I'd heard about his larger-than-life personality. I'd heard about his shoot-from-the-hip style. But I'd never heard . . . Never heard . . ."

Here, the Governor hesitated. It was brief and passed quickly, but he seemed definitely to lose his place momentarily. Anyone not watching for signs of strain or stress might have missed it entirely. But the Tycoon and McNelis did not.

They exchanged a glance.

"Let's just say I'd heard a lot of things about him, but it turned out I hadn't heard it all," the Governor continued. "What I've learned in the last few days . . . well, you just wouldn't believe."

"Is he going off script?" the Tycoon asked. "I don't remember that wording in the draft we approved."

McNelis opened his laptop and attempted to find the final version of the document.

"I have to tell you . . ." the Governor continued. "While our party's nominee was getting to know *me*, I was getting to know *him*. I was taking the measure of my running mate. Doing some observing. I've seen the way he treats the people who work for him, and how he treats the people he meets for the first time. Now, I can't hide the fact that he can be a little rough when debating politicians on a stage. He seems like he could eat them alive, right? But I've got to know this man one-on-one, and I'm here to assure you that he cares! He is utterly devoted to his family! He is committed to making America great again!"

Applause echoed through the arena.

"That line about eating them alive wasn't in the original," said McNelis, gazing at his glowing laptop screen. "He's sticking to the script generally, but that line was ad libbed."

The Tycoon furrowed his brow.

"Family is important to my running mate, but I want you to know it's important to me as well," the Governor continued. "Even if you do the honor of making me the next Vice President of these United States, no title anybody can give me will ever mean more than those three special letters, D-A-D."

The audience applauded. McNelis nodded to say this was all as scripted. The Tycoon frowned in satisfaction.

"And even if I am sworn-in and Vice President on Inauguration Day," the Governor continued, "no day in my life will ever be more important to me than the day 31 years ago when I first met my lovely and talented wife. She has been my best friend and my strongest asset. There are those in the liberal media who like to scoff at me because I won't eat women other than my wife . . . eat *with* women other than my wife . . . but I will always be a traditionalist when it comes to my values."

McNelis looked at the Tycoon over the top of his computer.

"*What?*" the Tycoon said. "He misspoke. It happens to everybody. I do it all the time. You yourself said it makes me relatable!"

McNelis chose to remain silent, but looked direly concerned.

"Now I can't address this upcoming election without talking about our opponent," the Governor continued to a round of boos. "I know, I know. Just at the moment when America cried out loudest for a new direction and new leadership, they've gone and picked the most predictable name possible! The embodiment of the status quo! The first lady of the failed establishment! Do I even *need* to say her name?"

A new flurry of boos assured the Governor that he did not.

"So we have a choice to make," he continued. "We have to choose where we want to go, and who we trust to get us there. We have to . . . We have to . . .make the decisions. The hard decisions that will protect . . . that will protect this nation, and lead . . . and . . . and lead to economic prosperity. Now, I . . . I . . ."

The Governor began to falter in a serious way.

"What the fuck is this?" the Tycoon demanded angrily as the Governor descended further into stammers. (The audience, for its part, was patient, and seemed willing to allow the man time to find his place.)

McNelis scanned the array of television screens as if looking for a clue.

"He's not even looking at the teleprompters anymore," McNelis shrieked. "It's like he can't focus. He's just staring down at the crowd at the foot of the stage. What's he looking for? Do we have an angle on it?"

And then McNelis saw, and the Tycoon did too. Once they found the right monitor—the one that showed a camera angle from somewhere above and behind the Governor's shoulder—it was impossible to miss.

In the first row, amongst the delegates from Indiana, was a man with the biggest, baldest head either of them had ever seen.

Immediately, the Tycoon recognized the symptoms.

"Oh no," the Tycoon said. "He's got the brain frenzy. Got it bad, from the looks of it. Fight it, damn you! Fight the urge!"

"Brain frenzy?" McNelis said.

"You wouldn't know a thing about it," the Tycoon said. "No zombie is completely immune, but it hits the newer among us hardest of all. What was anybody thinking, putting a man with a head like that right in front of him!?"

On the screen, they watched as the Governor lost his place again and again. He no longer seemed aware of where he was. He only stared into the first row. He seemed to have lost the ability to blink. He began to lick his lips.

"Okay," McNelis said, rising to his feet. "We have to fix this."

He gripped a walkie-talkie and began barking orders into it.

"Clear the first row! Do you copy? Clear the first row of the audience. Get them all out of there now. Yes! You heard me right!"

McNelis ran his hands through his hair. His eyes flickered back and forth between the concerned Tycoon and the screen where the Governor lingered, unmoving and transfixed.

"Should we have Secret Service rush him, like we did for you?" McNelis asked. "Make it look like a security threat? Should—"

Then the Tycoon screamed.

It was not like a scream of terror or pain. It was the noise a man makes when he puts his life savings on a horse that has fallen over a few feet short of the finish line.

"Nooooo, damn you!" the Tycoon cried, his eyes glued to the monitors. They showed him the fresh unfolding horror from every possible angle.

Without further ceremony, the Governor leapt into the audience like a stage-diving rocker. At the same moment, a confused team of Secret Service emerged from the wings and attempted to secure the front row. However, the Governor proved more aerodynamic than anybody had imagined. Sailing through the air, he landed squarely atop the small business owner from Westfield, Indiana with the enormous, sweaty head. Both men tumbled to the floor. Before anyone knew what was happening, the Governor tucked in. The small businessman screamed as the Governor bit him at the brow. Yet the cries were lost in the general chaos that erupted.

The Tycoon hung his head and mumbled something.

"What did you say?" McNelis asked urgently.

"I said he's an amateur," the Tycoon remarked. "The way he's trying to bite right into the skull? See that? A first-timer mistake. Heads are much stronger than the horror movies lead you to believe. He's going to find that out the hard way."

"Erm, yes," said McNelis. "In the meantime, how the hell do we play this? Quick! We need a dossier on the bald man being eaten. Was he an enemy of the Governor? Could he be a terrorist assassin? Did he have a criminal past? The Governor was . . ."

McNelis gesticulated wildly in the air as he attempted to compose a narrative.

"The Governor was *protecting* the rest of the delegation from this man, yeah?" McNelis announced proudly. "The candidate was bravely sacrificing himself—interrupting his own convention speech, even—in order to protect everyone from . . . from . . . Well, I'm sure we can find something on this guy. We'll plant something if we have to. A gun, a knife, a bazooka if that's what it takes."

On the monitors before them, the Governor continued to gnaw. The bald man was fighting back now, but the Governor remained firmly attached by the incisors. The Governor was crazed, and he would not unclench his jaw. As the Secret Service peeled him off, the Governor took with him a long thin strip of the man's temple and forehead. Blood gushed. Onlookers screamed. The cameras did not cut away.

McNelis got back on his walkie-talkie and resumed barking.

The Tycoon frowned and shook his head. Then his phone vibrated. His picked it up, checked the caller, and put it to his ear.

"Hello," he said.

"Are you watching this?" a voice came back.

"Of course I am," the Tycoon replied.

"We're going to hold you to your word," it said. "Initiative X. You know what you have to do."

"Do . . . do you really think—" the Tycoon asked.

"I'll ask again; are you watching this?"

The Tycoon confirmed that he was.

"Good," the voice said. "We expect action. Tomorrow at the latest."

The call disconnected.

The Tycoon placed his phone back into his pocket. He looked at the bank of monitors. They showed a convention devolving into fear and chaos. Now the Governor was being led away by bewildered-looking security. His face was bathed in gore. He sported a goatee of blood. His eyes rolled wildly. He gnashed his teeth and snapped at the air, bestial and aimless.

The Tycoon knew these images would shortly festoon the front pages of every paper in the world, and that the tape would play in an endless loop on the networks.

"Rabies!" McNelis called into his walkie-talkie. "The future vice president contracted rabies in the course of performing charity work in . . . in . . . wherever the last place he went was. You know? That mission work his church did? Hang on. Let me come over there."

McNelis ran out of the room, leaving the Tycoon completely alone.

THE REPORTER

It was late the next morning when Jessica Smith was finally able to take a break. The twelve hours since the Governor's violent meltdown had been the busiest and most surreal of her life. It all still felt very much like a dream or fantasy from which she might suddenly awaken.

She and an equally-exhausted George Cutler allowed themselves to rest for a brief moment together at a table in their press room. Neither had slept. Though George was too old for Jessica (and, moreover, not her type) the two both exuded the spent bewilderment of people who had just gotten laid.

"See," George said in the intervening silence. "I *told* you there was no way he could win."

"You were right about that," Jessica said.

"It's funny," George said. "I thought for sure I'd seen it all. I've been doing this so long, you know? But you've *never* seen it all."

"What, you've never seen a pair of zombies running for president?" Jessica teased. "Oh come on. That must have happened at least once before. Like a really long time ago. You know, like back in the 1990's."

George smiled and shook his head.

"No," he said. "What I meant is, I never thought I'd see a cub reporter who was about to win a Pulitzer Prize. And I'll be doubly damned if I even thought she would be sharing it with a blogger from . . . what was it again?"

"TruthTeller," Jessica said.

"Ah yes," George said. "Suppose I ought to memorize it. My God, these are strange times. But you've done more than win a Pulitzer, my dear. Think of what you have done for the republic. Think of what those people—not even people—those *things* might have accomplished if they had been allowed to proceed. Now it will all be investigated. The candidates. The Uneeda Society. I'll be impressed if most of them aren't in jail before the end of the month."

Details were hazy—and had remained hazy since the chaos on the convention floor—but it seemed that the Secret Service would *not* confirm that it currently had the Governor in any kind of custody. The precise location of the Tycoon was also not something that could be confirmed. The convention had ended after the Governor's attack, and the Tycoon seemed to have somehow slipped away.

"The only question is, does this kill the whole party?" George said. "They haven't cancelled the final night of the convention, but look for that any second now. And then what's left for them? They regroup and . . . what? *Appoint* a new candidate? Throw it to whoever came in second in the primaries?"

Jessica lowered her head to the table.

"I don't even remember who that was right now," she said after a long sigh.

"No . . ." said George. "It's over. They'll nominate someone before the general, but it will be a safe choice. No one will like it. They're going to lose every state. Maybe the Libertarians will actually have a shot this year, because these guys certainly don't. *Maybe* the party will survive. In eight, twelve years—if they *totally* clean house—they could come back. They might have to change the name."

"If they do, I hope they bring back the Whigs," Jessica said idly, contemplating her Pulitzer. "I don't remember who the Whigs were or what they stood for, but I always thought it sounded good."

George nodded to say that there might indeed be worse titles for political parties.

"I've also been meaning to apologize," George suddenly said. "I didn't mean to be curt with you earlier in the week. If I'd only known what you were working on . . . Err, scratch that. That's a lie, and we ought to be honest with one another. If you'd really told me what you were working on, I'd probably have fired you on the spot. There's no way I would have believed you. I guess . . . I guess what I'm trying to say is that you did the right thing."

"No hard feelings," Jessica said. "I think I might have fired me too."

"There's still so much more work to be done," said George. "God knows, we're all going to be connecting the dots for weeks and months to come. What you got from Bob Hogson? The footage of Cornelius Van Bergen from your friend? Not to mention the role of the Knights of Romero—those guys, we're still fact checking, but still . . . This is one of the biggest conspiracies in American history, Jessica. A small secret society of cannibal monsters trying to install themselves in the highest echelon of power? It's almost too fantastic to believe. But now people *will* believe it. Because of *you*."

"Thanks for saying that," Jessica told George. "But I think I was just in the right place at the right time. Or maybe the wrong place, depending on how you look at it."

George smiled and shrugged.

"I'm so exhausted I'm shaking a little bit," Jessica said. "But I also feel like I can't take a nap. My email inbox has exploded, every TV network wants to interview me, and my voicemail is full to bursting. But check this out. Before it filled up, I got a voicemail from my mom . . . who is now worried that I'm going to be assassinated."

George shrugged.

"You could tell her that being assassinated is better than being eaten by a zombie. Probably."

Jessica rolled her eyes.

"Frankly, I might be a little more concerned about your friend Tim," George added. "Doesn't he truck with the extremist crowd?"

"I think that he's probably safer because of that," Jessica said. "If anybody knows about black-ops and the ways they'd come after you, it's him."

George shook his head to say that all of this was moot.

"I think you're quite safe, young lady," he said. "The story is out there. The pictures are out there. The video is out there. Getting rid of the reporters doesn't accomplish anything at this point."

"I hope you're right," Jessica said. "To be honest with you, I'm almost too tired to care about assassins."

Suddenly, there was the sound of raised voices in the hallway outside. Someone said: "Jessica Smith is not receiving visitors at this time."

"Oh gawwwd, they've found us," Jessica drawled. "I seriously can't talk to anyone else right now, George. I can hardly lift my head."

"Don't worry," George said. "Our friends aren't letting anybody in."

The moment these words were out of his mouth, there was the unmistakable sound of a cheek being slapped. A moment later, Jay McNelis threw open the conference room door and barged inside. He looked around until his eyes lit upon the two exhausted reporters, piled like heaps at the end of a table.

Jessica lifted her head and said: "Oh shit."

McNelis—who had also not slept—made his way over. He did not look as if he intended violence, but with him, you never knew for sure.

"You're not supposed to be in here," George said, wearily rising to his feet. "What the hell is wrong with you?"

McNelis ignored this completely, and sidled up next to Jessica.

"Is your phone working?" he asked her.

"I've had to turn it off ever since it started ringing every two minutes," Jessica told him.

"You have voicemails—" McNelis began.

"My voicemail filled up five hours ago," she cut him off. "I think the system stops at twenty messages."

McNelis forced himself to wait for her to finish. When it was clear that she had, he repeated: "*You have voicemails* from the next President of the United States. Several. He wants to see you."

"What?" Jessica said, rubbing her eyes and blinking.

"He wants to talk with you," McNelis said. "Come along. I'll take you to him. Please."

"Where exactly *is* your party's nominee at the moment?" George said. A reporter's notepad and pen had seemingly materialized in his hands.

"Nice try," said McNelis. "Jessica, will you come?"

She glanced over at George. At this moment, there was no interview in the world more desirable than the Tycoon. Even so, she had already done a Herculean amount of reporting in the last twelve hours. Nobody would blame her for tagging out at this point.

George seemed to sense her hesitation.

"There are other people we can send if you're not feeling up to it," he said.

Jennifer ignored this and stared at McNelis.

"Did you just slap one of our people?" she asked harshly. "You come here slapping folks, and then expect me to go with you."

"That man slapped himself," McNelis said.

"Why?" asked Jennifer.

"Because I told him to," replied McNelis. "I can be very persuasive. Ask anyone."

Jennifer looked him up and down, trying to detect the slightest indication that McNelis might be joking. It appeared that he wasn't.

"Let's just get this over with," Jennifer said.

"Very good," McNelis replied. "There's a car waiting for us just outside. Follow me."

Jessica forced herself to stand and gather her things. George began to do the same.

"Nope," said McNelis. "Just her."

"What?" George said.

"No deal, otherwise," he said. "You want the hottest interview in the universe right now, you only send her."

"Now wait a minute," George said. "A second ago you were practically begging us to come. Now you're making rules?"

"I wasn't begging you," McNelis said. "Just her."

"And what if I want to come?" George said.

"Then I just might have to make you slap yourself," McNelis said. As insane as this sounded to Jessica, George looked at McNelis as though he might possess precisely such a power. George did not seem willing to test it.

"I'm fine to go alone," Jessica said. "It's all right."

"Call me if you need anything," George said.

Then he looked back at McNelis. And the strain of having been awake for so many hours became all too apparent.

"If you guys hurt her, I will fucking put you in the ground— you damn criminal fucks!" George all but screamed, his voice cracking. "When my family came over on the boat, we weren't called Cutler. Our name was fucking Coriglione. Don't think I don't know people who can find the most powerful man in the country and take him out. Because I do. And they would do it out of love. Love for me! Which is something you horrible rats will never even understand."

Jessica could not believe what she was hearing. McNelis only blinked rapidly several times.

"Whatever happened to the impartiality of journalists?" he eventually said.

"Go fuck yourself," George answered. "Jessica, be careful."

Jessica followed McNelis out of the conference room, past a pair of informal sentries (one of which had quite possibly just slapped himself), and then out into the hallway, where a few sad-eyed conventioneers and security made a grim patrol. Jessica kept her head down and tried to avoid being recognized.

McNelis passed through an exit door and she followed him out into the dawn light.

THE FAKE NEWSMAN

Tim Fife—who had *not* summoned the strength to stay awake all night—awoke to a vigorous rapping on his hotel room door.

He started, and his mind raced.

Had it all been a dream? A fantasy? The final culmination of a life spent marinating his brain in conspiracy theories?

But then he heard Ryan's voice.

"Hey, open up Tim. You're not going to believe what the boss sent over."

Then Dan.

"Yeah man, it's pretty sweet. Open the door."

Tim felt as though he had been hit by a truck.

He glanced at the bedside table, and saw his bottles of prescription sleep and anxiety aids—which he only took in cases of great emergency—resting beside his keys and wallet. These pills always left him feeling thick-headed and forgetful the next day, but sometimes he needed them. Though he could not recall opening the bottle, it certainly felt right that last night must have been one of those occasions.

Tim rolled out of bed and waddled over to the door. He opened it to reveal Dan holding a large, technology-based gift basket, and Ryan with a stack of boxes containing extra large pizzas.

"Here," Dan said, handing over the basket. "This was addressed to you specifically."

"Yeah," added Ryan, "but I assumed the pizzas had to be for all of us. There were a lot of them. This is just part."

"Pizza?" Tim said, as they pushed past him into his room. "It's—what?—eight in the morning."

"It's breakfast pizza," Ryan pronounced, sitting at the small desk and opening the box on top. "See? Eggs and sausage."

"The basket has a card," Dan said. "I went ahead and read it. The boss is really pleased."

"Yeah," Ryan said between bites. "He ought to be. You just killed the fake news label forever. This is something that takes an outlet from zero to hero overnight, like when TMZ had the Mel Gibson DUI exclusive back in 2006 . . . only ten times bigger! Of course the boss is happy. You just increased what he can charge for ads by about fifty-fold."

"I dunno," Tim said thoughtfully. "People who want to hate us will still hate us. And they'll say it was really all Jessica. That everything was her idea."

"A gray area is not necessarily a bad thing," Dan said. "It keeps us edgy. Keeps us outsiders. Albeit, outsiders who can charge fifty times more per ad."

"Maybe our salaries will go up," Ryan said as he chewed. "Not fifty times, but, you know. A little would be nice."

While Ryan and Dan chatted and ate, Tim opened his laptop and began sifting through the ruins of the two-party system.

"Christ," he said, rubbing his eyes. "I shouldn't have fallen asleep. Jesus!"

"What?" said Ryan.

"I have ten thousand emails," Tim said. "How am I supposed to . . . My phone!"

Tim went for his phone in its charger.

"Yeah, this is pretty much destroyed too," he pronounced.

"If it's any consolation, I think the boss sent you a new one in that basket," Dan said. "Along with a new laptop, a hoverboard, and lotsa other cool things."

"Want some of this pizza?" Ryan asked.

"No," Tim said. "I'm too freaked out to be hungry. I . . . I suppose I ought to write something new for the site. Last night seems so much like a blur. A dream. Jesus."

"What exactly happened to you?" Dan asked. "We were monitoring the feed from your cameras, but we kind of lost track when things went to shit and the Governor of Indiana started eating people."

"First of all, it got crazy up in the suite when Van Bergen realized the Governor was a zombie," Tim said.

"Yeah, we saw that part," Ryan said.

"It just got crazier from there," Tim continued. "Van Bergen lost it. So did the guys up there with him. I busted out of there as fast as I could. All of them were screaming and upset and . . . my mind is foggy on the details. I guess I should watch the tape."

"Sure, I'll hook you up with it," Dan said. "Email you a link to the raw feed recording."

"I remember trying to connect with Jessica afterwards . . . to make sure she had everything she needed," Tim continued. "But I was so freaked out. Van Bergen had this security guy, and I thought for sure he was going to kill me. I don't normally get panic attacks, but when I do they're awful. I guess I came back here and took some pills. I don't remember much. Christ. When did you lose the feed from my recorders?"

"About then," said Dan. "About when you commenced to running in cowardly terror."

"Dude, if you'd been there, you would have done the same thing," Tim said.

"I know," Dan said. "Just razzing you. We're all real proud. And I should let you know, a bunch of people want to talk to you, if you can't tell from your phone and email. Reporters from other outlets keep stopping by our table downstairs . . . when they can find it."

"Yeah," Ryan said. "Now you're one of those reporters who makes themselves into the news. I think officially that means we're supposed to hate you, but only because we're secretly envious? That's what I heard, at any rate. You sure you don't want any of this pizza?"

"No, I'm good," Tim said. "What about Jessica? Has she checked in?"

"We haven't seen her, but she might be around," Dan said. "She was filing stories all night."

"Then maybe I can catch up to her before she collapses from exhaustion," said Tim. "Look, can you guys clear out and let me take a shower and put on a clean shirt? I'll meet you back downstairs in ten."

"Yeah, that's fine," Ryan said, grabbing a trio of slices for the road. "And hey, congrats again. This really is something special."

"Thanks guys," Tim said.

He watched Ryan and Dan file out. As soon as the door shut behind them, Tim collapsed back onto his bed for a moment. He felt horrible, as he always did when he took sleeping pills but did not give himself eight hours in which to actually sleep. Swearing he would never do it again—this time, for real—Tim grabbed a clean-looking shirt and fresh-ish underwear from his suitcase and headed to the small hotel bathroom. He turned on the shower, fiddling with the unfamiliar knob before finding the hot water. Then he took off his shirt and threw it to the floor, fumbled for his toothbrush on the counter, and began to brush his teeth. The mirror slowly fogged as the water behind him heated, and so he nearly missed the long scrape along his right shoulder.

Nearly.

Tim lowered his toothbrush and spat into the sink. Then he fished around for a hand towel, and used it to wipe a small circle in the moisture-covered mirror. He leaned in close to take a look.

A long, deep furrow had been torn down the side of his shoulder. It started at the top of his arm and extended several inches down along his back. It was like something done by a nail. Or—Tim thought with mounting anxiety—a *finger*nail.

He began to feel lightheaded. He braced against the sink to steady himself. The previous evening, when the Governor had gone crazy and Tim had attempted to flee the skybox, there had been so much chaos. But now, as his head gradually cleared, it seemed to Tim that he could remember more. Van Bergen and his men had tried to keep him there, at least at first. He'd had to fight his way out. Everyone had been so confused. He remembered all of them—*including Van Bergen*—tugging at him, pulling at him, and all the rest.

The hidden cameras he'd worn had been forward-facing. There might be no record of who or what had injured his shoulder. Except for his own slowly-recovering memory.

But could it actually have been Van Bergen? At first glance, the old zombie seemed far too frail to do such damage as this. Yet Tim remembered the strength of the branchlike arm that had held him in his seat, and the way his wizened hands appeared to have devolved into something like claws. Maybe he had learned to use them like claws too.

Tim turned off the shower and wiped the whole mirror clean. Once more, he inspected the deep scrape. Everyone knew that zombie bites were a surefire means of transmitting the infection, but scratches were a grey area.

"Fuck . . ." Tim said out loud. "Fuuuuuuuuuck."

There was only one thing to be done. He had to know.

He left the bathroom and crept to the nightstand where his wristwatch rested beside the pill bottles. He brought the watch up close to his face. He stared intently at the second hand tick-tick-ticking past.

Then he took a deep breath and held it.

THE TYCOON

Deals.

The Tycoon knew *all* about them.

He made deals in New York real estate all the time (which, he had been assured, was among the toughest places to do them). He made deals in his personal life, and when negotiating rights on his reality television show. He had literally written a book about deals. (Well, not really. But a reporter who'd once interviewed him had ghostwritten it, which was almost as good. Better, probably. Maybe that was the ultimate demonstration of skillful dealing. Make a good enough book deal, and you don't even have to write it!)

As the Tycoon sat in the empty office in the warehouse and waited for Jessica Smith to arrive, he reminded himself that this was just another deal. Everything was a dealmaking if you thought hard enough. Everything. And he was the master.

Sometimes you made deals from positions of strength, and sometimes you made them when you were flailing and on the ropes, but you could always do it. You could always deal. That was the creed by which the Tycoon had always worked. Accord could always be found if both sides looked hard enough. Parties could always come up with ways to help one another.

Hiccups happened, sure. Setbacks? Yeah, absolutely. That was true for a major Manhattan construction project, and for a project of any size. It did seem to the Tycoon that the bigger the project, the more setbacks you could expect. Experience had taught him that. And becoming leader of the free world was the biggest project of all. So of course he ought to have expected this, he told himself. Of course there would be huge setbacks. *Huuuuge* setbacks. But setbacks, he had found, could always be handled . . . with further dealing.

And deal he would.

Deals were his art form. He was their Michelangelo. He reminded himself of all of this, repeatedly and aloud, until he became aware that someone was approaching.

"What the hell is this place?" he heard Jessica Smith distantly query.

The next voice belonged to McNelis.

"He can tell you that."

"No, you tell me," she insisted. "Or I can just turn around and leave. Get an Uber back to the hotel. Don't test me, McNelis. You know I'll do it."

The political operative sighed.

"This building is owned by a very significant donor to the campaign," McNelis said—now close enough that the Tycoon could hear their footsteps. "He has allowed us to use it while the campaign recharges and regroups."

"Recharges?" said Jessica. "I guess that's one way to put it."

If McNelis made any response it was not verbal, but McNelis's barely-contained rage was palpable as he opened the door and stepped into the small office room. Jessica followed.

The Tycoon stood.

"Hello, Ms. Smith," he said. "Thank you for coming. Would you like to have a seat?"

Jessica sat at one of the two visitor chairs that faced the desk. Instead of seating himself behind the desk, the Tycoon sat down right beside her.

"All right, McNelis," the Tycoon said. "You can leave."

"I'll be right outside," McNelis replied.

The Tycoon waved his hand to indicate that this was already too much information. McNelis silently exited.

The Tycoon turned his attention back to the reporter. She had already produced a laptop from her bag, and was now preparing to set up her recorder. She had bags under her eyes and looked ten years older than her online pictures. No doubt, this was a natural consequence of the previous 24 hours.

The Tycoon spoke delicately.

"I wonder if, *before* we go on the record—and we certainly will go on the record—you would permit us to first have a small, informal exchange."

Jessica flashed him a look that said she had not let herself be dragged all this way for anything informal. Nonetheless, she leaned back in her chair and looked at him like a woman resigned. The Tycoon realized he was being allowed to proceed.

"Thank you," he said. "I just want to, well, do something I make it a practice *never* to do. And that's apologize. I'm sorry that it was necessary to be so tricky. I hope that what I can do here today is show you *why* it was."

"Did you know your running mate was a zombie?" Jessica asked. "And you better believe this is on the record."

"It's almost impossible to answer that question," the Tycoon began.

"Okay, I didn't come here for prevaricating, doublespeak bullshit," Jessica said. She closed her laptop, stood up, and started gathering her things.

"It's almost impossible . . . because I knew him both before and after he became one," the Tycoon added.

Jessica slowly sat back down.

"Before and after?" she asked.

"Yes, before I made him into one," the Tycoon said.

Without taking her eyes off of his, she slowly opened her laptop again.

"*You* made him into . . ."

"Yes, that's correct," the Tycoon said. "Into a zombie."

"So you are definitely a zombie?" Jessica asked.

"Of course," the Tycoon said. "Had you really not figured that out yet?"

Jessica remained cautious.

"And so why are you telling me this now?" she said. "What do you hope to accomplish?"

"What do I hope to accomplish?" he said. "The same thing I hoped to accomplish when I started this campaign!"

"To . . . become president?"

"To save the world," he said. "From *her*."

Jessica screwed up her face.

"From . . . your opponent you mean?"

"Of course," said the Tycoon. "Who else?"

"I don't see how being a zombie . . . I mean . . . Why would . . ."

"Vampires," the Tycoon said.

" . . . "

"Is it *so* hard to believe?" the Tycoon pressed. "My opponent and her running mate are also members of the living dead, only a different kind. They are vampires."

The Tycoon reached onto the desk where a manila folder had been positioned innocently among paperweights, invoices and bric-a-brac. He picked it up and tossed it into Jessica's lap.

"Here," he said. "In case you don't believe me."

The Tycoon watched as the reporter carefully opened the folder and began to sort through the printed images inside. They were candid shots, always taken from a distance, and always in situations that made it clear the subjects were unaware. Jessica knew less about vampires than she did about zombies, but there was no missing it. The opponent baring her fangs during an argument. Levitating off the ground in her pantsuit. Appearing to feed at the neck of one of her unlucky aides.

"She can't go very long without fresh blood," the Tycoon explained as Jessica flipped between photos. "You saw when she passed out the other day before her handlers could get her into that van? It wasn't the flu-bug all the press releases said it was. That was a vampire that's gone too long without feeding. Between you and me, I think the protective makeup she wears was also coming off. You know, the kind that allows a creature like her to go out into the sun? It's all very hi-tech now, as you must be able to imagine."

"This . . . this is almost unbelievable," Jessica said, continuing to flip from photo to photo. "A few days ago I *wouldn't* have believed it. But if one party can be zombies . . ."

"Yes," said the Tycoon. "The other can, unfortunately, be vampires. I say 'unfortunately' because our two kinds are so bigly different. Huuuuge difference. The American people have a very important choice to make in this election; perhaps a more important choice than they've ever made."

"*What?*" said Jessica, aghast. "You can't believe that the election will still take place in light of . . . I don't even know what to call this. Don't you see that these disclosures change everything?"

"That's where you're wrong, kiddo," the Tycoon said with a grin. "It changes nothing. It only makes the differences between the candidates and their parties easier for the public to see."

Jessica looked at the Tycoon as if he had gone deeply, irreparably insane.

The Tycoon rose slowly, then began to pace around the room.

"Vampires are the wrong choice for America because they are natural globalists and elitists," the Tycoon began. "Picture a vampire. What do you picture? This person is wealthy. This person is finely attired—probably spends more on a single suit of clothes than most hardworking Americans earn in a month. This person likely speaks with a *foreign* accent. This person has snuck his or her way into the upper-crust of society; they rub elbows with kings, queens and world leaders."

"You're mostly describing yourself," Jessica interjected. "You realize that, right?"

"Then picture the zombie," the Tycoon continued as though she had said nothing. "Stalwart, plucky, hardwork-ing—and totally free from being fancy and pretentious. The zombie is local. It rises out of the ground where it has been planted—literally the soil of its home country, how patriotic is that?—and then it sticks around. If it travels at all, it travels real slowly. A zombie doesn't care how it looks. Personal appear-ance is not even on the radar. But it displays an all-American sticktoitiveness that vampires lack completely. A zombie is, simply, not capable of giving up. No matter how hard things get. No matter how the odds may be stacked against it. No matter how poorly it's doing in the polls. A zombie will never give up. It believes in itself.

"If my opponent—she and the other vampires—if they win, then the globalists win. They are in it for other power-ful vampires all around the world. They will use our nation's highest office to consolidate that power. They will make it into a place where favors are done for their *kind*—vampire and globalist, both! Loyalty will no longer be to the hardworking, soft-spoken, men and women of the soil! Instead, they will be made to serve those who are already elite, to help them to advance their obscure and decadent projects. Huuuge betrayal of the American people. Very, very bad deal."

"Most of the country isn't vampires, but they're not zom-bies either," Jessica interjected, clearly struggling to see his point.

"Not technically," said the Tycoon, with a shrug to show this objection didn't matter much. "But they *are* slow mov-ing. Americans get more sedentary every day. But they're also really, really self-reliant. On some level, they all crave a smaller government that will get off their backs and let them do their thing—whether that thing is eating brains, practicing their faith, or engaging in free trade. Americans are uncomfortable with the confusing, gender-ambiguous sexuality of vampires. They want something that is slow, straightforward, and easy to understand. A zombie's all of these things. It is the Joe Six-Pack of the monster world. He's not above you. He's one of you. There's no comparison to vampires. No way."

The Tycoon sat back down. Jessica's eyes searched the corners of the room.

"So you brought me here because I exposed your side as what you actually are . . . and now you expect me to do the same for her—for the vampires?"

"No," said the Tycoon, gently taking the folder of images from her hands and placing it back on the desk. "That is the opposite of what I would like you to do."

"Just when I thought I couldn't be more confused," Jessica said.

"It may have been a mistake not to tell everybody why I was really running for president," the Tycoon said. "But I'll fix that this evening when I deliver my remarks."

"You . . . ? You're still going to accept the nomination tonight? The convention is still happening?"

"It is. Trust me. My people are seeing to all of that. McNelis and his boys are making sure. But listen. My point is that I want to be the bigger man. I'm going to come out and admit who *I* am. Then we'll see if *she* has the guts to tell the American people the truth and admit who she really is."

"So, you have all this intel on her . . . and you're not going to use it?" Jessica asked.

"No," the Tycoon said. "And I'm going to ask you not to use it either. Not for the moment, at least. What I *am* going to do is ask you to give me a chance. I know you don't like me. Let's be blunt. You probably hate me, or *think* you hate me. But I'm asking you to get to know me. To understand what my project is. What I'm trying to do for this country. If you do that—"

"My personal feelings don't enter into this," Jessica said. "As a journalist, I have certain duties and responsibilities."

"Journalists withhold information all the time when it's in the interest of national security," the Tycoon reminded her. "Your own news outlet has done it during every war fought in the last hundred years. How is it not a matter of national security to see whether a major political candidate will *admit* that she drinks the blood of living people and flies around like a bat?"

And for the first time, the Tycoon saw precisely what he wanted to see. Hesitation. The Tycoon could see Jessica pausing to consider the way forward. He knew she was considering calling someone for advice on how to proceed.

"All I'm asking is that you report on what I have to say tonight honestly and fairly . . . If you can agree to do that, then I am prepared to offer you unprecedented access during the general election. And I don't mean you'd get the press releases an hour before everybody else. I mean that you'd be embedded with me personally. Tonight, for example—if you want—you'll be with me backstage. This campaign is going to be all about openness, from this moment forward. We want the public to see our commitment to making America great again. From here on out, we have nothing to hide."

This was the moment of truth. The line was in the water. The Tycoon waited to see if he would get a bite.

Jessica appeared to consider this offer. Then she spoke.

"I still have so many questions. *When* did you become a zombie? How? Why? Which of the stereotypes I've heard about zombies are true? How many other zombies are in politics, or in Manhattan real estate? Why are the Knights of Romero so dead set on destroying you? Why—"

"There'll be time for these questions," the Tycoon said. "I assure you, I'd love to sit down with you and go over them one-by-one. At the moment, however, I have much to do before my speech. We'll go over them at a later date, okay? Like tomorrow maybe?"

Jessica looked as though this might be acceptable to her.

"Yes, I think I can make that work," she finally pronounced. "But look . . . If we do this. I'm not going to pull punches. I'm a real journalist, and I'm going to ask you real questions."

"Of course you are," the Tycoon assured her. "And of course you will. That's what I'm planning on."

"All right then," Jessica said. "So long as we're clear."

"Crystal . . . like on the chandeliers that hang in the lobbies of my many fine properties," the Tycoon said with a grin. "Okay. I think we are finished here. I need to prepare. McNelis will arrange to have you transported back to the arena."

"What is preparation like for you?" Jessica asked, even as she gathered her things. "Do you need to rest? To sleep?"

"All these things in good time," the Tycoon said. "For the moment, I can't see much past this evening."

"A lot rides on your speech, if they even still let you give it," Jessica said, preparing to depart.

"Oh, they will," the Tycoon said.

"How can you be so sure?" Jessica asked.

"Because those words—'they' or 'me' or 'I'—have less and less meaning as time goes by. Every day, I become they, and they become me. I am the party right now. There is no other option, and they know it. If I go down, it goes down too. And you can print that I said that."

"Don't worry," Jessica responded. "I will."

The Tycoon had not been lying about the time crunch. He really did have an inhuman amount of work ahead if he planned to be ready to deliver his speech that same evening. Yet, as the young reporter exited, the Tycoon allowed himself a long and satisfied smile. It was very different from the fake smile he had carefully honed in front of mirrors to use at building dedications and in press photos. It was a deep and ugly smile. The smile of satisfaction one only gives when unobserved.

The Tycoon was a dealmaker. He had just made another deal. It was who he was. It was what he did.

This deal had possibly just saved him. It would make possible all the deals he would ever make in the future.

The Tycoon leaned back in his chair and put his hands behind his head.

Would he ever stop winning? Now it seemed unimaginable that he had ever doubted it. He vowed that he would only win from this point on. That there would be no further setbacks. He would only win. And win and win and win.

He began softly repeating the word to himself, like an adherent to meditation repeating a mantra. The sound echoed softly through the office, out the door, and into the cavernous warehouse beyond.

With McNelis stepping away to find Jessica Smith a car, it was only the Tycoon's security guards who heard it clearly. The pair had heard and seen unbelievable things in their years of service, but never quite something like this.

"Win! . . . Win! . . . Win!"

One of the guards lowered his sunglasses enough to exchange a glance. The other guard smiled and gave the smallest shrug. Then the two men resumed their stoic expressions, listening to the softly echoing incantation that seemed as though it would go on forever.

THE REPORTER

When the car dropped Jennifer back at the arena, the first of the international news agencies were just beginning to arrive. The convention had already been news, but now it was something epic. Something for the ages. Once-in-a-lifetime stuff was happening. Every newspaper, TV network, blog, and web channel wanted to bring it to their audiences firsthand.

Beyond this extra press, the crowd outside had swelled to almost unbelievable proportions because of curious onlookers. This was the kind of crowd you called out the National Guard to handle. Blocks around the arena were swelled with foot traffic, and it was difficult for vehicles of any kind to get through. At first glance, the general demographics of the crowds seemed not much changed from the days prior, but now a strange and intense madness possessed them. Conventioneers, gun rights enthusiasts, and fervent foes of political correctness all walked the streets and sidewalks as if on patrol.

But for what? Jessica wondered: Were they looking to hunt zombies, or protect them?

As she neared the arena entrance, she began to see free-lance groups decked out in body armor. They carried rifles and wore bandannas across their faces, and they did not seem affiliated with any particular law enforcement agency. One of them carried a riot shield hastily painted with a zombie inside a red circle and slash. One of them smoked a cigar. All seemed wild-eyed.

Police were also present, but none of them seemed partic-ularly excited about enforcing laws. They were there because they had to be. They obviously did not understand what was going on or why. (Jessica imagined that when your leaders were revealed to be literal bloodthirsty monsters, the urge to serve and protect them was probably diminished.) Most peo-ple simply looked right through the law enforcement profes-sionals still present.

It made Jessica think of her childhood summers in the northeast. Sometimes both parents would come, but at the very least Jessica, her sister, and her mother would annually retire to a coastal enclave in Maine for the hottest parts of July and August. It was a small community with a dodgy power grid that seemed to fail at least once a summer. Whenever that happened, the whole town suddenly stopped. The residents would emerge from their homes and from the business along Main Street, no matter the hour. People chatted. They carried drinks with them out of the bars, and food out of restaurants. It was the strange space apart from reality. It appeared magi-cally, and only lasted for the hour or so it took to get the grid back online. That hour might have been Jessica's favorite part of the summer. In that odd ethereal timeout, all bets were off.

The rules and customs that had ruled moments before did not apply. It was as if everyone was "not playing" in the same way Jessica might advise her friends that she was "not playing" when they declaimed that the floor was lava or a giant conifer was a crash-landed spaceship.

As Jessica opened the door to one of the arena entrances and stepped inside, she saw that same "not playing" on the faces of the men and women who had—less than a day before—known quite precisely their purpose and responsibilities. The convention delegates were dead-eyed and running on automatic pilot. (Jessica stopped just short of thinking of them as "zombified.") The representatives from organizations and causes looked like they had given up. A few had already started tearing down their displays. The souvenir vendors were unsteady and cautious. Perhaps their t-shirts emblazoned with the candidate's face had just become collectables that would go for ten times their face value on eBay. Or perhaps they were worthless. (One enterprising vendor had taken a marker and given the portraits of the Tycoon and the Governor he sold a zombified aspect. Jessica wondered if these revised versions were selling better than the originals. A news item for another time, perhaps.)

The only people who seemed energized and purposeful were the reporters. Fully half of the media onsite were now new arrivals. They were well-slept and full of vim. (For these qualities alone they could be immediately distinguished from the veteran hacks.) Because so many of those in attendance were now alert newsmen and newswomen, Jessica was recognized almost immediately. With the exception of the Tycoon, the Governor, and the senior officials of their party, no person was now the subject of more interest than Jessica Smith herself. Once recognized, she was forced to nearly sprint down the hallway to the conference room where she hoped George and other friendly faces still waited. A peloton of other reporters trailed after her as she loped down the changed, strange hallways.

Finally, blessedly, the correct door came into view. A couple of folks from her organization were still milling around in front of it. Jessica acknowledged them with a nod and said: "Keep these turkeys outside."

She ducked in and shut the door behind herself.

Back at their table, Jessica found that George was indeed there waiting for her. But he was not the only one. Tim's two associates from TruthTeller were there. Yet Tim himself was nowhere to be found.

"Hey, are you okay?" George asked, hopping up from his chair. "What happened?"

"I met with him," Jessica said. "There's a whole lot, but the short upshots are that he confessed to being a zombie, said he's still going to deliver his speech tonight, and . . . and he wants to give me unprecedented inside access to his campaign."

"What?" said George. "I . . . I don't know what part of that to ask about first."

"There's actually more," Jessica said.

She told George and the others about the photos she'd seen of the former first lady levitating and draining necks.

"So . . . wait?" George said. "Did he give you these photos?"

"No," Jessica said. "He said he's not going to leak them. Instead, his idea is to get her to . . . I suppose the word would be 'confess.' To being a vampire, right? I think he's going to challenge her to talk about it when they have their debates."

"Can you back any of this up, Jessica?" George asked. "Obviously, I don't doubt you personally, but with all that's happened we need multiple solid sources and people who can confirm things. Every word you write from here on out is going to be fact-checked to death, both coming and going. You have to know that."

"I recorded our conversation, but I didn't have time to take pictures of the vampire photos. If you want, I could—"

Suddenly, one of the reporters stationed outside burst through the door.

"It's still on!" the young woman shrieked as though she could not believe the words as she spoke them. "They've just announced it! They're going to hold the rest of the convention tonight."

"And the final speaker will be . . . ?" George said, breathless.

"They haven't announced that," the young woman told him. "The press release doesn't say. But I'll try to find out."

She rushed back out of the room.

"It's got to be him," Jessica said. "He said he was still going to accept the nomination tonight, and I think he wasn't bull-shitting. Also, he said I would have full access to him tonight. Backstage, everything. He said he'd be giving me that access for the rest of the campaign."

George nodded carefully.

"Have you thought about *why* he is doing that?" George asked. "What *he* gets from it? Isn't it a little suspicious that the man who has been running on a platform of hating and discrediting the press now wants you on his hip. What if Nixon had said to Woodward and Bernstein, 'Hey, I'm not so bad. I'll let you shadow me so you'll agree.' It'd be outrageous."

"I may be young, but I'm not stupid, George," Jessica replied. "I'm not saying that this changes anything. I'm just telling you what he offered. Sure, he wants me to provide a certain kind of coverage—to 'humanize' a zombie, is my guess—but that doesn't mean I have to do it. Tactically, I think he's trying to set a precedent for access now that his cat is out of the bag. We know he's a zombie. He wants to dare the other campaign to let us get close enough to show that their candidate is a vampire."

"Hmm, that actually makes a bit of sense," George said. "It's a smarter idea than I'd usually give him credit for."

"I'm with you there," Jessica said. "So many times in this campaign, he does things that are so crazy and flailing. I'd started to wonder if that was because he had something to hide. Now that that's been taken away, we might see an entirely new candidate."

George fell silent for a moment, considering this possibility. Ryan and Dan used the opportunity to insinuate themselves into the conversation.

"Jessica, have you heard from Tim today?" Dan asked.

"I haven't been in touch with him since sometime last night," Jessica said. "Have you guys lost track of him?"

"Uh, we saw him this morning," Ryan contributed. "We brought him some gifts and pizza. It was breakfast pizza. Anyhow, he was going to take a shower and meet us downstairs. But that was like hours ago. He's not answering his phone or emails."

"I'm sure his phone and email got overrun with messages, like mine did," Jessica said. "He's probably still sifting through them."

"Yeah," Ryan said. "But when we went back upstairs to check on him, he wasn't in his room either."

"Gaining access to a room in a big hotel like this is not as much of a challenge as they'd like you to believe," Dan added ominously.

"We can't find him anywhere," Dan complained. "It's not like him to disappear. We were kind of hoping he was with you."

"No," Jessica said. "Sorry."

"Okay," Ryan said. "Well if he comes back, send him over to the TruthTeller desk. Tell him if he can force his way to the center of the mob, he'll eventually find us. He's as famous as you are now. We're getting staked-out by everybody. They want the details on how we pulled it off."

"It's crazy, right?" Dan added. "It's like the people haven't used hidden cameras and recorders before. What do they even teach in journalism school these days?"

"Um, other things, I guess," Jessica said with a shrug.

"Whatever," Dan said. "Just tell him to find us if you see him."

With that, the representatives from TruthTeller departed.

Jessica looked up at George with eyes that had seen into vast, unimaginable distances in the past 24 hours . . . and were also very tired.

"I think I need to sleep before tonight," she told him. "I can feel my body starting to shut down. I think I'll pass out if I don't."

"I thought that might be the case," George said. "I've had some cots brought in and set up in the adjacent conference room. You can reach it through the side door. I thought going back out there to get to your hotel room might be too crazy."

"Bless you," Jessica said, already beginning to move toward the side door. "Can you wake me up in just a couple of hours?"

"I'll do my damnedest to," George said with a grin. "But if I remember from the plane, you're a sound sleeper. Bit of a snorer, too."

"Okay, thanks," Jessica said.

Now that the idea of rest had been made actionable and real, she felt a new wave of exhaustion sweeping over her that seemed supernatural in scope. Enormous. Irresistible.

Jessica opened the door in the conference room's collapsible wall. There was indeed a side room where several movable hotel cots had been placed side-by-side. The mattresses were thin and the sheets were rough, but at that moment they looked like fourposters with extra memory foam. Jessica was aware that the slight amount of makeup she had applied that morning to make herself look less tired was probably smearing onto the cot. She did not care. She closed her eyes the moment her head touched the miniature pillow. She concentrated on the sound of her own breathing, trusting sleep to come soon. She shifted slightly. Then, for whatever reason, she chanced to open her eyes again. And that was when she saw that she was not alone.

Sitting in the far corner of the room was a woman Jessica recognized. It was the woman with long black hair from the Knights of Romero. She was looking at Jessica intently. As Jessica watched, she rose from her chair and crept over to shut the door between the conference rooms. Then she edged to the row of collapsible beds. Jessica forced herself to sit up.

"You?" Jessica said. "How did you get in here?"

"Never mind that," the Knight replied. "I'm the one asking the questions. Have you been to see *him*? What happened?"

"So what if I have?" Jessica said. "I meet with people. I write down what they say. It's my job."

"You mean that even after what you know? After all that we in the Knights have been able to prove . . . ?"

"Journalists interview everybody," Jessica said. "We talk to serial killers and rapists. We talk to people we personally find abhorrent."

"Your story you wrote last night—the one that everyone's talking about—it's not enough," the Knight said.

"Not enough!?" Jessica said incredulously. "It's just ruined an entire political party. It's taken down some of the most powerful men in the country."

"It's not enough," the Knight repeated.

"Do *you* want to talk to me?" Jessica shot back. "Do *you* want to go on record?"

"You know I can't do that," the woman said. "That's not how our organization works."

"You guys don't even know the whole story," Jessica said.

"What?" the Knight said. "What don't we know?"

"I know you aren't much for zombies, but where does your organization stand on vampires?" Jessica asked.

"What?" the woman said. "Vampires? They're a myth. Zombies are *real*."

"What if I've seen evidence that both are real?" Jessica told her

She gave the Knight a quick version of what she had seen in her meeting with the Tycoon.

The Knight looked confused, but said: "Of course, *he* would tell you that. He'd show you fake photos he'd had doctored. He'll do anything do stay in the race. That's what makes him so dangerous. He's not only a zombie, he's power-mad and insane. You have to see that. This is just him muddying the water again."

"I don't . . ." Jessica began, then restarted. "What do you want me to do? Why are you here? I'm still not clear on how you got past George."

"Based on what I'm hearing, I think I'm here to warn you," the Knight said. "Zombies are the enemy. Everybody has to pick a side when it comes to them. If you think we're going to stand by and let that happen, you're crazy."

"OK, you're *really* afraid this man is going to become president?" Jessica said sarcastically. "They were saying he had no chance *before* all this happened. It doesn't make sense that he could win now . . . unless you *do* think those vampire accusations are real."

"Just watch yourself," the woman replied.

And with that she left the room, walked out purposefully through the adjacent conference room (where George dozed with his head in his hands), and let herself out into the hall.

Jessica shook her head. Normally she would have done something, said something more, but all she could think about was sleep. Jessica laid her head down on her pillow. Surely some rest would help everything make more sense.

She closed her eyes.

Before she could wonder if she was asleep, she was.

THE FAKE NEWSMAN

Tim Fife was *not* feeling like himself. Not at all . . .

THE TYCOON

Absurdly, the Tycoon found himself able to concentrate on everything *except* his speech, mere moments away. The Tycoon lounged in the backstage area, in a green room designed especially for him, and waited to be told that it was time. So much rode on what he did next that no brain—zombie or human—could truly grasp the scope of it. Perhaps this was a mercy. For failure would not only mean the end of him, but also the end of many others like him. He could be remembered as a credit to his caste, or as the man who undid it utterly.

Outside the green room, McNelis flitted about like a large hummingbird powered by Adderall and scotch. Though McNelis had composed the draft of the remarks that afternoon, the Tycoon had made several substantial changes known only to himself and the teleprompter operator.

Instead of musing on his soon-to-be-determined fate, the Tycoon regarded the patriotic embellishments some thoughtful soul had placed in the green room. In addition to an American flag cake and red, white, and blue table setting, there was a long ribbon that ran along the walls. It too bore patriotic colors, and was also decorated with the faces of prominent presidents.

There was always a first, the Tycoon thought to himself. We had a first Catholic president. A first handicapped president. A first black president. And now, we would have a first zombie president.

They would find him not so different than the others, the Tycoon thought to himself. Not if they really thought about it.

U.S. Presidents had literally killed men. Some had done it wholesale, on a massive scale, dropping bombs from planes while fighting in wars. Others had kept it personal, dueling with enemies *mano a mano*. The American people knew this. They knew this and voted for these men anyway. The urge to kill, at least occasionally, was not inhuman. Rather, it was *entirely* human. Voters would not shy from it, the Tycoon assured himself. Alone in the ballot box with nobody looking, they would *relate* to it. They would remember that it was *who they were* as well.

The Tycoon's eyes slowly worked their way along the ribbon. It showed him many men of great inherited wealth. It showed him skirt-chasers. Bigots. Gamblers. Drunks. War-mongering expansionists. Men who had used every form of deception to get ahead.

Yet if one thing struck the Tycoon about these celebrated personages set before him, it was that *they were not better than him.* They were *like* him, but not better. The things they had done were things he could do. He seemed to know this innately. Their accomplishments were all within his wheel-house. Given the right advisors and assistants, and how hard could it be? Probably, the Tycoon mused, he could outper-form these men in all the real, meaningful ways. Many U.S. Presidents had made mistakes. They had shown weakness. They had started fights they could not finish.

These men were not better than him. If anything, he was better than them.

The Tycoon heard McNelis's frantic footsteps approach-ing. Time was short. The Tycoon stepped back and looked at all the presidents on the ribbon together. It seemed, for just a moment, that they were looking back.

"You're not so special," the Tycoon said. "You're not so smart! You did it back when it was *easy.* You were like those athletes from olden times. Sure, Babe Ruth could hit all those homers because nobody could throw ninety yet. Well I've got to do it *today.* I've got to run with the liberal media dead set against me. In a world where everything I do is recorded. I've got to campaign when every person has a phone in their pocket, and every phone has a camera in it. I make one mistake, and it's preserved forever. Then they can put it online and the whole country sees it immediately! Is that the world you campaigned in? I've got news for you. It wasn't!"

The Tycoon made a slow circle of the room. He extended a finger and pointed it accusingly at the ribbon of faces.

"You will not judge me. You will not keep me out of your club just because I am a zombie. I built my own club, did you know that? And people pay six figures just to join. They *beg* to join. There's a waiting list. You were not so different from me. Hell, you *were* me. And I am one of you. I will make this country greater than any of you could ever imagine."

The Tycoon heard someone clear his throat. He turned in a slow circle and scanned the faces. Who had it been? Washington? Lincoln? FDR?

Then the Tycoon rotated to face the door to his green room and saw that it was only McNelis.

"Sir, ten minutes 'till—"

The campaign manager's face fell.

"Your m-makeup," McNelis stammered. "You aren't wearing your makeup."

"Tonight, the American people are going to meet the real me," the Tycoon said. "I want that to be true in every way possible, so I told the makeup lady she could go home. The hair fella too. Combed it myself. I think it looks all right."

"But sir, you're *known* for your makeup," McNelis said. "What's more, everybody wears it on television, not just you. Hell, *I* wear it when I go on the talk shows to campaign for you."

"Well, I don't wear it anymore," the Tycoon said, crossing his arms.

"Remember the Nixon/Kennedy debate? Nixon refused the makeup and Kennedy didn't. They say it cost Nixon the election."

"I don't care," said the Tycoon. "My mind is made up."

"Sir . . . I say this to you because I love you," McNelis managed, swallowing hard. "Without your makeup, you look scary. Your skin is . . ."

"Like a cadaver?" the Tycoon said. "Like a ghoul? You're getting warmer, McNelis. I look like *what I actually am*."

"It's just that I don't know if the voters . . ." McNelis tried again.

"The voters will understand," he said to McNelis. "That's all I can tell you. I've made the decision. It's done."

McNelis hung his head.

"Now, what were you saying?"

"It's ten . . . nine minutes until you go on," McNelis said, glancing at his watch. "We ought to move you into place."

"Very well," the Tycoon said. "Lead the way."

McNelis did, conducting the Tycoon through a backstage area and onto the red X marked in tape by the side of the stage. As they moved into place, the Tycoon noted that the entire arena—both out in the audience and their area behind the scenes—felt somehow devoid of life. The seats were full, but the conventioneers were quiet.

"This feels like the walkthroughs, the rehearsals we did," he whispered to McNelis.

"People still aren't sure what is happening," McNelis said. "Folks are edgy. Understandably."

"It looks like most of the floor is still filled—out there, I mean," the Tycoon said, gesturing to the audience.

"Yes," McNelis said evenly. "We had some defections, but those have been compensated for. Some new supporters have arrived. These newcomers like you more *because* you are a zombie."

"Outstanding," said the Tycoon.

"They are your most extreme supporters," McNelis said. "The kind of people, for whom, you can do no wrong. They really like you . . . and they really hate *her*."

"Ahh, the kind that read that website. What's it called? TruthTeller?"

McNelis nodded.

"Yes," McNelis said. "Initially, it was thought that Truth-Teller's coverage regarding your differently-alive status might be a negative. But as you see, they love you all the more for it. They post online about how other candidates can eat their opponents alive *figuratively*, but you can do it *literally*. They've come to view you as superhuman because of it. We've granted that outlet unprecedented access, accordingly."

"Speaking of unprecedented access," the Tycoon said as a small figure in a rumpled two-button powersuit emerged from the shadows.

"Hello there," Jessica Smith said. "Sorry I'm late. I had a hard time waking up."

"You're here, and that's what matters," said the Tycoon.

Jessica looked him up and down.

"Are you all right?" she asked. "You're not sick are you? You look . . . different."

"Zombies don't get sick," the Tycoon said dismissively. "And I'm feeling fine. Now, are you ready to see a politician deliver the most important speech in American history?"

Jessica did not immediately respond.

"Whether or not you're ready, it's what you're about to see," the Tycoon asserted. "Believe me. What I'm going to do tonight. It's going to be big. The biggest *ever*."

"We're all excited for your speech," Jessica said neutrally.

"Good," the Tycoon replied. "You should be. *Everyone* should be if they know what's good for them. And afterward, like I said before, you can ask me anything you want."

Jessica nodded and stepped away.

Then the Tycoon noticed another familiar—albeit unexpected—face standing off to the side of the backstage area. Several paces behind Jessica. It was a man known to him, and, indeed, to most of the world. The actor was Hollywood royalty. Famous for playing the tight-lipped lead in Westerns and cop films of the 60's and 70's, he was now an elder statesman of Tinseltown, still making films as a director. He was also a member of the Uneeda Society, and had been for several years.

A longtime supporter of the Tycoon's party, the actor could probably go anywhere he liked at a political convention—even backstage. But his presence on this evening was no good-natured show of support. The Tycoon understood immediately that it was quite the opposite.

As if to confirm this, the actor dropped his hand to his hip and came up with an invisible double-action six shooter. He levelled it at the Tycoon, cocked it, and pulled the trigger—bucking slightly under the imaginary recoil. Then he gave the slightest wink.

There was no mistaking the message. If the Tycoon did not pull this off, he was dead. The Uneeda Society had had a good thing going for several decades. Now, that was probably all fucked up. Even the failsafe device meant for these sort of situations—Initiative X—was probably fucked up. (The Initiative called for a member of the Uneeda Society to identify him or herself as a member of the undead publicly, while disavowing any association with the society. It was meant to be like jumping on the grenade to save the entire platoon.) If the Tycoon did not right things tonight, then the next gun pointed in his direction would not be imaginary.

"Okay," McNelis said, turning to the podium where a successful tech venture capitalist was introducing the Tycoon. "It's almost go-time. Ms. Smith, we'll talk to you again after the speech."

As was customary before big speeches, McNelis faced the Tycoon to give him one final going-over, brushing away lint and looking for cowlicks. But staring up into his wan, pale face, it was clear to McNelis that this was not a normal speech. The Tycoon was doing things in his own way. His appearance was so stark and startling, that McNelis decided some cowlicks might do him good.

The venture capitalist at the podium drew to a close. McNelis and the Tycoon listened in.

". . .which is why I'm so proud to introduce him. I give you a man who is not just a thinker, but also a do-er. The man you have chosen as your nominee. In ways that no one has expected, he has come to define the new face of what is possible in America. He is an extraordinary man, in every sense of the word. He is here to earn your trust and earn your vote. I could not be more proud to present you with . . . the next president of the United States!"

"Go get 'em," McNelis said, giving the Tycoon a final pat on the back.

The venture capitalist intercepted the Tycoon halfway to the podium. The men shook hands and smiled for the crowd, but the Tycoon had time to see the capitalist's face fall (and stay fallen) the moment he stepped past. This man was here out of obligation. Now, that obligation had ended. In a few short minutes the man would be on his private jet headed back to Silicon Valley, and that would be that.

As the Tycoon strode out to the podium and heard the applause building, it was as though he were carried along by legs that were not his own. The clapping and cheers continued. He stood ready to begin his speech, patriotic music blaring and American flags waving behind him. Yet the Tycoon could see hesitation on the faces of many in the audience. Where was their bright, shining orange hero? What was this pale, sickly ghost standing in his place? This poor imitation?

The crowd continued to applaud and to wiggle in the air the signs that bore his name, but it all seemed hesitant and halfhearted.

No matter, thought the Tycoon. In a moment they would see. In a moment they would understand.

The Tycoon looked into the teleprompter and began to speak.

"Friends, delegates, and fellow Americans, I am here tonight to accept your nomination for the presidency of the United States. But I'm also here to do more than that. When I announced my candidacy one year ago, we were living in a very different world. America was different, you were different, and I was different too.

"Throughout my life, I have grappled with the question of my own identity. The question of who I truly am. Perhaps this is because I've been so many things. I've been a successful businessman. I've been a philanthropist. I've been a television celebrity who got amazing ratings, just amazing; they were just unbelievable. I've been all of these wonderful things . . . but I still had questions about who I truly was, and how to share that truth with the American people.

"And so I did what you do when you're looking for something important. I went on a quest. A very, very important quest. A quest for my party's nomination. In undertaking this quest, I discovered you all. I discovered America. I discovered places I had known, but in most cases never visited before. And I met people. Wonderful people. People who accepted me even though I was different from them. I met people who were of different faiths than me. People who saw me as a city-slicker who dated supermodels, went to gallery openings, and lived in a skyscraper. I had never been to a tractor pull or gone bow hunting. But even so, these wonderful people showed me love. They looked straight into my eyes and said that even though I was different, I was their man. My skills as a dealmaker and negotiator might not be the same as skills like skinning a buck or running a trotline, but they didn't care. They wanted me to put *my* skills to work for them, and for the entire country.

"I realized I had found what I was looking for. I had found myself. Looking into the faces of the Americans from coast to coast who welcomed me with open arms, I realized that it was okay for me to be different. In fact, it might even be *preferable*. Because I could bring my different skills and talents to do the work that will make America great again!"

Here, the Tycoon paused because the volume of the applause had become overwhelming. The audience was responding to his message. Despite his new appearance and lack of orange glow. They were connecting with his words.

The Tycoon forced himself to wait for the clapping and cheers to die back down. A quick glance over his shoulder into the wings showed him McNelis beaming. The Tycoon had jettisoned his favorite speechwriter's words, but all that mattered was he had the audience now. They were with him.

"So you see," the Tycoon continued, "where . . . at first . . . I had hesitated to let people at events and campaign stops see 'the real me,' I realized that, the more I dropped my guard, the more they liked it. The more certain they became that I was their man for the job. And that is why I am here today not just to accept the nomination, but to say something I've never said publicly. Something that I believe will position our party to crush all opposition in November and take back the White House. Today, I am here to tell you my truth . . . that I am a Zombie-American."

And the Tycoon paused again.

A more cowardly candidate would have continued on, hurrying to frame this stark admission in positive terms. But the Tycoon knew that to do so would be already to admit defeat and failure. To show he found it necessary to employ the kind of subterfuge and skullduggery he had so lately forsworn.

And so the Tycoon let it linger. He let the word reverberate off of the rafters at the top of the arena. Zombie-American.

The cat was really out of the bag. The bag was empty. That was it. Now his whole being—his whole future and everything else—truly did hang in the balance.

Then the sound.

Uttered from the mouth of a young man. (Probably, one of these new supporters from the internet McNelis had been telling him about.) One sound. Not even a real word. Just a sound.

"Ow!"

But it was no exclamation of pain. It was the kind of "Ow!" one said after a band member had finished a particularly spectacular guitar solo at a heavy metal concert. It said "rock on" and "keep it up" and "more of that."

Did they want more?

He would give it to them. Oh yes he would.

The Tycoon smiled.

"Some in the biased liberal media have questioned whether our party should be holding this final night of this convention, or whether I should still be the nominee. I am here tonight to tell you that nobody, but nobody, can do the job that I can. I will lead our party back to the White House. I will do it as a Zombie-American, yes, but more importantly, I will do it as an American!"

More cries of support. More cheers. Then a slow swell of applause. It washed over the Tycoon like a warm bath. Like a magical wave that healed all that was broken within him, removed all doubts, and restored him to former and future glory.

"Under my administration, we will be a country of law and order again!" he continued. "Attacks from outside our nation, and out-of-control crime in our inner cities, both threaten our way of life. Anyone who does not grasp that is not fit to lead. I tell you, I grasp that bigly! The crime and violence that afflict our nation will soon come to an end. Believe me, when I am president, evildoers will fear me. When *I* am president, order will be restored!"

Thunderous applause.

"And I don't have to tell you that times are tough in America right now. Things are hard for working men and women. But when I am president, Americans will come first again. Other nations will treat us with respect. I tell you, it's us against them! Big business, the liberal media, and elite donors are all lining up behind my opponent because they know she will keep the rigged system in place. She is the status quo. Her message is that things will *not* change. My message is that things *have to change*, and I am the one to change them. I am your voice. I am the laid-off factory worker struggling to put food on the table. I am the weeping mother who has lost her children to drugs and violence. I am the zombie shambling across the plains and mountains and deserts of America. I will give a voice to all Americans—rich and poor, male and female, alive and undead. Now, nobody is forgotten. Now, everybody has a voice."

More cheers and applause.

"Not to harp on my opponent here . . . but when a Secretary of State illegally stores her emails on a private server, deletes over 33,000 of them so the authorities can't see her crime, lies about it in every different form—and, I might add, is *strongly* rumored to be a vampire—I know that corruption has reached a level like never before. That's right. You heard me. I didn't misspeak. Over 33,000. Also, a vampire. You know, back in the good old days, they would have taken care of someone like her with a stake. But now you have to be politically correct."

The cheers came and they did not stop coming.

In a trice, the Tycoon saw it all unfolding before him. This would work. This was the way forward. His "honest" approach would be effective.

Now nothing would stop him. Nothing at all.

As he continued his speech, he only became more certain of it. He could already taste victory. It might not be brains, but it was still damned delicious.

THE REPORTER

Jessica had seen many remarkable things since landing in Cleveland, but the spell weaved by the Tycoon as he accepted the nomination might have been the most remarkable of all.

There were moments in life where you had to decide if you were okay with something. And Jessica knew that what one decided one was "okay with" could determine the fate of men and nations. Were you okay with a little corruption? Were you okay with a little tyranny (as long as it was less than in the neighboring country)? What about with just a little bit of zombie presence? Just a little?

Jessica's head swam as she listened to the Tycoon outline his plan for the future. Her thoughts went immediately to a date she'd had in J-school. A blind date her friend had set her up on. She'd arrived at the Morningside Heights bistro to find that the man awaiting her was handsome, kind, had a great sense of humor . . . and was fifteen years her senior. Also, he had a kid. And she had thought to herself, "Wait, do I do this? Do I, Jessica Smith, date men who are fifteen years older than me and have kids? Am I okay with this?"

Quite abruptly and unexpectedly, she had been confronted with whether or not she would cross a line.

In her online dating profiles, Jessica capped the age limit at a hard 29. But in the presence of this charming, urbane

Human Resources manager for a Fortune 500 company, everything suddenly felt negotiable. And Jessica had decided she *was* okay with it.

Her thoughts went to that handsome HR manager because she realized something even more surprising and remarkable was happening here in Cleveland. She was watching the electors of a major American political party indicate that they were "okay with" a zombie as their president.

The electorate had not blanched as the Tycoon had lampooned the disabled, bragged of groping women, and called for protestors at his rallies to be taken out and beaten. The Tycoon's supporters had been "okay with" these things. But the candidate's being a zombie? Literally a blood-drinking, brain-eating zombie? Surely, one imagined, that would be a bridge too far.

But no. From the look and sound of things, they were absolutely *loving* it.

Was there no bridge too far?

Perhaps there was not. Perhaps this man really would win. Perhaps the country would discover something new about itself. Or something old and hidden. Something long forgotten. That the American people could be "okay with" all sorts of dark bargains.

Standing near Jessica was an ancient movie actor, famous since before she was born. He was also watching the Tycoon's performance, and he was smiling from ear to ear.

Then another man approached and stood near her, lingering in the shadows. Close, but not too close. It took a moment for Jessica to recognize him in her peripheral vision.

"Omigod, Tim," she whispered. "Where have you been? Are you seeing this?"

"I sure am," he said in a voice that sounded uncharacteristically flat.

"You think there's something that will be too far . . . or too much, right? And then he goes there, and it's not too much. I just can't believe it."

"Uh, yeah," Tim said. "It's . . . yeah."

Something was wrong. Beyond a natural adverse reaction to what they were seeing on the stage, Tim seemed not right.

Jessica forced herself to tear her eyes away from the Tycoon. Tim did not look like himself. He was deathly pale. More alarmingly, the front of his face and the top of his t-shirt were covered in blood.

"Tim," Jessica said, putting her hand to her lips. "What is—"

"A new kind of political costume," Tim said. "People are dressing up like zombies to show support for him. Crazy huh?"

"Well isn't that a little inappropriate for you to do, seeing as how you're a member of the media?" Jessica asked.

Then she smiled and turned back to watch the candidate's speech.

"That's sort of why I'm here," Tim said. "I don't know if I can go on in the same way anymore. I'm not the same, Jessica."

Jessica turned back to him.

"I know how you feel," she said. "The past twenty-four hours have changed things for me too. I never thought the world could be like this. All of it seems impossible, unbelievable—but here we are. And you and I are kind of at the center of it. It's crazy."

"I've changed, Jessica," Tim continued.

"Tell me about it," she replied.

"No, I don't think you fully understand," said Tim, taking a step back.

The portly reporter seemed to fumble with something in his pocket. Jessica looked down and realized that he was holding a handgun. She froze.

"Tim!" she whisper-shouted, glancing frantically. "What are you doing? You can't have that back here. The Secret Service will literally kill you."

"Knowing what I know now—what I've discovered in the last few hours—I . . . have to do this, Jessica," he whispered back.

"Jesus," Jessica said. "That's not a costume you're wearing, is it? That's not fake blood! I don't understand. I don't . . ."

Tim did not respond verbally, but his grip on the .357 seemed to tighten.

"Tim, you can't," Jessica continued, serious as a heart attack. "Whatever they've done to you, however you feel right now, this is not the way. I can't believe this, Tim. No! You'd shoot him? What the hell?"

"No," Tim said icily. "This is not for him, Jessica. This is for *you*."

"Tim, what—"

"Now that I've seen the other side, I understand everything," he told her. "What this man is doing will make America unstoppable for years to come. Maybe for centuries. It's the best thing anyone has ever done, ever. Now that I'm *like him* I can see it all—everything he's going to do—like it's a movie playing out in my head. I can see every part of it, clear as day."

"Tim, why are you pointing that at me?"

"Because you're the only thing that stands in his way," Tim said. "That's what I've realized. It's you. You're the only one with the experience. You know the Knights. You're the only one who has gotten close enough to his camp to actually bring him down."

Tim's eyes looked inhuman and insane. Jessica began to believe that Tim really would use the gun. She waited for security, for the Secret Service, for *someone* to notice what was happening in the dark wings of the stage. But there was no response. Not even the movie actor seemed to have noticed Tim's firearm. Jessica wondered how long she could stall. Someone was bound to help her soon.

Weren't they?

"If you shoot me, they'll put you in jail," Jessica tried. "You can't eat anybody's brains in jail. At least I don't think you can."

"I don't think the rules about what we can or can't do are set in stone just yet," Tim said. "Besides . . . I'm sort of counting on a presidential pardon."

Then he raised the weapon and pulled the trigger.

Jessica would, in later years, be unable to say precisely how conscious her reaction to the weapon had been. She had flinched and screamed. The same thing almost everybody does when they are about to be murdered. And in what seemed to be the same instant, two Secret Service (who, at the last minute, had noticed the armed Tim Fife) had raced over and thrown themselves onto his back.

Tim had wobbled, but not gone down right away. He staggered like a bull fighting to maintain focus under the jab and bite of the picador's lance. The Secret Service punched him violently, and his legs began to give. Sensing that it was now or never, Tim did his best to flail his arm in Jessica's direction. Then he squeezed the trigger hard.

The report was very loud, but the bullet went nowhere near Jessica. A moment later, Tim was on the ground—choked, unconscious, and/or merely a zombie playing dead. A cry of alarm went up from the audience. Jessica spun around to see the Tycoon on the floor of the stage. The bullet had hit him squarely in the chest and knocked him off of his feet.

For the third night in a row, pandemonium reigned at the convention.

Then Jessica—and the rest of the nation—watched in astonishment as the Tycoon got back up. He pushed away the Secret Service who had rushed to form a circle around him. These men and women looked on disbelievingly as the Tycoon fingered the hole in the front of his chest where the bullet had gone in. At one point a medical professional appeared to approach the Tycoon for a moment, examine him in bafflement, and shrug as the zombie assured him that no assistance was needed.

With the stage still crowded, cries of "We got him!" and "Over here!" boomed from beside where Jessica still stood. She watched as the limp form of Tim Fife was carried away by men and women in black suits.

Then Jessica glanced back in the direction of the stage, because the Tycoon had resumed speaking into the microphone.

"Is everybody all right?" he asked. "The bullet didn't hit anybody else, did it?"

Indeed, there seemed to be no other injured. The crowd's murmurs of alarm began to die away. People found their seats once again.

"Headshots, somebody should have told him!" the Tycoon said through a good-natured smile. "*Headshots* kill zombies. Everybody knows that!"

He stuck his finger into his chest to the second knuckle, then held it up for the crowd's amusement. They loved it.

"I told you I was tough!" he said. "I wasn't lying, was I?"

The cheers were unearthly and deafening.

Impossibly, the Tycoon had presented his audience with one more miracle. With one more dazzling display of who they would get if they voted for him. If Jessica had not known better, she would have said the Tycoon had staged the event himself.

But it was real. All of it.

The Tycoon.

Tim Fife.

Zombies.

All of it was real.

THE FAKE NEWSMAN

Tim Fife's punishment was *especially* harsh.

As the months went by and the Tycoon took office— and then gradually began to implement his policies—Tim Fife was probably the lone zombie who failed to enjoy the magnificent changes being made to the United States. Confined to a cell for an indeterminate period, Tim knew only privation and hunger. A zombie could subsist nearly forever without eating, though it was by no means a pleasant existence. The human food brought to his cell sickened him. He never touched it, and after some time the guards got permission to cease feeding him entirely.

His access to television and radio were spotty, but he heard quite a bit through guards' palaver.

It sounded like a brave new world. For zombies.

As president, the Tycoon had begun with executive orders mandating the closure of the country's southern border entirely. Then regulations of every kind were rolled back. International, globalist agreements fettering the United States to other nations were severed wholesale. A new nationalism reigned.

But what kind of nation would it be?

There seemed to be new freedoms everywhere. New opportunities. New amendments. (It felt like every day, the Tycoon was decreeing something or the other.) And in all of them, the zombies were given primacy.

During this period, the ardently faithful Vice President was keen to remind the nation of the Bible's promise that the last should one day be first. And the last, by his reckoning, could be nothing other than the zombie. They had been kept low for so long. They had been forced to exist in the shadows for centuries. Killed on sight, most of the time. (And they were slow enough that they were often literally last in any kind of race they ran.) But all of that—with the lord's blessing, the Vice President assured the nation—was now beginning to change. Precisely as had been foretold.

As Tim languished in his cell, the world around him metamorphosed. Zombies outside killed at will. Humans came more and more to accept their lot as convenient meat for the the undead.

Even to a zombie, it was sometimes difficult for Tim to credit the tales he heard of the outer world from the talkative prison guards. (At times, he wondered if they were exaggerating in order to intentionally titillate him, and thus make his imprisonment all the more painful.) But the most unbelievable part was not just how good it was getting for zombies. The most unbelievable part seemed to be that the Tycoon had gotten Americans of all stripes to accept the changes.

In the Tycoon's America, firearms regulations had been relaxed even further. Now, age limits and waiting periods were entirely a thing of the past. Prohibitions for the drug addicted and insane were lifted too. Enthusiasts of personal freedom had never been so ecstatic. The only thing the Tycoon had asked in return was that the penalty for violence upon a zombie should be immediate death. It was a bargain Americans urged their legislators to make.

The new President had next legalized all drugs and formerly banned substances. His only sticking point had been that "human brains" be included among these substances made newly-legal to consume. The request seemed so modest—and enthusiasts of drug legalization so adamant—that, again, the bargain was struck. ("It probably won't be *my* brain that gets eaten," the constituents told themselves—and urged their representatives to support the law.)

Healthcare was also gutted. If zombies did not require it, then how important could it be? Besides, the new President pointed out in a famous Rose Garden address, 90% of people who died, died in hospitals. Did it not then follow that they were dangerous places that the country would be better off without? To many Americans, this logic seemed unassailable.

In area after area, the nation was being reduced for humans . . . and enhanced for zombies. All with the willing consent of the majority.

Was there opposition? From what Tim could ascertain from inside his cell, there surely was. But the Tycoon's masterstroke had been the insinuation that his opponent in the

general election had also been a member of the undead—albeit
a slightly different variety. This new world of zombies might
be bad . . . but bad compared to what? A bunch of decadent,
elitist bats flying around and sucking your blood sounded
worse to most people. (Zombies, at least, you could mostly
outrun.) The fact that his opponent showed no evidence of
actually *being* a vampire—and that the Tycoon was believed
to have used doctored photos to convince reporters (Jessica
Smith, among them) of her initial battiness—did not seem to
sway the voters back in her direction. In fact, her every attempt
to prove her humanity—garlic soup, wearing crosses, bathing
in holy water—only showed the voters that she was protest-
ing too much. Trying too hard. And the Tycoon had set the
precedent that these tests could be faked with his stethoscope
trick. "That's not even real garlic soup" the voters said. And
so, feeling that they were to have an undead leader no matter
what, the American people had chosen the zombie.

A year into the Tycoon's first term, America was truly
shaping up into a wonderland for the undead. The prison
guards Tim overheard said that the growing levels of zombie
invasion and contagion were different from city-to-city and
state-to-state, but it was all rather hard to gauge because of
the changes to the media. Any news outlet that characterized
zombies in a negative light was swiftly labeled a hate group by
the White House and just as promptly shut down by executive
order. There were also simply more news outlets than there
had ever been before, many of which offered "alternative facts"
about the "alternatively alive." It all made it quite difficult for
anybody trying to keep things straight. Was the next county
over beset with a plague of the undead, or was it experiencing

a vibrant cultural revival? The answer depended very much on which networks you watched or which papers you read.

The only thing that seemed certain was that it was now a land by and for zombies, and would remain so henceforward. The undead walked unafraid in sunlight. They fed upon whomever they wished, whenever they wished. Shooting them was a crime, and speaking out against them was downright un-American.

Zombies were putting the red back in the good old red, white, and blue. The tree of liberty was being watered with the blood of tyrants, yes, but also the blood of just anybody the zombies happened to feel like eating.

And poor Tim Fife?

He was missing it *all*.

ABOUT THE AUTHOR

Scott Kenemore is the author of the horror novels *The Grand Hotel*; *Zombie, Indiana*; *Zombie, Illinois*; and the bestselling *Zombie, Ohio*, as well as the *Zen of Zombie* series of undead-themed satire books. He is a graduate of Kenyon College and Columbia University. A member of the Horror Writers Association and the Zombie Research Society, Scott lives in Chicago and is the drummer for the musical band The Blissters.